Recent praise
for David Shields

Salinger (with Shane Salerno)

· *New York Times* bestseller
· *LA Times* bestseller

Revealing ... [A] sharp-edged portrait.

MICHIKO KAKUTANI, *The New York Times*

There are riches here ...

LEV GROSSMAN, *Time*

... Hugely impressive ...

JOHN WALSH, *The Sunday Times of London*

... *Salinger* is the thorny, complicated portrait that its thorny, complicated subject deserves ...

LOUIS BAYARD, *The Washington Post*

Salinger gets the goods on an author's reclusive life ...

DAVID L. ULIN, *Los Angeles Times*

Juicy ... *Salinger* is full of fascinating revelations....

ANDREW ROMANO, *The Daily Beast*

The reclusive author's story, thrillingly told ...

KYLE MINOR, *Salon*

... refreshingly frank about [Salinger's] many shortcomings and how they might have affected his work ...

LAURA MILLER, *Salon*

How Literature Saved My Life

...These rigorous, high-octane, exhaustive yet taut ruminations on ambivalence, love, melancholy, and mortality are like an arrow laced with crack to the brain.

KRISTY DAVIS, *O, The Oprah Magazine*

...Wonderful, vastly entertaining book.

EUGENIA WILLIAMSON, *Boston Globe*

Concise, fearless, urgent. A soulful writer, a skillful storyteller, and a man on the hunt for the Exquisite.

MINNA PROCTOR, *Bookforum*

A generation from now, when we pick up our flex-tablets or digi-goggles or whatever and read about literature at the turn of the twenty-first century, there's a decent chance we'll see it referred to as the David Shields era.

MARK ATHITAKIS, *Barnes & Noble Review*

Shields has an uncanny ability to tap into the short attention span of modern culture and turn it into something positive.... *How Literature Saved My Life* presents a way forward for literature in new forms.

KEVIN MCFARLAND, *The A.V. Club*

Shields is a stunning writer. Within this book lies significant passion and revelation.

THE HUFFINGTON POST

Uncompromisingly intelligent, blisteringly forthright, and eschewing convention at every turn.

A. J. KIRBY, *New York Journal of Books*

There is no more interesting writer at this precise moment than David Shields.

JEFF SIMON, *Buffalo News*, Editor's Choice

... altogether fascinating.

PUBLISHERS WEEKLY, starred review

Quintessential genre-defying Shields. His writing gives you [a] sense of vertigo. It's energizing and weird, and it works.

EMILY GOGOLAK, *The Village Voice*

Shields's ideas about literature come from a place of deep love; he's not trying to destroy but rebuild what is already broken.

CRAIG HUBERT, *ArtInfo*

I find David Shields unavoidable. A lot of that is a matter of style—I enjoy fragmentary writing, and few are more adept at it than he is.

GUY CUNNINGHAM, *Bookslut*

Reality Hunger: A Manifesto

· Named one of the best books of the year by more than thirty publications

Maybe he's simply ahead of the rest of us, mapping out the literary future of the next generation.

SUSAN H. GREENBERG, *Newsweek*

I can't stop recommending it to my friends.

EDWARD KING, *The Times of London*

[I am] grateful for this beautiful (yes, raw and gorgeous) book.

SUSAN SALTER REYNOLDS, *Los Angeles Times*

This is the most provocative, brain-rewiring book of 2010. It's a book that feels at least five years ahead of its time and teaches you how to read it as you go.

ALEX PAPPADEMAS, *GQ*

I find Shields's book absorbing, even inspiring. The ideas he raises are so important, his ideas are so compelling, that I raved about this book the whole time I was reading it and have regularly quoted it to friends in the weeks since.

JAMI ATTENBERG, *Bookforum*

Thank goodness for David Shields and his new book, *Reality Hunger: A Manifesto*, which, among other things, is a literary battle cry for the creation of a new genre ... brilliant, thoughtful, and yes, original ...

CATHY ALTER, *The Atlantic*

David Shields's radical intellectual manifesto, *Reality Hunger*, is a rousing call to arms for all artists to reject the laws governing appropriation, obliterate the boundaries between fiction and nonfiction, and give rise to a new modern form.

ELISSA SCHAPELL, *Vanity Fair*

I don't think it would be too strong to say that Shields's book will be a sort of bible for the next generation of culture-makers.

DAVID GRIFFITH, *Bookslut*

Reality Hunger ... heralds what will be the dominant modes in years and decades to come.

LUC SANTE, *The New York Times Book Review*

As is true of any good manifesto, [Shields] clocks or locks a feeling in the air, something already everywhere, familiar but not fully formed.

ALEXANDRA JUHASZ, *The Huffington Post*

Essential reading for both readers and writers.

STEPHEN EMMS, *The Guardian*

... an important book ... a provocative and entertaining manifesto.

BLAKE MORRISON, *The Guardian*, "Book of the Week"

David Shields has written yet another stunning book ... Why is this man always writing the most interesting books?

FREDERICK BARTHELME

The Thing About Life Is That One Day You'll Be Dead

· *New York Times* bestseller
· Named one of the best books of the year by *Amazon.com*, *Artforum*, *Salon*, *Seattle Times*, and *TimeOut Chicago*

Many writers aim to capture the human condition in all its variety, audacity, and contradiction, but few can claim to get as close to their target as Shields.... [A] truly original vision brought to fruition.

JOSH ROSENBLATT, *The Austin Chronicle*

... a terrible beauty of a book is born.

THOMAS LYNCH, *Boston Globe*

Enthralling ... Fascinating ...

MEREDITH MARAN, *San Francisco Chronicle*

An edifying, wise, unclassifiable mixture of filial love and Oedipal rage.

LEV GROSSMAN, *Time*

Mr. Shields is a sharp-eyed, self-deprecating, at times hilarious writer. Approaching the flat line of the last page, we want more.

STEPHEN BATES, *The Wall Street Journal*

A primer on aging and death for those who take theirs without the sugar. … There's a comfort to be found in this sober investigation of mortality, in Shields's clear-eyed look at the ways in which we come undone.

BENJAMIN ALSUP, *Esquire*

Library of Congress
Cataloging-in-Publication Data

Shields, David, 1956– author.
Life is short; art is shorter: in praise
of brevity / by David Shields and
Elizabeth Cooperman.
pages cm
Includes bibliographical references.
ISBN 978-0-9893604-5-6

1. Literature–Philososphy.
2. Discourse analysis.
3. Authorship.
4. Short story.

I. Cooperman, Elizabeth, 1981–
author.
II. Title.

PN45.S393 2014
801–DC23
2014020263

Hawthorne Books
& Literary Arts

9 2201 Northeast 23rd Avenue
8 3rd Floor
7 Portland, Oregon 97212
6 hawthornebooks.com
5 *Form*:
4 Adam McIsaac/Sibley House
3
2 Printed in China

Set in Paperback

Life Is Short–
Art Is Shorter

In Praise of Brevity
David Shields and
Elizabeth Cooperman

HAWTHORNE BOOKS & LITERARY ARTS
Portland, Oregon | MMXV

Contents

Life is short.
Art is long.

  HIPPOCRATES

LIFE IS SHORT – ART IS SHORTER

Introduction

Short Stuff

BOBS, TEMPERS, COLLEGE REJECTION LETTERS, KINDS of love, postcards, nicknames, baby carrots, myopia, life flashing before eyes, gummy bears, the loser's straw, Capri pants, charge on this phone battery, a moment on the lips (forever on the hips), caprice, velvet chokers, six months to live, penne, some dog tails, how long I've known you though it feels like a lifetime, even a complicated dive, tree stumps, a shot of tequila, breaking a bone, a temp job, bobby socks, when you're having fun, a sucker punch, going straight to video, outgrown shoes, a travel toothbrush, just missing the basket, quickies, some penises, lard-based desserts, catnaps, staccato tonguing, a sugar rush, timeouts, Tom Cruise, a stint, brusque people, stubble, the "I'm sorry" in proportion to the offense, fig season, grammatical contractions, bunny hills, ice cream headaches, dachshunds, –ribs, –stops, –hands, –changed, … but sweet.

Failing the Test of Literature

IT WAS THE best of times, it was the worst of times, it was the age of wisdom, it was the age of foolishness, it was the epoch of belief, it was the epoch of incredulity, it was the season of Light, it was the season of … [1]

Imagine, for a moment, that you have fallen asleep while reading a great book. Suppose that the book is *War and Peace* or

---

1   Charles Dickens, *A Tale of Two Cities*

Crime and Punishment or *Moby-Dick*; it doesn't matter, so long as the book carries with it a crushing weight of cultural prestige. But somehow, toward the middle, your attention flags, or you're not up to the challenge, or you're tired and irritable. Whatever the cause, you've fallen asleep. The huge book you've been reading falls to the floor. Because it's a big book, it makes a resounding thud when gravity finally has its way with it. The sound shocks you awake. You look up, dazed. You feel guilty (again). You have failed, at least temporarily, the Test of Literature. Something is wrong (you have always known it) with your attention span.[2]

The world of remarkable individuals making moral decisions across a long span of time is often what passes for profundity in literature. Greatness, we in America especially think, has to do with sheer size, with the expansion of materials, but one is entitled to have occasional doubts.[3]

What if length is a feature of writing that is as artificial as an individual prose style?[4]

As it happens, in the tradition of Western literature we have come to believe that, at least with the novel, length is synonymous with profundity (this is a confusion of the horizontal with the vertical, please notice) and that most great literature must be large. But what if length, great length, *is* a convention not always necessary to the materials but dictated by an author's taste or will, a convention that runs parallel to expansionism, empire-building, and the contemplation of the heroic individual? It may simply be evidence of the writer's interest in domination.[5]

Get fat and you will call hunger one of the virtues.[6]

I didn't have time to write a short letter, so I wrote a long one instead.[7]

2   Charles Baxter, "Introduction," in *Sudden Fiction International: Sixty Short-Short Stories*, ed. Robert Shapard and James Thomas (New York: Norton, 1989)
3   Baxter
4   Baxter
5   Baxter
6   James Richardson, *Vectors: Aphorisms and Ten-Second Essays* (Keene, NY: Ausable Press, 2001)
7   Blaise Pascal, *Provincial Letters*, no. XVI

All work is the avoidance of harder work.[8]

Try painting a landscape on a grain of rice.[9]

If you don't know the whole truth, you might as well keep whatever you have to say short. You might as well puncture the pretense of sheer size.[10]

It is as if the titanic ego of fiction itself has been brought down to a human scale.[11]

The Invention of Brevity

WHAT IF VERY short short stories are products of mass societies in which crowding is an inescapable part of life? The novel is, spatially, like an estate; the very short story is like an efficiency on the twenty-third floor. As it happens, more people these days live in efficiencies than on estates.[12]

It is as if all the borders, to all other realms, have moved closer to us, and we ourselves are living in tighter psychic spaces.[13]

In college I was once accused of owning only six objects.[14]

In my dating days, as soon as I anticipated going to bed with someone, I found it absurd, irrational, to further resist the inevitable.[15]

One common contemporary approach: cut to the quick.

Jettisoning content – temporal, material, or textual – makes me feel good all over.[16]

At this point, I must make a sort of confession: I, too, have fallen asleep over several famous authors. And I have woken up feeling that the fault must be mine and wondering, vaguely, about the convention of length in literature.[17]

---

8   Richardson
9   Jay Ponteri, "On Brevity," unpublished manuscript
10   Baxter
11   Baxter
12   Baxter
13   Baxter
14   Sarah Manguso, conversation with David Shields, *Believer*, June 2010
15   Manguso
16   Manguso
17   Baxter

I'm bored by plot; I'm bored when it's all written out, when there isn't any shorthand.[18]

If there's a good line in a book, I'll happily copy out the line and sell the book to the Strand.[19]

Value yourself according to the burdens you carry, and you will find everything a burden.[20]

The short-short story isn't a new form; it's not as if, in 1974, there sprung from the head of Zeus the short-short story.

Think of the shortest story you know.[21]

Perhaps it's just an anecdote.[22]

Or a joke.

"A wife is like an umbrella," says Freud, citing an Austrian joke; "sooner or later one takes a cab."[23]

Short-shorts are similar to algebraic equations or lab experiments or jigsaw puzzles or carom shots or very cruel jokes. They're magic tricks, with meaning.

Many people's reaction nowadays to a lot of longer stories is often *Remind me again why I read this*, or *The point being?*

If you don't know the whole truth, you might as well keep whatever you have to say short.[24]

Quite a few critics have been worried about attention span lately and see very short stories as signs of cultural decadence – bonbons for lazy readers, chocolates stuffed with snow.[25]

No one ever said that sonnets or haikus were evidence of short attention spans.[26]

Kafka, who was unusually susceptible to textual stimuli, read only a couple of pages of a book at a time, he read the same

18   David Salle, quoted in Janet Malcolm, "Forty-One False Starts," *New Yorker*, July 11, 1994
19   Manguso
20   Richardson
21   Baxter
22   Baxter
23   Heather McHugh, *Broken English: Poetry and Partiality* (Middletown, CT: Wesleyan University Press, 1993)
24   Baxter
25   Baxter
26   Baxter

relatively few things over and over, his reading habits were eccentric, and he wasn't a completist.[27]

The short-attention-span argument seems to have been invented by Anglo-centric critics who are nostalgic for the huge Victorian novel as the only serious form of literature, and talking about the short attention span is a form of blaming-the-reader.[28]

Duration of attention doesn't seem as important as its quality.[29]

Many undergraduate writing students have an admirable impatience with the Dickensian model; they want, instead, to be commanded by voice.

We are all mortal. We are existentially alone on the planet. We want art that builds a bridge across that abyss. We want to read work that shows how the writer solved the problem of being alive.

Tell a story about the relation between literature and life, between art and death.

The way to write is to throw your body at the mark when all your arrows are spent.[30]

In the best short-shorts the writer seems to have miraculously figured out a way to stage, in a very compressed space, his or her own metaphysic: *Life feels like this*. Or at least: *Some aspect of life feels like this*.

Isn't what grips us emotional and intellectual depth charge? What else matters?

Jonathan Franzen and Ian McEwan are antiquarians; they're entertaining the troops as the ship goes down. Their writing is pre-modern.

On or about December, 1910, human character changed.[31]

Whether it's a story, a short lyric essay, or a prose poem, something about the very nature of compression and concision forces a kind of raw candor.

---

27   Manguso
28   Baxter
29   Baxter
30   Emerson
31   Virginia Woolf, "Mr. Bennett and Mrs. Brown," in *The Virginia Woolf Reader*, ed. Mitchell A. Leaska (San Diego: Harcourt Brace Jovanovich, 1984)

The short stories, lyric essays, and prose poems gathered in this volume seem to gain access to contemporary feeling states more effectively than the conventional story does. As movie trailers, stand-up comedy, fast food, commercials, sound bites, phone sex, bumper stickers, email, texts, and tweets all do, short-shorts cut to the chase.

Let us merge criticism and imagination, fact and dream.

Let us obliterate the distinctions between fiction and nonfiction and create new forms for a new century.

Here, in a page or a page and a half, I'll attempt to unveil for you my vision of life...

Let us create an explosion on every page, in every paragraph.

I don't want to be bogged down by the tangential, irrelevant, or unnecessary. Stick a spear straight to my heart – stick it straight to my brain.[32]

The Fascinating Question of Art: What Is Between A and B?

ONE GOOD THING about my impending death is that I don't need to fake interest in anything. Look, I'm dying![33]

We are all getting tired of the Village Explainers. Explanations don't seem to be explaining very much anymore. Authoritative accounts have a way of looking like official lies, which in their solemnity start to sound funny.[34]

Exposition is a very Windexed window.[35]

We say: begin or end in the middle; begin at the ending or end with the beginning, but do not, do not begin at the beginning or end with the ending.[36]

In these stories, there are no prolonged, agonizing reappraisals, disquisitions on psychology. The situations don't permit it because both time and space have run out simultaneously.[37]

I like to imagine a brush fire, deep inside a national park.

32   Tara Ebrahimi
33   Manguso
34   Baxter
35   McHugh
36   Ponteri
37   Baxter

The reader is a firefighter, and the writer's job is to drop that reader directly at the edge of the blaze to encounter the flames and smoke immediately. There is no time for the long hike in.[38]
— the turn without the long straightaway, the take-off without the mile of runway.[39]

How much can one remove and still have the composition be intelligible? This understanding, or its lack, divides those who can write from those who can really write. Chekhov removed the plot. Pinter, elaborating, removed the history, the narration; Beckett, the characterization. We hear it anyway. Omission is a form of creation.[40]

The fascinating question of Art: What is between A and B?[41]

Two prisoners told each other the same jokes so many times that they resorted to numbering the jokes and just mentioning numbers to each other. One prisoner turned to his bunkmate and said, "Hey: number 27." The other one didn't laugh. "Why didn't you laugh?" "I didn't like how you told it."

The line of beauty is the line of perfect economy.[42]

I say: when you dip a single toe in cold water, a shiver runs through your entire body.[43]

What the detail is to the world of facts, the moment is to the flow of time.[44]

Perhaps it is the nature of small things to flow together, forming something larger.[45]

In the very brief works collected here, there is precious little time between beginnings and endings, between entrances and departures.

Brevity is unluxurious. It can't afford to lose the point, unless, of course, losing the point is the point.

38 Dinty W. Moore, "On Brevity, and Parachuting into a Literary Brush Fire," *Creative Nonfiction* 27 (2005)
39 Richardson
40 David Mamet, "Writers on Writing; Hearing the Notes That Aren't Played," *New York Times*, July 15, 2002
41 Mamet
42 Emerson
43 Ponteri
44 Baxter
45 Pagan-themed website, quoted by Ponteri

The ending of a short-short is crucial. It should provide "retrospective redefinition" – that is, it should force the reader to process anew what she has just read.

The whole thing again, but with a difference.

The river we stepped into is not the river in which we stand.[46]

The pressure to lift great weight in a short span resembles the work that must be done in the final couplet of a sonnet – the two-line *volta* or "turn" that should flip the poem, disorient the argument.

Because, by the end of the story, poem, or essay, it becomes fairly transparent whether or not the writer can "perform," the short-short is highly nervous-making.

There's no time to relax in a short text. It's like resting during the hundred-yard dash. It's ridiculous even to consider. One should instead close the book and just watch television or take a nap.[47]

When students write very short compositions (as opposed to, say, a fifteen-page story that's flawed from the get-go and flounders on and on in that state), the author has nowhere to hide. Instructors can much more effectively critique – both in class and in written comments – these shorter works.

So, too, in an hour-long class, a teacher can identify and trace for students the way in which each gesture or silence adds up in one or more of this book's forty-seven essays and stories.

Intelligent intensity has nothing to do with scale. It has to do with the quality of a person's attention.[48]

I like the focus that working on small things brings. I must be exact and careful and pay attention to nothing but the little stuff in front of me. I don't focus on details in most areas of my life, but here is one place I must pay deliberate, patient attention.[49]

There is the night a student reads a fictive description of a plane crash … the torn limbs pile up … [50]

46   Heraclitus
47   Manguso
48   Baxter
49   Card designer Bekki Witt, quoted by Ponteri
50   Amy Hempel, "Captain Fiction," *Vanity Fair*, December 1984

A simple hair across a scoop of ice cream will do much to repel people.[51]

A reviewer said about a collection of linked stories, published twenty years ago, that if the author kept going in this direction (i.e., toward concision), he'd wind up writing books composed of one very beautiful word.

The reviewer meant it as a putdown, but to the author it was wild praise.

Dissect, disassemble, break the short-short down.

Discuss it word for word, as if it were a geometric proof.

These stories provide an observable canvas that can be held in the hand and examined all at once.

Your mind can encompass a very short story in the way it can't grasp a novella or a novel – like a hand closing over a stone with the word *sadness* painted on it.[52]

It is my ambition to say in ten sentences what everyone else says in a whole book – what everyone else does *not* say in a whole book.[53]

What is creation made of, and what do we make of it?[54]

The sun is one foot wide.[55]

A bow is alive only when it kills.[56]

Practically every week, physicists proclaim the existence of a subatomic particle that is smaller and shorter-lived and more elusive than the particle thought to be the fundamental building block of matter the day before.[57]

It is the space that defines the words, the skull the kiss, the hole the eye.[58]

Ah, what can fill the heart? But then, what *can't*?[59]

51   Gordon Lish, quoted in Hempel
52   Ponteri
53   Nietzsche
54   McHugh
55   Heraclitus
56   Heraclitus
57   Bernard Cooper, "Train of Thought," in *In Brief: Short Personal Takes on the Personal,* ed. Judith Kitchen and Mary Paumier Jones (New York: Norton, 1999)
58   McHugh
59   Richardson

I. Object

Welcome to the world. You are a newborn baby. You are an object.

Object

TROW'S FEDORA. WOODMAN'S WALLET. THERNSTROM'S painting. Merkin's scarf. No ideas but in things, as William Carlos Williams reminded us. We live through specifics or not at all. Objects are real. Details matter – to the devil and to everyone else, including and especially writers. Specifics are at the absolute center of a composition: the exact image, the exquisitely rendered insight, the physicality of being on planet Earth. In each of these four essays – two of them very, very brief – the author anchors his or her meditation in a very specific object.

Your assignment is, similarly, to write a story or essay or prose poem (500 words or fewer) in which you, too, place an object at the center of your composition, but be sure to use it as a way to rotate the object outward, into something larger. This isn't a sixth-grade writing assignment in which you describe vividly your pencil sharpener. The object is meant to be a metaphor, a gateway to get at something you want to say about the human condition.

A psychology experiment – in which participants were asked to handle clothing that supposedly belonged to an ex-lover, a victim of hepatitis, or someone famous – concluded that most people faced with such a proposal operate according to what is called a "magical law of contagion." According to researcher Carol Nemeroff, we believe that objects carry the positive and negative qualities associated with their former wearers/owners and that those qualities are transmittable via touch. Few of us would deign to put on, for example, Hitler's hat, for fear of some evil residue.

Trow uses a fedora to explore the way his father sees this hat as the very mark of civilization, whereas for Trow, "irony has seeped into the felt of any fedora hat I have ever owned … A fedora hat worn by me without the necessary protective irony would eat through my head and kill me." Notice the insidiousness implied by the word "seep." For Trow, the objectionable aspects of his father's way of life *literally* (as opposed to symbolically) inhabit the fedora, possess it. We know that when the father takes the hat off at the end of the workday and puts it on his young son's head, he passes him more than the hat. Consequently, when the adult Trow "tortures" a fedora out of shape, he enacts a very real rebellion.

In one brilliant sentence, Trow enacts the entire essay, expressing in oddly Latinate, high-church prose, his desire to be more informal: "My father had had his first fedora at the age of nine, but he said he recognized that the circumstances of his bringing up had been different from the circumstances of mine (it was his opinion that his mother, my grandmother, had been excessively strict in the matter of dress), and he would not insist on anything inappropriate or embarrassing." Trying to tell us that he is not his father's son, he also makes sure we can see by his formality that he is; whether or not he dons a fedora, Trow has been bred and educated in "the traditional manners of the high bourgeoisie" that he would like to escape. The syntax and diction tell you he never will, but does he know this? Maybe.

Merkin uses a lost scarf to get at two kinds of people: those who obsess over loss and those who don't. She is, of course, as are your present editors, one for whom "the only true paradise is lost paradise" (Proust). The way in which people obsess over lost objects is revealed to be a dress rehearsal for dealing with more important losses throughout their lives – the loss of loved ones and, ultimately, the loss of their own lives. Merkin: "Which of us, to put it bluntly, would be happy to have our own deaths got over too quickly?" The Gerard Manley Hopkins poem Merkin quotes only in passing, "Spring and Fall," opens with a young girl contemplating a "goldengrove unleaving" (i.e., the falling, autumn leaves) and ends with that child awakening to the fact that someday she, too, will die ("it is Margaret you mourn for," writes Hopkins in the final line). Merkin's use of scale is similar: she transitions from the smallest, most particular of losses – the paisley scarf that is meant to be "draped, shawl-like, over (rather than under) a coat" – to a meditation on her fear of the final, largest, most abstract of losses: her self. The tone of the final sentence, even, is unapologetically childlike: "I want everything back," she says, refusing to stop the tantrum. Intelligent, vivid, and alert to its own delusions, Merkin's essay bears down upon the lost scarf until it yields emotional meaning; she shows that you can take the most trivial incident and blow it up until it becomes nothing less than a meditation on love and death.

Thernstrom obsesses over a David Smith sculpture her grandmother promised to give to her upon her death, but she never does, and it becomes clear that this truly horrible woman promises and rescinds the promise as a way to endlessly test and torture Melanie. We are in *King Lear* country. For Thernstrom, the sculpture represents the possibility of a life devoted to art – the sculpture is worth millions – whereas the grandmother wants to make sure that Melanie doesn't have more freedom to pursue art than she herself did. The great charm of this essay is its candor; Thernstrom doesn't lie about the reality of love and its relationship to money. She is emotionally naked, and she doesn't cover herself in moral clover. Her strength/her weakness is her endless ambivalence: Melanie both loves and doesn't love the grandmother; she both does and doesn't want the sculpture. The sculpture matters most to her as lost object, as would-be talisman, as salvation; it's not at all clear that it would have been worth as much as she thought it would. It's now sitting in the basement of the Cleveland Museum of Art, valued at four million dollars, and mislabeled.

Allen Woodman's wallet is also misplaced, misidentified; it's loaded up with debris – expired coupons, losing Lotto tickets, a stale fortune cookie fortune. The "worthless articles" in the old man's trick-wallet portray a life spent, dried up, laid to waste. In this case, the physical object is used as bait to recover something extremely intangible: the father's grasp on what remains of his own youth and verve. The son waits in the car, acting as his father's "wheelman," supporting him in his effort to recover this sense of vitality. In the end, the older man runs out of the mall, shouting for his son to "drive fast, drive fast," full of piss and vinegar. "There will be time enough for silence and rest," Woodman writes, echoing Andrew Marvell's call for action in "To His Coy Mistress": "Had we but world enough, and time, / This coyness, lady, were no crime / … But at my back I always hear / Time's winged chariot hurrying near; / And yonder all before us lie / Deserts of vast eternity." In Woodman's story, the father senses that "vast eternity" of death and makes off like a (literal) bandit, becoming the bad guy instead of the victim, which is more interesting/exciting/erotic than being good. There is no effort to recover lost objects (e.g., the real, pickpocketed wallet); rather, the attempt is to reenact and revise the crisis of loss – to disturb the universe rather than to play out "the same old story," as prophesied by the fortune in the stale cookie. It's when his father loses the wallet that the son is revivified, as is his love for his father. As is the father.

Perhaps it's wrong to say that we live through objects. Maybe we live most through *lost* objects, through the missing signifier. As Elizabeth Bishop wrote in her villanelle "One Art" – first sincerely and, by the final lines, with the sting of irony – "the art of losing isn't hard to master; / so many things seem filled with the intent / to be lost that their loss is no disaster." Consider writing your essay/story/prose poem about the object just out of reach. All four of these selections are very much about that.

George W. S. Trow

Within the Context of No Context (excerpt)

WHEN I WAS VERY YOUNG – FOUR YEARS OLD, THAT IS, and five – it was my habit in the late afternoon to stand at a window at the east end of the living room of my family's house, in Cos Cob, Connecticut, and wait for my father to come into view. My father commuted on the New Haven Railroad in those days, and walked home from the station. When I spotted him, I waved. I usually saw him before he saw me, because my eyesight was much better than his. When he saw me, he waved back and walked (I believe) at a faster pace until he was at our door. Once inside, he put down the bundle of newspapers he carried under his arm (my father, a newspaperman, brought home all three evening newspapers and, often, one or two of the morning papers as well), and hugged my mother. Then he took his fedora hat off his head and put it on mine.

It was assumed that I would have a fedora hat of my own by the time I was twelve years old. My father had had his first fedora hat at the age of nine, but he said he recognized that the circumstances of his bringing up had been different from the circumstances of mine (it was his opinion that his mother, my grandmother, had been excessively strict in the matter of dress), and he would not insist on anything inappropriate or embarrassing. He said that probably it would not be necessary for me to wear kid gloves during the day, ever. But certainly, he said, at the end of boyhood, when as a young man I would go on the New Haven Railroad to New York City, it would be necessary for me to wear a fedora hat.

I have, in fact, worn a fedora hat, but ironically. Irony has seeped into the felt of any fedora hat I have ever owned – not out of any wish of mine but out of necessity. A fedora hat worn by me without the necessary protective irony would eat through my head and kill me. I was born into the upper middle class in 1943, and one of the strange turns my life has taken is this: I was taught by my parents to believe that the traditional manners of the high bourgeoisie, properly acquired, would give me a certain dignity, which would protect me from embarrassment. It has turned out that I am able to do almost anything but act according to those modes – this because I deeply believe that those modes are suffused with an embarrassment so powerful that it can kill. It turns out that while I am at home in many strange places, I am not free even to visit the territory I was expected to inhabit effortlessly. To wear a fedora, I must first torture it out of shape so it can be cleaned of the embarrassment in it.

Daphne Merkin

Count Your Losses

SEVERAL WEEKS AGO I BRIEFLY CONSIDERED RISKING my life – or, at least, a limb or two – in order to retrieve a scarf I had left in the taxi that was just pulling away. I was with a friend, and the two of us had become engaged in a conversation about the Gulf War with our opinionated and well-informed driver. The scarf in question was newish, one of those vast challis paisleys that are meant to be draped, shawl-like, over (rather than under) a coat. I might add that it was the first such scarf I owned; prior to it, I had a drawer full of haphazardly gathered, skimpy silk squares, most of which I never wore.

I am in general not the sort of person to go in for elaborately conceived fashion, but having admired for some time the effect of almost military elegance that was achieved when women wore scarves this way, I decided I was ready to try it myself. I had just the coat for the purpose, too: a simple but well-styled black cashmere-and-wool with a shawl collar. The scarf had been purchased in one of those tiny, exquisitely organized stores that can seduce you into thinking it matters less what you wear than how you accessorize what you wear, and the scarf came in just the noncolor colors that I like: mustard and khaki and taupe, shades of dun, nothing too vivid, yet subtly enlivening.

I have traced the etiology of this object the better to convey the irrational significance of its loss. I ran after that cab for a good long stretch – across 79th Street and over to Fifth and then down a few blocks; I got honked at and sworn at as I raced fearlessly, without regard to red lights or oncoming traffic, toward my fast-disappearing scarf. I gave up only when I lost track of the cab in a sea of yellow. As I hurried back to my waiting friend, the foolish bravado of my effort struck me: my kingdom for a horse, maybe, but my life for a scarf? It didn't, on the surface, make sense.

It continued to not make sense when I, a native and therefore untrusting New Yorker, hung on the phone the next day trying to get in touch with the taxi lost and found. The ways of this establishment, for those who have never got in touch with it, are labyrinthine: when the Muzak finally stops and a living person comes on the line, it is only to inform you that there is no longer a general lost and found; anything left in a taxi has to be brought in to the police station closest to the drop-off point by the not only honest but deeply enterprising driver. Short of this highly unlikely sequence of events having taken place, I was welcome to arrange to come in to look at a photographic lineup of drivers.

No, I didn't make an appointment to study the physiognomy of thousands of Manhattan cabbies. I did, however, wend my way back to the store to check first if they had another of my scarf in stock, and then, with fading hope, if it could be reordered. (It couldn't.) If time is money, as the saying goes, the worth of my scarf had been expanded tenfold. Then again, it should be clear at this point in my mini-saga that we're not talking scarves. We're talking loss, the disappearance of anything – big or little, inanimate or human – that helps moor us in what George Eliot in *Middlemarch* called "the largeness of the world." To grieve over such a loss, one might say, is to grieve over all losses. I think what I must have had somewhere in mind as I bounded toward the taxi that sped along, oblivious to my scarf abandoned on the back seat, was an act of redemptive harakiri: if I could undo this one loss, I could undo all the losses I'd suffered. If I could have my scarf back, in its generous, enveloping softness, it was possible that nothing else was gone forever, either.

A list of the losses I've incurred in the past year or so would include, in no particular order of importance: a job; a pair of earrings; a piece of my work (the paperback copies of my novel were recently shredded); a literary mentor; that damn scarf; and one of my most kindred-spirited friends.

It could be argued that some of these were ordinary losses and that others were necessary, but what I know for certain is that sooner or later all of them – people and objects alike – will turn up, deep at night, scattered across my dreams. In dreams my friend is sitting on a beach chair again, discoursing avidly about books in his dry, humorous voice, and I am back in my office again, under the fluorescent lights, juggling calls, and there, plain as can be, folded neatly on a shelf, is my challis scarf. I have yet to have the perfect dream of retrieval, in which everything is found in one blissful spot, but there is always the next night.

For as long as I can remember, I have been an assiduous counter of losses – the sort of person who remembers, with a stab of pain, that which is missing. I realize, of course, that this sort of raging about a scarf strikes many people as incomprehensible. In that mental exercise whereby we try to divide people into arbitrary categories, I suggest a valid division would be those who cut their losses versus those who keen over them. For those of us who fit the latter category, every loss is tinged with mortality: the valence of a scarf, as weighed on the scales of the psyche, is not all that different from the valence of a worthier object; both are eligible for the Pantheon of Losses. Listen to one such implacable soul expound with poetic intensity on the loss of a pin – a pin, she is at pain to point out, that she bought for $30 at a "junky, secondhand shop": "I loved that pin. From the day I found it to the day I lost it, I was the happiest person. Ever since I lost it, I wander around looking for it." Given such longing, who's to argue the source?

As a rule, I tend to gravitate toward people who don't take even minor losses lightly, who fight and kick and scream. It seems to me that there is something admirable about their defiance. And yet, although there may be greater health in adapting to loss than in becoming fixated on it, in the end we have one loss self-protectively in mind. And which of us, to put it bluntly, would be happy to have our own deaths got over too quickly?

The world is full of wisdom – folk and otherwise – about how best to respond to loss, much of it hortatory in nature. And with good reason: the human condition is so full of spilled milk that if we cried too much each and every time, we'd never move on. Most of us have learned by adulthood to reserve our feelings of desolation for the really tragic losses – the deaths of loved ones most signally. It is only in very small children, who haven't yet caught on to the fact that losing and more losing is, as the poet Gerard Manley Hopkins said, "the blight man was born for," that we catch glimpses of our uninured primal selves, inconsolable over the most trivial of privations.

Some years ago, when I was a graduate student, a professor quoted a literary critic as follows: "The only paradises are lost paradises." I think the critic was French and that the reference was to Proust – who, God knows, is unbeatable as far as the plangent evocation of loss goes. In any case, liking the sound of it, I immediately wrote the quote down in my notebook. It's a line I recall often: I'm always looking for antidotes to my inborn nostalgia, and this seems as sprightly a perspective on the matter as any. Still, I'm not sure I believe it, or how much difference it makes. When I am dead and buried I suppose I shall not care at all about the red suede glove I dropped in Central Park 15 years ago. Meanwhile, I want everything back.

Melanie Thernstrom
The Inheritance That Got Away

IT WAS AT MY GRANDMOTHER'S MEMORIAL SERVICE THAT a friend of hers mentioned that my sculpture – the one my grandmother had always promised to leave me – was worth $4 million. It was one of the few moments in my life I found myself wordless. It was her memorial service! I already disliked how the service seemed to resemble an art opening, with toastlike speeches, projected slides of her work and wine and cheese in the Art Students League building. And now we were talking about money?

Yet, in the midst of the floating emotions of the hour, the different kinds of grief, love and disappointment, here was something new: a number. It was as if I had been looking at a paperweight snow globe watching miniature snow petals fall in the miniature world and suddenly someone had flipped it over and exposed the price tag. My sculpture had represented so many things, incorporating so many realms of feeling, but here was a meaning I hadn't contemplated. And I knew that no matter how much I tried to banish the thought and right the globe, it would never look the same again.

The first time Grandma Dorothy suggested she might not leave me my sculpture was in a French restaurant a few blocks from her lower Fifth Avenue apartment. It was a gay late-April evening. I had just arrived from upstate, where I was in graduate school, and my grandmother embodied for me all the glamour of Old New York life. We took a turn in Washington Square Park, and then, sitting in Café Loup, I watched the elegant 87-year-old drink a glass of Lillet. With her dancer's posture and flapper's haircut and a topaz brooch at her throat, she looked far too attractively lofty to be interested in her plate of spaghetti.

"I am thinking of leaving 'Dorothy Taking Bath in Wheelbarrow' to the Cleveland Museum of Art," she announced. "It's an extremely valuable piece, and there's a young curator there who'd love to have it."

My sculpture is a small bronze abstraction of my grandmother as a young woman bathing in a wheelbarrow. Her first husband, David Smith, made it in 1940 on their farm in the Adirondacks. It's a remarkable piece. The woman whose body forms the cup of the wheelbarrow is not wholly human. Her head bulges forward like an insect, and she has multiple arms and tentacles for breasts. The work seems to summarize the narrative of their stormy 23-year marriage: she wanted to be an artist, and he wanted her to be art. Throughout her life, the sculpture sat in the entrance hall of her apartment, surrounded by dried red leaves; it was the first thing and the last thing I'd see on my many visits there. And for as long as I could remember, I'd always thought of it as mine.

Dorothy Dehner was my mother's stepmother from the time my mother was a teenager – her wicked stepmother, Dorothy liked to say, with a wicked look. And although she did treat my mother shabbily, she always bestowed her best attentions on me. I was her favorite, her real relative, she often told me conspiratorially – the next bather in the wheelbarrow. At dinner that night, she mentioned my rival heir – the museum – so coyly, it sounded less like a decision than a ploy of some kind. But what kind?

Did she want me to beg her for it? To tell her that it was my favorite favorite thing, that my heart was set on it and could not be reset? Or was this more of a King Lear test: would insisting that I wanted nothing but love from her prove me worthy of the marvelous thing?

I was 23 then and fancied myself a Cordelia type. I was infatuated with the idea of renunciation. I was Della, who cut off her hair in "The Gift of the Magi" and received true love in return. I was not someone whose treasure was something rust and moths could find. (I was studying Marxist literary theory, after all.) But since, unlike my literary heroines, I was actually filled with resentment, my speech came out like a parody of renunciation.

"What a good idea!" I declared. "The people of Cleveland will appreciate it! Why put a cultural treasure in private hands? Just because I'm your granddaughter doesn't mean I'm entitled to anything." As a final flourish, I picked the check off the table, saying, "Oh, let me." The tab came to $84, I still recall. I took my time counting out the bills: a dollar for almost every year of her life. Loving her was like that, I thought: always having to pay for things that happened long before you were born.

The word "grandmother" has a noble ring. People – we like to think – improve with time. Older people are said to be at peace with their pasts, as memory loses its razor focus, blurring into an Impressionist painting of the happiest occasions and the best weather. Striving, vanity and ambition pass and are replaced by love – selfless love, charitas, giving. Had my head not been so stuffed with idealized grandmother images, I might have seen my grandmother for who she was.

Whenever I'd visit her, the light in her room would flicker on and off until dawn. She'd get up to pour herself Lillet. Her eyesight was failing; she no longer had books for company. A century of loss, she would sometimes say, the wars merging in her mind with the early death of her family. And this: two fortunes – large fortunes, belonging to the two central figures in her life – had slipped through her open fingers. She went over the details in her mind, again and again, telling herself she didn't care; some people care about money, but not Dorothy.

The first fortune belonged to her Aunt Cora. Dorothy was born in Cleveland to a wealthy old American family of Dutch and German heritage on Christmas Eve, 1901. Her parents and two siblings died by the time she was in her early teens, leaving her in the care of her maiden aunts – Flo, the kind one, and Cora, the terrible. Cora – the one she was close to – was a hot-tempered beauty involved in a long affair with a railroad baron who wouldn't leave his wife. Dorothy decided to become an actress and moved to New York to play an ingénue Off Broadway while she took classes at the Art Students League. At her boarding house she met David Smith, an aspiring artist from Decatur, Indiana.

"David was the first penniless man I married," Dorothy would say. "Your mother's father was the second. But I didn't care. My life wasn't about money – it was about art."

In all the times that she repeated this story, only once did I say, "But you had inherited money from your mother to live on."

"I sewed all our clothes at Bolton Landing! And grew vegetables and canned peaches and tomatoes while David sculpted."

It was clear to me, even as a teenager, that the sewing and growing were more ideology than necessity: they were Communists, like many of their peer group. (My grandmother always maintained that Stalin was the victim of unfair propaganda.) The income from her inheritance from her mother was always enough to live on, and even during the Depression, they never had to worry.

Their farmhouse on Lake George in the Adirondacks was landscaped with his colossal industrial-steel monuments. Dorothy wanted to make sculpture but didn't dare try while they were together. They visited the city frequently, hanging out at the Cedar Tavern with John Graham, Arshile Gorky, Adolph Gottlieb, Mark Rothko and Jackson Pollock – the whole macho gang of Abstract Expressionist pioneers. Dorothy was "one of the wives." "Oh, the wives!" she would say, with a sigh.

Like others in the gang, he had affairs. He began beating her, she said, and in 1951, when she was 50, she left him. Although she felt in his shadow professionally throughout her life, her work began to flower once she moved away. In her later years, her paintings and sculpture were sometimes clustered with other overlooked Abstract Expressionist-era wives like Lee Krasner and Elaine de Kooning.

After Dorothy left David, her Aunt Cora wanted her to move

back in with her. Cora was an extremely rich woman by this point. Her baron lover had died, leaving her his railroad millions. But Dorothy didn't want to - she had just gotten out from her husband's domination. Cora was very offended. When she died soon after, she left her entire fortune to a mentally disabled girl from a poor family who had been put in her care.

But Dorothy lost an even greater fortune from the Smith estate. Like his friend Pollock, David died driving his car off the road, and the art whose production she had supported all those years was immensely valuable. Everyone advised Dorothy - who had never accepted alimony - to contest the will. She had a few drawings and sculptures that David had given her, but he left the entirety of his estate to his two young daughters from his second marriage.

"I didn't want the money," she would tell me over and over and over. "My life is about art. Money means nothing to me, you see."

As I got older, I began to see, but I didn't tell her what I saw. Although she didn't need the money, the fact that the two most important people in her life had left her nothing kept her awake nights.

Most people's grandparents aren't wealthy; many people support their parents in their old age. My father's parents didn't have money, although his mother, my Grandma Bea, left me some very fine English blue-pansy china and an Art Deco diamond engagement ring that I wear now. Last year, I made the decision to use the china, too, and it makes me happy, several times a day. Since Bea didn't have money, money wasn't part of our relationship. And if my sculpture had been a teacup, maybe Grandma Dorothy would have given it to me. But when your teacups are David Smiths, what then?

From the night in the restaurant until the day she tumbled down some stairs to her death six years later, the fate of my sculpture was always an unspoken question. She seemed to toy with the idea of giving it to me, slipping sometimes into calling it "your sculpture," as in "Your sculpture has always been my favorite of all David's works." My heart would beat faster whenever she said this, but I steadfastly refused to respond. I knew she knew how badly I wanted it. I refuse to be manipulated, I told myself. I have pride. I don't care, I said, like Pierre to the lion.

This wasn't the first time I'd pretended not to care about something she owned. When I was in college, my grandmother's building went co-op, and she was offered the insider price on her apartment. But as it was rent-controlled and her payments wouldn't decrease, she didn't want to buy it. My mother suggested she and my father might want to purchase it for me to live in after Dorothy died. It was the apartment my mother had grown up in, in which her own mother had died. But Dorothy said no; she didn't like the idea of anything being lived in after her death – "or anybody living," my mother added sardonically when she told me the story. I remembered how stunned I was. I didn't say anything to my grandmother (the idea of "unseemliness" held such weight with me then), but I kept asking my mother if she could have misunderstood. Didn't Grandma want me to have a life like hers? A life in which – from the vantage point of an antique and art-filled cordial-stocked apartment on lower Fifth – I, too, could say all I cared about was my art, and creating it without commercial considerations. Hadn't she always told me I was her heir in all senses of the word?

I liked all the same – costly – things she did. I liked accompanying her to the summer Bach festival in Madeira. And I would have liked to pop into delightful little bistros every night of the week dressed in splashy fabulous or cool drapey clothing with Victorian jewelry. Or spend my first years of marriage in the Virgin Islands and in Europe, as she and David had, and then buy 86 acres upstate. And even though I was still in college then, I already knew it took a great deal of money for money to be no object at all.

Yet she was always Lady Bountiful to people outside her family. She was godmother, honorary aunt or grandmother to literally dozens of others. "So delightful," they would tell me. "And so generous!" She especially relished wooing my boyfriends. Some of her gestures toward them were so provocative that it was as if she was daring me to say something. My college boyfriend and I loved one watercolor she made in the '40s. It was a playful, feminine work of delicately sketched squares melting into clouds of orange and violet. "I'll give it to you as your wedding present," my grandmother would always say. We weren't engaged, so the remark annoyed and embarrassed me, but that was a grandmother's prerogative, my boyfriend said. She was mad for that boyfriend, a writer, and she constantly compared us with her and David (a comparison we never quite knew what to make of). When we broke up, he moved to the Adirondacks near where my grandmother and David had lived. When he married, she told me that she sent the painting to him and his new wife to hang over their kitchen table.

She was every bit as seductive with my graduate-school boyfriend. She'd put on red lipstick and African jewelry, serve Mumm in Art Deco glasses and play the piano, determined to be more fabulous than any grandmother he had ever met. And although my sculpture was already on the scales by then, she seemed to have no hesitation about giving him a watercolor. Other paintings went to subsequent boyfriends.

Then a couple of years after our dinner, something unusual happened. Grandma had promised a Smith painting to my mother when she was a graduate student, if she finished her dissertation. Nineteen years passed. My mother was now a professor, the author of several books. The work was large, with dark splashes of paint resembling a flock of angry, impersonal birds. My mother didn't especially admire it – she had, in fact, taken a dislike to modern art per se, and defiantly decorated her own walls with representational work my grandmother sniffed at. But she felt cheated. The slight grew in her mind, symbolizing all the ways the relationship had duped her. Finally, during a visit, she did something radical: she asked for it. And Grandma gave it to her.

Why didn't I just ask for my sculpture? I wondered at the time. Why didn't I plead or argue or even get angry, and acknowledge what Grandma never would – that priceless art has a price and she had power for having it? While I knew she wanted me to ask, I didn't want to have to. I wanted her to have the kind of love that would make her want to give it to me.

But tests of love always end badly. Cordelia didn't get what she wanted. When I read "The Gift of the Magi" now, it seems to me a story about loss. I thought my grandmother was the one with the misbegotten tests, but I was testing her, too, with my silence.

Sometime around a year before she died, my grandmother was hospitalized for several weeks. I must have been 28 or 29, teaching in Boston. I was quite withdrawn from her by then. Although I called her every week and visited every month or two, I kept my boyfriends away and met my friends on the street rather than taking them in to meet her. My presents became cheap. On her 90th birthday, one of her godsons sent her 90 pink roses; I picked up my bouquet at the corner grocer.

She looked small in the hospital bed that day; her sightless blue eyes stood out against her pale hospital gown. I hadn't thought she had noticed the change in our relationship, so I was surprised when she said plaintively: "Remember how you wanted to be just like me! You adored me."

"I love you," I said in a voice that doubtless revealed exactly what that love had become: a fact, not a joy.

"But it's different now," she said. "You don't look up to me anymore."

I was startled. I hadn't known she was capable of such emotional honesty. Just when I thought we were getting somewhere, she interjected: "Do you want the sculpture? Take it, really. Take it home with you tomorrow."

She is trying to bribe me, I thought – as in one of those deathbed conversions priests used to indulge for a price. I was staying in her apartment to visit her in the hospital; I had looked at it just that morning, and the bather looked more like a praying mantis than a woman. I could go back right now and stuff it in my backpack, I thought. But she might change her mind when she recovered, and I'd be stuck taking it back on the train, tricked again.

"Forget it," I said. "I don't want it."

"You didn't really want the sculpture, anyway," my boyfriend at the time tried to console me after her lawyer called and informed me what was in the will. The will called for her money to be divided among family members (I've blocked out the exact amount that I received, but I think it was around $30,000), but she had left the art – including her own work – to charity and museums. The codicil that had given my sculpture to the museum had been added only that year – after the conversation in the hospital. I was crushed. I was also upset at myself for being upset about the will. I felt degraded by thoughts of money in the midst of mourning. And although the way toward the will had been a long one, I still didn't really understand how she had arrived there. Everyone had theories.

"While she identified with your creativity, she was also competitive with you," my mother suggested.

"She wanted you to write about her, but you were always writing about something else," a friend of hers commented.

"You only wanted the sculpture because it had sentimental value," my boyfriend insisted. "What you really wanted was your grandmother's love," as if the two were separable. When she was alive, I would have said the same thing, but now the words rang false. They sounded, I realized, like the very pieties that kept me from getting – or even trying to get – my sculpture.

It amazes me now that I never wondered what it was worth, but I had thoroughly internalized the taboo against drawing any connections between love and money. It's a curiously modern taboo – you can hardly find a 19th-century novel whose subject is not the thickness of that very connection.

Yet as soon as I found out the sculpture's worth, its meaning metamorphosed. Suddenly I wanted the sculpture not only for the sentiment but also for the freedom it could have bought me – especially because, as it turns out, I, too, am marrying an impoverished artist.

If the woman at the memorial service was correct and my

sculpture was really worth $4 million (while some of Smith's work has sold for millions, others have sold for hundreds or tens of thousands), I'm certain now that I would have sold it. I would have sold it and used the money to finance my life – my writing and my fiancé's art – because my future is more important to me than her past.

I think sometimes about the life I could have had – the life my grandmother had – if I simply had said yes that day in the hospital. Especially if I had asked for the large, lower Fifth Avenue, classic-six, prewar, doorman, original-molding, million-dollar apartment. Might she have given me that as well? I could have sold it, bought a loft with my fiancé in Williamsburg, where real artists live, and lived on the difference. What if I had talked her into throwing in some of her art collection, which included an unusual Smith oil that also went to the Cleveland Museum of Art and an outstanding John Graham that went to the Phillips Collection in Washington? I could have sold all that and kept the apartment and my sculpture. Then my beautiful sculpture would be sitting in the entrance hall just where it always was, instead of in its final resting place: in permanent storage – mistitled "Bather" – in the basement of the Cleveland Museum.

Allen Woodman
Wallet

TIRED OF LOSING HIS WALLET TO PICKPOCKETS, MY father, at seventy, makes a phony one. He stuffs the phony wallet with expired food coupons and losing Florida Lottery tickets and a fortune cookie fortune that reads, "Life is the same old story told over and over."

In a full-length mirror, he tries the wallet in the back pocket of his pants. It hangs out fat with desire. "All oyster," he says to me, "no pearl."

We drive to the mall where he says he lost the last one. I am the wheelman, left behind in the car, while my father cases a department store.

He is an old man trying to act feeble and childlike, and he overdoes it like stage makeup on a community-theater actor. He has even brought a walking stick for special effect. Packages of stretch socks clumsily slip from his fingers. He bends over farther than he has bent in years to retrieve them, allowing the false billfold to rise like a dark wish and be grappled by the passing shadow of a hand.

Then the unexpected happens. The thief is chased by an attentive salesclerk. Others join in. The thief subdued, the clerk holds up the reclaimed item. "Your wallet, sir. Your wallet." As she begins opening it, searching for identification, my father runs toward an exit. The worthless articles float to the floor.

Now my father is in the car, shouting for me to drive away. There will be time enough for silence and rest. We are both stupid with smiles and he is shouting, "Drive fast, drive fast."

2. Prose Poem

You are neither an infant nor a child. You are a toddler, betwixt and between.

Prose Poem

THE PROSE POEM (A TRICKY CONTRADICTION IN TERMS) looks like prose but sounds like poetry; it tends, to an uncanny degree, to both embody and explore paradox.

Along with other French symbolist poets, Charles Baudelaire is thought to have innovated the prose poem form as we understand (or struggle to understand) it today. In 1869, he wrote, "Which of us, in his ambitious moments, has not dreamed of the miracle of a poetic prose, musical, without rhyme and without rhythm, supple enough and rugged enough to adapt itself to the lyrical impulses of the soul, the undulations of the psyche, the prickings of consciousness." In his introduction to the anthology *Great American Prose Poems: From Poe to the Present*, David Lehman describes how the prose canvas became a particular kind of refuge for the poet burdened by poetry: "Liberated from the implacable requirements of formal French verse, Baudelaire wrote with a sort of infernal energy that the prose medium helped release."

The birth of prose poetry sounds not unlike the birth of modern dance, the originators of which enacted a rebellion against the constraints of classical ballet – abandoning the duck-like, outward rotation of the hips, permitting the feet to flex, chucking the stiff, satin pointe shoes – while retaining techniques from the mother form. Lehman writes, "As soon as you admit the possibility that verse is an adjunct of poetry and not an indispensable quality, the prose poem ceases to be a contradiction of terms. Verse and prose are the real antonyms."

Russell Edson says that prose poetry appeals to him because "it is a poetry freed from the definition of poetry, and a prose free of the necessity of fiction." According to Sarah Manguso, Edson's prose poems exemplify defining techniques of the genre, such as inappropriate understatement, omission, and restraint; inappropriate loquacity or overwriting; use of incorrect reasoning/illogic; and failure to accumulate sense. While the prose poem isn't properly a poem – written, as it is, in sentences rather than lines – it isn't proper prose, either. More like prose behaving badly. For Edson, it's "a small, complete work, utterly logical within its own madness."

Madden us with your own prose poem, 500 words at the most. In honor of the hybrid spirit of the form, stage your prose poem in such a way that you get at what is to you one of life's crucial paradoxes.

In "The Poet's Husband," Molly Giles first evokes what we think is the boorish husband of what we assume is going to be the sensitive poet – embodiments as it were of the prosaic and the poetic, respectively; Giles then evokes the insipid solipsism of the poet, proceeding to sketch each of them in his or her moment of vulnerability, need, love; and at the end of the story, we see the husband looking through the smudged windowpane (which his wife has cleaned desultorily) at the moon. Is he acting boorishly again, or is he – with his "clear eyes that don't blink" – the poet? If so, what does that make her?

In Jamaica Kincaid's "Girl," a Caribbean mother advises her daughter to behave and misbehave, especially toward her colonial overseers; she chastises her and caresses her; the monologue is spoken by the mother, but the daughter occasionally interrupts. Kincaid writes with the kind of "infernal energy" Lehman ascribes to Baudelaire. The language seems possessed of some inner, lyrical contagion. Certain nouns and imperative phrases catch in the flow of the mother's litany and, sentence by sentence, are carried feverishly down the page: "This is how to make a bread pudding; this is how to make a doukona; this is how to make pepper pot;

this is how to make a good medicine for a cold; this is how to make a good medicine to throw away a child before it even becomes a child." Kincaid merges literal-minded instruction (how to cook) with more threatening instruction (how to be or not be a slut), which creates vertigo in the listener and in the reader. Everything seems fraught; all instruction comes to seem dangerous. The mother transmits this "wisdom" at a pace that feels unstoppable. Have we come here to bury the daughter or praise her, save her or doom her?

Jayne Anne Phillips's "Stripper" is an erotic dirge about the terror and error of eros, an ode to and protest against experience's inevitable violation of innocence. Notice how brilliantly Phillips threads black-and-white imagery throughout the story, how related this is to innocence and knowledge, and how pitilessly she connects this to the psychology of sex underlying father-daughter love ("Every daddy wants his daughter," cousin Phoebe instructs during the opening scene). In the last section, Phillips breaks from prose into spooky song lyrics – "Baby stick em up Baby don't touch … I got you Baby I got you Let go" – that evoke the lover as the child, and vice versa.

Flat, legalistic, mathematical, pointy-edged: Lydia Davis's "The Old Dictionary" is a witty, acerbic dissection of the extraordinary care the speaker takes with her dictionary, as compared to the relative carelessness with which she treats people (especially her son) and other objects (especially plants).

Distance, apparently, is a crucial vector on love's grid. When Davis writes, coolly, "The plants make one or two demands," she is consciously crafting a chilly voice; you are meant to be struck by the speaker's detachment from the creatures she cares for, to understand that she is probably not the kind of person – unlike your editors – who would try to perk up houseplants with a little Mozart concerto.

Invoking her own curiously inverted Darwinian ladder of living (and inanimate) things, Davis's narrator launches into a meditation on the difficulties of love. Perhaps for her it is more challenging to love life than language. It seems that you're meant not to hate her but to find her slightly tragic in the way that you find yourself slightly tragic.

What is James Tate's "Desperate Talk" – revolutionary manifesto, anti-revolutionary manifesto, deism, deicide, praise-song to paradox? In this poem, Jasper and the narrator begin by believing in revolution; they then accept that the revolution is flawed, then doomed; they go on to acknowledge the tendency of revolutions and people to self-destruct; they wind up believing in no utopias, including God or heaven. Kant: "Out of the crooked timber of humanity, nothing straight was ever made."

Molly Giles

The Poet's Husband

HE SITS IN THE FRONT ROW, LARGE, A LARGE MAN WITH large hands and large ears, dry lips, fresh-cut hair, pink skin, clear eyes that don't blink, a nice man, calm, that's the impression he gives, a quiet man who knows how to listen; he is listening now as she sways on the stage in a short black dress and reads one poem about the time she slit her wrists and another poem about a man she still sees and a third poem about a cruel thing he himself said to her six years ago that she never forgot and never understood, and he knows that when she is finished everyone will clap and a few, mostly women, will come up and kiss her, and she will drink far too much wine, far too quickly, and all the way home she will ask, "What did you think, what did you really think?" and he will say, "I think it went very well" – which is, in fact, what he does think – but later that night, when she is asleep, he will lie in their bed and stare at the moon through a spot on the glass that she missed.

Jamaica Kincaid

Girl

WASH THE WHITE CLOTHES ON MONDAY AND PUT THEM
on the stone heap; wash the color clothes on Tuesday and put
them on the clothesline to dry; don't walk barehead in the hot sun;
cook pumpkin fritters in very hot sweet oil; soak your little cloths
right after you take them off; when buying cotton to make yourself a nice blouse, be sure that it doesn't have gum on it, because
that way it won't hold up well after a wash; soak salt fish overnight
before you cook it; is it true that you sing benna in Sunday school?;
always eat your food in such a way that it won't turn someone else's
stomach; on Sundays try to walk like a lady and not like the slut
you are so bent on becoming; don't sing benna in Sunday school;
you mustn't speak to wharf-rat boys, not even to give directions;
don't eat fruits on the street – flies will follow you; *but I don't sing
benna on Sundays at all and never in Sunday school*; this is how to
sew on a button; this is how to make a button-hole for the button
you have just sewed on; this is how to hem a dress when you see
the hem coming down and so to prevent yourself from looking
like the slut I know you are so bent on becoming; this is how you
iron your father's khaki shirt so that it doesn't have a crease; this
is how you iron your father's khaki pants so that they don't have
a crease; this is how you grow okra – far from the house, because
okra tree harbors red ants; when you are growing dasheen, make
sure it gets plenty of water or else it makes your throat itch when
you are eating it; this is how you sweep a corner; this is how you
sweep a whole house; this is how you sweep a yard; this is how you

smile at someone you don't like too much; this is how you smile at someone you don't like at all; this is how you smile to someone you like completely; this is how you set a table for tea; this is how you set a table for dinner; this is how you set a table for dinner with an important guest; this is how you set a table for lunch; this is how you set a table for breakfast; this is how to behave in the presence of men who don't know you very well, and this way they won't recognize immediately the slut I have warned you against becoming; be sure to wash every day, even if it is with your own spit; don't squat down to play marbles – you are not a boy, you know; don't pick people's flowers – you might catch something; don't throw stones at blackbirds, because it might not be a blackbird at all; this is how to make a bread pudding; this is how to make doukona; this is how to make pepper pot; this is how to make a good medicine for a cold; this is how to make a good medicine to throw away a child before it even becomes a child; this is how to catch a fish; this is how to throw back a fish you don't like, and that way something bad won't fall on you; this is how to bully a man; this is how a man bullies you; this is how to love a man; and if this doesn't work there are other ways, and if they don't work don't feel too bad about giving up; this is how to spit up in the air if you feel like it, and this is how to move quick so that it doesn't fall on you; this is how to make ends meet; always squeeze bread to make sure it's fresh; *but what if the baker won't let me feel the bread?*; you mean to say that after all you are really going to be the kind of woman who the baker won't let near the bread?

Jayne Anne Phillips
Stripper

WHEN I WAS FIFTEEN BACK IN CHARLESTON, MY COUSIN
Phoebe taught me to strip. She was older than my mother but she
had some body. When I watched her she'd laugh, say That's all right
Honey sex is sex. It don't matter if you do it with monkeys. Yeah
she said. You're white an dewy an tickin like a time bomb an now's
the time to learn. With that long blond hair you can't lose. An don't
you paint your face till you have to, every daddy wants his daughter.
That's what she said. The older dancers wear makeup an love the
floor, touchin themselves. The men get scared an cluster round,
smokin like paper on a slow fire. Once in Laramie I was in one of
those spotted motels after a show an a man's shadow fell across
the window. I could smell him past the shade, hopeless an crack-
lin like a whip. He scared me, like I had a brother who wasn't right
found a bullwhip in the shed. He used to take it out some days and
come back with such a look on his face. I don't wanna know what
they know. I went into the bathroom an stood in the fluorescent
light. Those toilets have a white strip across em that you have to rip
off. I left it on an sat down. I brushed my hair an counted. Counted
till he walked away kickin gravel in the parkin lot. Now I'm feelin
his shadow fall across stages in Denver an Cheyenne. I close my
eyes an dance faster, like I used to dance blind an happy in Pop's
closet. His suits hangin faceless on the racks with their big woolly
arms empty. I play five clubs a week, $150 first place. I dance three
sets each against five other girls. We pick jukebox songs while the
owner does his gig on the mike. Now Marlene's gonna slip ya into

a little darkness Let's get her up there with a big hand. The big hands clap an I walk the bar all shaven an smooth, rhinestoned velvet on my crotch. Don't ever show em a curly hair Phoebe told me, Angels don't have no curly hair. That's what she said. Beggin, they're starin up my white legs. That jukebox is cookin an they feel their fingers in me. Honey you know it ain't fair what you do Oh tell me why love is a lie jus like a ball an chain. Yeah I'm a white leather dream in a cowboy hat, a ranger with fringed breasts. Baby stick em up Baby don't touch Baby I'm a star an you are dyin. Better find a soft blond god to take you down. I got you Baby I got you Let go.

Lydia Davis
The Old Dictionary

I HAVE AN OLD DICTIONARY, ABOUT ONE HUNDRED AND twenty years old, that I need to use for a particular piece of work I'm doing this year. Its pages are brownish in the margins and brittle, and very large. I risk tearing them when I turn them. When I open the dictionary I also risk tearing the spine, which is already split more than halfway up. I have to decide, each time I think of consulting it, whether it is worth damaging the book further in order to look up a particular word. Since I need to use it for this work, I know I will damage it, if not today, then tomorrow, and that by the time I am done with this work it will be in poorer condition than it was when I started, if not completely ruined. When I took it off the shelf today, though, I realized that I treat it with a good deal more care than I treat my young son. Each time I handle it, I take the greatest care not to harm it: my primary concern is not to harm it. What struck me today was that even though my son should be more important to me than my old dictionary, I can't say that each time I deal with my son, my primary concern is not to harm him. My primary concern is almost always something else, for instance to find out what his homework is, or to get supper on the table, or to finish a phone conversation. If he gets harmed in the process, that doesn't seem to matter to me as much as getting the thing done, whatever it is. Why don't I treat my son at least as well as the old dictionary? Maybe it is because the dictionary is so obviously fragile. When a corner of a page snaps off, it is unmistakable. My son does not look fragile, bending over a game or manhandling the dog. Certainly his body is strong and flexible, and is not easily harmed by me. I have bruised his body and then it has healed. Sometimes it is obvious to me when I have hurt his feelings, but it is harder to see how badly they have been hurt, and they seem to mend. It is hard to see if they mend completely or are forever slightly damaged. When the dictionary is hurt, it can't be mended. Maybe I treat the dictionary better because it makes no demands on me, and doesn't fight back. Maybe I am kinder to things that don't seem to react to me. But in fact my houseplants do not seem to react much and yet I don't treat them very well. The plants make one or two demands. Their demand for light has already been satisfied by where I put them. Their second demand is for water. I water them but not regularly. Some of them don't grow very well because of that and some of them die. Most of them are strange-looking rather than nice-looking. Some of them were nice-looking when I bought them but are strange-looking now because I haven't taken very good care of them. Most of them are in pots that are the same ugly plastic pots they came in. I don't actually like them very much. Is there any other reason to like a houseplant, if it is not nice-looking? Am I kinder to something that is nice-looking? But I could treat a plant well even if I didn't like its looks. I should be able to treat my son well when he is not looking good and even when he is not acting very nice. I treat the dog better than the plants, even though he is more active and more demanding. It is simple to give him food and water. I take him for walks, though not often enough. I have also sometimes slapped his nose, though the vet told me never to hit him anywhere near the head, or maybe he said anywhere at all. I am only sure I am not neglecting the dog when he is asleep. Maybe I am kinder to things that are not alive. Or rather if they are not alive there is no question of kindness. It does not hurt them if I don't pay attention to them, and that is a great relief. It is such a relief it is even a pleasure. The only change they show is that they gather dust. The dust won't really hurt them. I can even get someone else to dust them. My son gets dirty, and I can't clean him, and I can't pay someone to clean him. It is hard to keep him clean, and even complicated trying to feed him. He doesn't sleep enough, partly because I try so hard to get him to sleep. The plants need two things, or maybe three. The dog needs five or six things. It is very clear how many things I am giving him and how many I am not, therefore how well I'm taking care of him. My son needs many other things besides what he needs for his physical care, and these things multiply or change constantly. They can change right in the middle of a sentence. Though I often know, I do not always know just what he needs. Even when I know, I am not always able to give it to him. Many times each day I do not give him what he needs. Some of what I do for the old dictionary, though not all, I could do for my son. For instance, I handle it slowly, deliberately, and gently. I consider its age. I treat it with respect. I stop and think before I use it. I know its limitations. I do not encourage it to go farther than it can go (for instance to lie open flat on the table). I leave it alone a good deal of the time.

James Tate

Desperate Talk

I ASKED JASPER IF HE HAD ANY IDEAS ABOUT THE COMING revolution. "I didn't know there was a revolution coming," he said. "Well, people are pretty disgusted. There might be," I said. "I wish you wouldn't just make things up. You're always trying to fool with me," he said. "There are soldiers everywhere. It's hard to tell which side they're on," I said. "They're against us. Everyone's against us. Isn't that what you believe?" he said. "Not everyone. There are still a few misguided stragglers who still believe in something or other," I said. "Well, that gives me heart," he said. "Never give up the faith," I said. "Who said I ever had any?" he said. "Shame on you, Jasper, it's important to believe in the cause," I said. "The cause of you digging us deeper into a hole?" he said. "No, the cause of people standing together for their rights, freedom and all," I said. "Well, that's long gone. We have no rights," he said. We fell silent for the next few minutes. I was staring out the window at a rabbit in the yard. Finally I said, "I was saying all that just to amuse you." "So was I," he said. "Do you believe in God?" I said. "God's in prison," he said. "What'd he do?" I said. "Everything," he said.

3. Image Becomes Metaphor

Enter early spring. Twigs and buds emerge. You are preadolescent.

Robin Hemley	Riding the Whip
Mary Robison	Pretty Ice

Image Becomes Metaphor

THE WORD "METAPHOR" COMES FROM THE GREEK WORD *metapherein*, meaning to transfer, to carry, to bear. In the classic, epiphany-based short story, there is a text, or plot, beneath which plays subtext or subplot. By story's end, the dominant image takes on a metaphorical property – that is, it becomes theme-carrying. Subtext penetrates the surface; the story's "aboutness" outs: plot and theme come together. This is precisely what happens in "Riding the Whip" and "Pretty Ice," but unlike in longer stories, the transformation happens so quickly that it feels to the reader less like watching your garden grow and more like a time-lapse film of flowers shooting up from the ground and blossoming all at once.

In "Riding the Whip," Jay, a boy who seems to be about twelve, is taken to a carnival by Rita, fifteen, and her aunt, Natalie, to distract him from the fact that his older sister lies in a hospital room after attempting suicide (she dies the next day). Whereas – for the sake of creating conventional suspense – another writer might have withheld for a while the cringe-worthy circumstances of Jay's visit to the carnival, Hemley conveys that information in the first two sentences. He begins at the dramatic pinnacle and then moves quietly and rapidly *away* from it (that is, away from the theatrics of plot).

When at first Jay tries to present heroically for Rita, on whom he has a crush, he says, "This Ferris wheel was so tame and small. There was nothing to be afraid of at fifty feet." (T. S. Eliot: "I will show you fear in a handful of dust.") Although for Jay there's plenty to be afraid of at fifty inches, he claims to be having "too much fun," and yet he knows he "shouldn't be." He and Rita go on a ride called The Whip. "That didn't make any sense to me. A whip wasn't something you rode. It was something to hurt you, something from movies that came down hard on prisoners' backs and left them scarred." It's crucial that the story is framed from the child's perspective; if the boy understood the situation correctly, the whip metaphor would seem rather blunt and it would ruin things. Here, via Jay's initial misunderstanding, Hemley sets up the final moments of the story. Jay wants to punish himself to expiate the guilt he feels as well as his intense identification with his sister, his terror that he's destined to become her. "In the middle of the ride something grazed my head. There was a metal bar hanging loose along one of the corners, and each time we whipped around it, the bar touched me. It barely hit me, but going so fast it felt like I was being knocked with a sandbag. It didn't hit anyone else, just me, and I tried several times to get out of the way, but I was strapped in, and there was no way to avoid it." He protests too much: it hits him because he wants it to hit him.

Rita looks at him as if he might see things through the same distorted lens his sister does. He bluffs, overplaying the gesture: "I don't even care what happens to her."

Crucially, Jay returns to the ride for more self-inflicted wounds: "I found the same seat. I knew which one it was because it was more beat up than the rest, with several gashes in its cushion, as though someone had taken a long knife and scarred it that way on purpose." We've come full circle: a whip *is* something to hurt you; it comes down hard on Jay's head, and it leaves him scarred, which is how Jay needs it to be. There is also more than a suggestion that Jay is a secret sharer with other masochists. "The man strapped us into our seat," Jay says, as he and Rita first mount the ride. That possessive pronoun will become universal in scope: certain others will mysteriously find this ride, this seat, this gash – in the seat and themselves. The Whip has become the story's very meaning; the image has become a metaphor.

In Mary Robison's "Pretty Ice," the protagonist, Belle (a beauty lacking a beast to unlock her), is also recovering from a suicide – her father's, fourteen years earlier. Her fiancé is arriving soon to visit, but what she's all atwitter about is finishing her taxes. She rails against her mother and her fiancé; she studies music, but she can't play, just as Will, her will-less fiancé, studies botany but can't get anything to grow. Both he and she are bereft of the creative principle, as opposed to her mother and her father, coincidentally also named William, though decidedly a grown-up version of the younger. Of course, the literal difference between the names "Will" and "William" is that crucial "I am," syllables that imply what Belle isn't – her light, her presence of being, having gone out permanently at age twenty, when her father shot himself in the dance studio.

He was larger than life, literally so; a tall billboard still advertises his studio, showing "a man in a tuxedo waltzing with a woman in an evening gown. I was always sure it was a waltz ... They [her father and mother] were both handsome – mannequins, a pair of dolls who had spent half their lives in evening clothes." Now, Belle (her mother is/was the true beauty) yearns for the large car her father used to drive, loves maps and atlases (though she herself doesn't drive), and wishes Will had put on a better shirt; she also notices the pen marks near his mouth, his lank hair, and his mittened hand, and sees that he has put on weight, girlishly, around his hips. It seems as if, when they finally meet at the train station, she can barely bring herself to touch the man she is planning to marry. "I let him kiss me," she says, indicating not an ounce of lust or even affection. In contrast to Belle's ice queen-ish passivity, her more vigorous mother greets Will by getting up on tiptoes and giving him a kiss.

Absolutely nothing happens in the story, and yet it closes as surely as a jewel box does. How does it do this? By the way in which the snow and ice move from white noise in the background to the story's main music. "My yard was a frozen pond ... The tires whined for an instant on the old snow ... Mother steered the car through some small windblown snow dunes and down the entrance ramp ... We passed a group of paper boys who were riding bikes with saddlebags. They were going slow, because of the ice." All of this is wallpaper. But then: "Behind the gates there was a frozen pond, where a single early-morning skater was skating backwards, expertly crossing his blades." This is the narrator, who is trapped in the past. The snow-and-ice imagery has gathered all the force of the narrator's inability to ever rejoin the flow of life following her father's suicide.

At the very end, Belle's mother says, "I know everybody complains, but I think an ice storm is a beautiful thing."

"It is pretty," Belle says.

Will says, "It'll make a bad-looking spring. A lot of shrubs get damaged and turn brown, and the trees don't blossom right."

The narrator concludes, "For once I agreed with my mother. Everything was in place, the way it was supposed to be, quiet and holding still."

In the very movement of the snow-and-ice-imagery, Robison masterfully tracks Belle's enclosure: she wants that bigger-than-life life back, and not able to retrieve it, she is forever encased in ice.

Write a brief story or essay (no longer than 1,000 words) in which you move background to foreground: create an image, develop the image into a motif, then "pay out" the image at the end as metaphor, as meaning. This assignment is similar to the one for "Object," except the image or object you choose is now in dynamic movement.

Robin Hemley
Riding the Whip

THE NIGHT BEFORE MY SISTER DIED, A FRIEND OF MY parents, Natalie Ganzer, took me and her niece to a carnival. I couldn't stand Natalie, but I fell in love with the niece, a girl about fifteen, named Rita. On the Ferris wheel Rita grabbed my hand. On any other ride I would have thought she was only frightened and wanted security. But this Ferris wheel was so tame and small. There was nothing to be afraid of at fifty feet.

When we got down and the man let us out of the basket, I kept holding Rita's hand, and she didn't seem to mind.

"Oh, I'm so glad you children are enjoying the evening," said Natalie. "It's so festive. There's nothing like a carnival, is there?"

Normally, I would have minded being called a child, but not tonight. Things were improving. There was nothing to worry about, my mother had told me over the phone earlier that evening. Yes, Julie had done a stupid thing, but only to get attention.

Still, there was something wrong, something that bugged me about that night, where I was, the carnival and its sounds. I was having too much fun and I knew I shouldn't be. Already, I had won a stuffed animal from one of the booths and given it to Rita. And usually I got nauseated on rides, but tonight they just made me laugh. Red neon swirled around on the rides and barkers yelled at us on the fairway. Popguns blew holes in targets, and there were so many people screaming and laughing that I could hardly take it in. I just stood there feeling everyone else's fun moving through me, and I could hardly hear what Rita and Natalie were asking me.

"Come on, Jay," shouted Rita. My hand was being tugged. "Let's ride The Whip." The whip. That didn't make any sense to me. A whip wasn't something you rode. It was something to hurt you, something from movies that came down hard on prisoners' backs and left them scarred.

"You can't ride a whip," I shouted to her over the noise.

She laughed and said, "Why not? Don't be scared. You won't get sick. I promise."

"Aren't you having fun, Jay?" Natalie asked. "Your parents want you to have fun, and I'm sure that's what Julie wants, too."

I didn't answer, though I was having fun. Things seemed brighter and louder than a moment before. I could even hear a girl on the Ferris wheel say to someone, "You're cute, did you know that?" One carny in his booth stood out like a detail in a giant painting. He held a bunch of strings in his hand. The strings led to some stuffed animals. "Everyone's a winner," he said.

The carnival was just a painting, a bunch of petals in a bowl, which made me think of Julie. She was an artist and painted still lifes mostly, but she didn't think she was any good. My parents had discouraged her, but I bought a large painting of hers once with some paper money I cut from a notebook. A week before the carnival, she came into my room and slashed the painting to bits. "She's not herself," my mother told me. "You know she loves you."

Now we stood at the gates of The Whip. Rita gave her stuffed animal to Natalie, who stood there holding it by the paw as though it were a new ward of hers. The man strapped us into our seat and Rita said to me, "You're so quiet. Aren't you having fun?"

"Sure," I said. "Doesn't it look like it?"

"Your sister's crazy, isn't she?" asked Rita. "I mean, doing what she did."

I knew I shouldn't answer her, that I should step out of the ride and go home.

"She just sees things differently," I said.

"What do you mean?" Rita asked. She was looking at me

strangely, as though maybe I saw things differently, too. I didn't want to see differently. I didn't want to become like my sister.

"Sure she's crazy," I said. "I don't even care what happens to her."

Then the ride started up and we laughed and screamed. We moved like we weren't people anymore, but changed into electrical currents charging from different sources.

In the middle of the ride something grazed my head. There was a metal bar hanging loose along one of the corners, and each time we whipped around it, the bar touched me. It barely hit me, but going so fast it felt like I was being knocked with a sandbag. It didn't hit anyone else, just me, and I tried several times to get out of the way, but I was strapped in, and there was no way to avoid it.

At the end of the ride I was totally punch-drunk and I could barely speak. Rita, who mistook my expression for one of pleasure, led me over to Natalie.

"That was fun," said Rita. "Let's go on The Cat and Mouse now."

My vision was blurry and my legs were wobbling a bit. "I want to go on The Whip again," I said.

Natalie and Rita looked at each other. Natalie reached out toward my head, and I pulled back from her touch. "You're *bleeding*, Jay," she said. Her hand stayed in mid-air, and she looked at me as though she were someone in a gallery trying to get a better perspective on a curious painting.

I broke away from them into the crowd and made my way back to The Whip. After paying the man I found the same seat. I knew which one it was because it was more beat up than the rest, with several gashes in its cushion, as though someone had taken a long knife and scarred it that way on purpose.

Mary Robison
Pretty Ice

I WAS UP THE WHOLE NIGHT BEFORE MY FIANCÉ WAS due to arrive from the East – drinking coffee, restless and pacing, my ears ringing. When the television signed off, I sat down with a packet of the month's bills and figured amounts on a lined tally sheet in my checkbook. Under the spray of a high-intensity lamp, my left hand moved rapidly over the touch tablets of my calculator.

Will, my fiancé, was coming from Boston on the six-fifty train – the dawn train, the only train that still stopped in the small Ohio city where I lived. At six-fifteen I was still at my accounts; I was getting some pleasure from transcribing the squarish green figures that appeared in the window of my calculator. "Schwab Dental Clinic," I printed in a raveled backhand. "Thirty-eight and 50/100."

A car horn interrupted me. I looked over my desktop and out the living-room window of my rented house. The saplings in my little yard were encased in ice. There had been snow all week, and then an ice storm. In the glimmering driveway in front of my garage, my mother was peering out of her car. I got up and turned off my lamp and capped my ivory Mont Blanc pen. I found a coat in the semidark in the hall, and wound a knitted muffler at my throat. Crossing the living room, I looked away from the big pine mirror; I didn't want to see how my face and hair looked after a night of accounting.

My yard was a frozen pond, and I was careful on the walkway. My mother hit her horn again. Frozen slush came through the toe of one of my chukka boots, and I stopped on the path and frowned at her. I could see her breath rolling away in clouds from the cranked-down window of her Mazda. I have never owned a car nor learned to drive, but I had a low opinion of my mother's compact. My father and I used to enjoy big cars, with tops that came down. We were both tall and we wanted what he called "stretch room." My father had been dead for fourteen years, but I resented my mother's buying a car in which he would not have fitted.

"Now what's wrong? Are you coming?" my mother said.

"Nothing's wrong except that my shoes are opening around the soles," I said. "I just paid a lot of money for them."

I got in on the passenger side. The car smelled of wet wood and Mother's hair spray. Someone had done her hair with a minty-white rinse, and the hair was held in place by a zebra-striped headband.

"I think you're getting a flat," I said. "That retread you bought for the left front is going."

She backed the car out of the drive, using the rear-view mirror. "I finally got a boy I can trust, at the Exxon station," she said. "He says that tire will last until hot weather."

Out on the street, she accelerated too quickly and the rear of the car swung left. The tires whined for an instant on the old snow and then caught. We were knocked back in our seats a little and an empty Kleenex box slipped off the dash and onto the floor carpet.

"This is going to be something," my mother said. "Will sure picked an awful day to come."

My mother had never met him. My courtship with Will had all happened in Boston. I was getting my doctorate there, in musicology. Will was involved with his research at Boston U., and with teaching botany to undergraduates.

"You're sure he'll be at the station?" my mother said. "Can the trains go in this weather? I don't see how they do."

"I talked to him on the phone yesterday. He's coming."

"How did he sound?" my mother said.

To my annoyance, she began to hum to herself.

I said, "He's had rotten news about his work. Terrible, in fact."

"Explain his work to me again," she said.

"He's a plant taxonomist."

"Yes?" my mother said. "What does that mean?"

"It means he doesn't have a lot of money," I said. "He studies grasses. He said on the phone he's been turned down for a research grant that would have meant a great deal to us. Apparently the work he's been doing for the past seven or so years is irrelevant or outmoded. I guess 'superficial' is what he told me."

"I won't mention it to him, then," my mother said.

We came to the expressway. Mother steered the car through some small windblown snow dunes and down the entrance ramp. She followed two yellow salt trucks with winking blue beacons that were moving side by side down the center and right-hand lanes.

"I think losing the grant means we should postpone the wedding," I said. "I want Will to have his bearings before I step into his life for good."

"Don't wait too much longer, though," my mother said.

After a couple of miles, she swung off the expressway. We went past some tall high-tension towers with connecting cables that looked like staff lines on a sheet of music. We were in the decaying neighborhood near the tracks. "Now I know this is right," Mother said. "There's our old sign."

The sign was a tall billboard, black and white, that advertised my father's dance studio. The studio had been closed for years and the building it had been in was gone. The sign showed a man in a tuxedo waltzing with a woman in an evening gown. I was always sure it was a waltz. The dancers were nearly two stories high, and the weather had bleached them into phantoms. The lettering – the name of the studio, my father's name – had disappeared.

"They've changed everything," my mother said, peering about. "Can this be the station?"

We went up a little drive that wound past a cindery lot full of flatbed trucks and that ended up at the smudgy brownstone depot.

"Is that your Will?" Mother said.

Will was on the station platform, leaning against a baggage truck. He had a duffle bag between his shoes and plastic cup of coffee in his mittened hand. He seemed to have put on weight, girlishly, through the hips, and his face looked thicker to me, from temple to temple. His gold-rimmed spectacles looked too small.

My mother stopped in an empty cab lane, and I got out and called to Will. It wasn't far from the platform to the car, and Will's pack wasn't a large one, but he seemed to be winded when he got to me. I let him kiss me, and then he stepped back and blew a cold breath and drank from the coffee cup, with his eyes on my face.

Mother was pretending to be busy with something in her handbag, not paying attention to me and Will.

"I look awful," I said.

"No, no, but I probably do," Will said. "No sleep, and I'm fat. So this is your town?"

He tossed the coffee cup at an oil drum and glanced around at the cold train yards and low buildings. A brass foundry was throwing a yellowish column of smoke over a line of Canadian Pacific boxcars.

I said, "The problem is you're looking at the wrong side of the tracks."

A wind whipped Will's lank hair across his face. "Does your mom smoke?" he said. "I ran out in the middle of the night on the train, and the club car was closed. Eight hours across Pennsylvania without a cigarette."

The car horn sounded as my mother climbed from behind the wheel. "That was an accident," she said, because I was frowning at her. "Hello. Are you Will?" She came around the car and stood on tiptoes and kissed him. "You picked a miserable day to come visit us."

She was using her young-girl voice, and I was embarrassed for her. "He needs a cigarette," I said.

Will got into the back of the car and I sat beside my mother again. After we started up, Mother said, "Why doesn't Will stay at my place, in your old room, Belle? I'm all alone there, with plenty of space to kick around in."

"We'll be able to get him a good motel," I said quickly, before Will could answer. "Let's try that Ramada, over near the new elementary school." It was odd, after he had come all the way from Cambridge, but I didn't want him in my old room, in the house where I had been a child. "I'd put you at my place," I said, "but there's mountains of tax stuff all over."

"You've been busy," he said.

"Yes," I said. I sat sidewise, looking at each of them in turn. Will had some blackish spots around his mouth – ballpoint ink, maybe. I wished he had freshened up and put on a better shirt before leaving the train.

"It's up to you two, then," my mother said.

I could tell she was disappointed in Will. I don't know what she expected. I was thirty-one when I met him. I had probably dated fewer men in my life than she had gone out with in a single year at her sorority. She had always been successful with men.

"William was my late husband's name," my mother said. "Did Belle ever tell you?"

"No," Will said. He was smoking one of Mother's cigarettes.

"I always liked the name," she said. "Did you know we ran a dance studio?"

I groaned.

"Oh, let me brag if I want to," my mother said. "He was such a handsome man."

It was true. They were both handsome – mannequins, a pair of dolls who had spent half their lives in evening clothes. But my father had looked old in the end, in a business in which you had to stay young. He had trouble with his eyes, which were bruised-looking and watery, and he had to wear glasses with thick lenses.

I said, "It was in the dance studio that my father ended his life, you know. In the ballroom."

"You told me," Will said, at the same instant my mother said, "Don't talk about it."

My father killed himself with a service revolver. We never found out where he had bought it, or when. He was found in his warm-up clothes – a pullover sweater and pleated pants. He was wearing his tap shoes, and he had a short towel folded around his neck. He had aimed the gun barrel down his mouth, so the bullet would not shatter the wall of mirrors behind him. I was twenty then – old enough to find out how he did it.

MY MOTHER HAD made a wrong turn and we were on Buttles Avenue. "Go there," I said, pointing down a street beside Garfield Park. We passed a group of paper boys who were riding bikes with saddlebags. They were going slow, because of the ice.

"Are you very discouraged, Will?" my mother said. "Belle tells me you're having a run of bad luck."

"You could say so," Will said. "A little rough water."

"I'm sorry," Mother said. "What seems to be the trouble?"

Will said, "Well, this will be oversimplifying, but essentially what I do is take a weed and evaluate its structure and growth and habitat, and so forth."

"What's wrong with that?" my mother said.

"Nothing. But it isn't enough."

"I get it," my mother said uncertainly.

I had taken a mirror and a comb from my handbag and I was trying for a clean center-part in my hair. I was thinking about finishing my bill paying.

Will said, "What do you want to do after I check in, Belle? What about breakfast?"

"I've got to go home for a while and clean up that tax jazz, or I'll never rest," I said. "I'll just show up at your motel later. If we ever find it."

"That'll be fine," Will said.

Mother said, "I'd offer to serve you two dinner tonight, but I think you'll want to leave me out of it. I know how your father and I felt after he went away sometimes. Which way do I turn here?"

We had stopped at an intersection near the iron gates of the park. Behind the gates there was a frozen pond, where a single early-morning skater was skating backwards, expertly crossing his blades.

I couldn't drive a car but, like my father, I have always enjoyed maps and atlases. During automobile trips, I liked comparing distances on maps. I liked the words *latitude, cartography, meridian*. It was extremely annoying to me that Mother had gotten us turned around and lost in our own city, and I was angry with Will all of a sudden, for wasting seven years on something superficial.

"What about up that way?" Will said to my mother, pointing to the left. "There's some traffic up by that light, at least."

I leaned forward in my seat and started combing my hair all over again.

"There's no hurry," my mother said.

"How do you mean?" I asked her.

"To get William to the motel," she said. "I know everybody complains, but I think an ice storm is a beautiful thing. Let's enjoy it."

She waved her cigarette at the windshield. The sun had burned through and was gleaming in the branches of all the maples and buckeye trees in the park. "It's twinkling like a stage set," Mother said.

"It is pretty," I said.

Will said, "It'll make a bad-looking spring. A lot of shrubs get damaged and turn brown, and the trees don't blossom right."

I put my comb away and smiled back at Will. For once I agreed with my mother. Everything was in place, the way it was supposed to be, quiet and holding still.

4. Lovers' Quarrel

Girls become women. Boys become men.
You are a teenager on the rollercoaster of love.

Tim Parks	Adultery
Jayne Anne Phillips	Sweethearts
Jayne Anne Phillips	Slave
Amy Hempel	In the Animal Shelter
Amy Hempel	The Orphan Lamb

Lovers' Quarrel

THE POINT IS OFTEN LOST UPON US IN LONGER WORKS, which may be "well made," but what we can pull from them remains obdurate. In some prose poems/lyric essays/short-shorts, we're told a simple and clear "story," but the writer has figured out a way to stage, with radical compression, his or her essential vision. Such works are often disarming in their pretense of being throwaways: at first glance they may feel relatively journalistic, but they rotate toward the metaphysical. Prose poems/lyric essays/ short-shorts frequently hold the universal via the ordinary. Said differently: working within such a tight frame, the writer needs to establish friction quickly; hence, many of these works unfold across a sexually charged tableau.

Perhaps it's appropriate that this section features two pairs of stories – two by Jayne Anne Phillips, two by Amy Hempel – and one essay by Tim Parks, as if the writer of the latter were contemplating two pairs of lovers. We start, therefore, with Tim Parks's "Adultery," a remarkably compressed yet nuanced meditation on a friend's passionate affair. The essay uses this affair to get at the very nature of the sexual imagination, its need for new data, new stimuli, its mad craze for reinvention. "One lives such a short time, yet wishes to do everything," says Parks, "and then to recapture everything." Marriage had become routine and sexually stagnant for Parks's friend; he finds himself invigorated by conversations with his young, intelligent, Italian mistress (experiencing "the delirium of all that information flowing back and forth – your own life retold, another life discovered"), as well as recharged, of course, by the fact that "sex was new again." Writes Parks, "They made love in Rome, Naples, Geneva, Marseilles. They made love in cars, trains, boats. They made love every possible way. Anal sex, water sports, mutual masturbation ... They adored each other's bodies inside and out." In contrast, the term this friend assigned to the dreaded task of sleeping with his wife was "duty-fucking."

Rereading the essay, we keep thinking of Chris Rock's injunction "You gotta recycle the pussy," by which he means lovers need to figure out how to infinitely reinvent or renew their sexual love; otherwise, each of us is doomed to endless search for the new. This is not moral admonition; it's psychic survival kit. In Parks's words: "The perfect union begins again. Another intimacy beautifully galvanized by the unbridgeable distance between men and women."

Note, too, the way that Parks has cleverly framed the story of his friend's extramarital affair within the context of a very brief history of marriage (and its accompanying legacy of temptation) to get much more mileage out of the central story. Parks begins with an anecdote about attending a brilliant lecture on marriage and adultery as depicted in Elizabethan-era tapestries and in Shakespeare's plays ("scenes of domestic bliss undermined by allusions to more disturbing emotions: serpents and harpies warning rapturous newlyweds of obscure calamities to come"). Once we know that the middle-aged lecturer's husband deserted her for a twenty-five-year-old (life imitating art imitating life), we view Parks's friend's story as if it has already been written–or, in this case, woven. Formally, the essay gives one that sense of cycling and recycling, which is also its subject.

Jayne Anne Phillips's best book is her first book, *Black Tickets*, from which both of these stories are taken. "Sweethearts" is a full geography of desire, taking us line-by-line into a new stratum, moving from movie fantasy to junior romance imagined from the point of view of younger kids to humdrum grown-up reality to grotesque sexual molestation. Students often debate the ending–does

Mr. Penny's pawing at the girls redefine all that goes before in a harsher light, or is it simply one of several strata of desire? Once we've left the first paragraph, we never meet those horny, bacchanalian teenagers again. Instead, as the story unfolds, it is the un-sexed (that is, the prepubescent "sweethearts") and the de-sexed (the old people) who become sexualized; the little, uninitiated girls hear fat-fingered Mrs. Causton's thighs rub together like candy wrappers, while Mr. Penny's sexuality gets revealed to them overtly, despite its inappropriateness. By story's end, he has become the focal point–his stained fingers, his arms, his heart, his smoker's whisper, his impulse, his life force.

As does "Sweethearts," Phillips's other story here, "Slave," takes us through all the stages of desire or of a relationship, but its greatness lies in its merciless examination of a particular woman's sexual imagination. For her, desire is connected unmistakably to absence and difference and distance; when she is "close" to someone else, there is no possibility of arousal: "He was so much like her. She already had what he had. She could get along without him, because when he came, there was no triumph of conquering their separation and winning him."

The key to the story is how virtually every sentence takes us deeper and deeper into her psyche. She is the grammatical subject of almost every sentence in the story–in fact, the word "she" appears no fewer than thirty-seven times in this single page of writing. The repetition anchors the reader each time in the woman's perspective, also creating a hypnotic prose rhythm. About halfway down the page, the language starts to feel choppy, as if we're on a rocky sailboat that until now had been cruising along smoothly. The point of view shifts from a tight focus on her to a contested, combative blend that includes the man's point of view. In the end, the man hangs up the phone and disappears (along with his POV), leaving her with the frantic, "bleeping" dial tone. The focus returns to her: "Alone, she could feel her power holding up," reads the penultimate sentence. She could make them come;

they couldn't make her come. This gives her the upper hand – and isolates her, turning her into a tragic figure.

So, too, Amy Hempel's two stories here trade between female and male POV. The first story, "In the Animal Shelter," is an extraordinarily precise unraveling of the way in which beautiful women, abandoned by men, go to the animal shelter to cuddle with "one-eyed cats," not only to imagine mothering these homeless pets in order to reverse the rejection they experienced by the men but also to return to the rejection and re-experience that rejection. It's a sad, discomfiting story. The women's question "Is Mama's baby lonesome?" captures their need to mother – the men don't want to get married and have children – but also their need to project their own rejection onto another creature.

With "Orphan's Lamb," Hempel switches targets and now it is the masculine ego that she sees through entirely: the way in which the man tries to frame his experience as caring, implying that he will care for her just as deeply. The female character sees right through that old ruse. In this marvel of a story, Hempel manages to dramatize birth, death, love, creation, and destruction in six sentences.

What is perhaps most impressive about these stories is how they trade hats: in each pair, the writer sees first through the female perspective, then through the male. Write two stories or essays, each 500 words long, in which you first see through the male perspective, then through the female perspective. Or, alternately, write a story or essay in which you are looking at both points of view. The key is to create a sexual tableau, keep exploring the tableau so that you are excavating the very nature of the relationship, and wind up with something with the effect of being an anatomy of sexual love. At the end of the composition, you should have arrived at what for you is a working definition, implicitly or explicitly, of the nature of desire.

Tim Parks
Adultery

A COUPLE OF YEARS AGO, I ATTENDED A LECTURE ON A somewhat abstruse theme: "Marriage Bedroom Tapestries in the Works of Shakespeare." It's not the kind of thing I would generally move heaven and earth to get to, but I was stuck in a conference at Lake Como, way out of town, it was raining heavily, and there was nothing else to do. As it turned out, I was spellbound. The speaker, a fine-looking woman in her fifties, used slides and video to illustrate the ambiguities of a series of images woven onto the upholstered bedsteads of the Elizabethan aristocracy. Particularly fascinating were scenes of domestic bliss undermined by allusions to more disturbing emotions: serpents and harpies warning rapturous newlyweds of obscure calamities to come. The speaker explained how Shakespeare had drawn on this material in his plays, but what she ended up giving us was a history of marriage, from its dynastic origins, when family was everything and sentiments were relegated to extramarital adventures, through the crisis sparked off by the tradition of courtly love, when husbands and wives began to leave their partners to follow their lovers, to the novel idea that marriage be founded on love rather than on family. This, the speaker claimed, was the subject of three plays she had selected for consideration, the underlying theme of the allegories in the bedroom tapestries: the huge gamble of placing love at the heart of marriage, the sad discovery, fearfully embodied in Othello, that love is even more fragile than dynasty. All it takes is an unexplained handkerchief, a jealous temperament, and, as Shakespeare put it, "Farewell the tranquil mind! farewell content!"

After the lecture, chatting with two elderly professors, I couldn't help praising the woman's marvelous dispatch, the energy and passion and relevance of her analysis of marriage. "A brilliant lecture," I insisted.

"No mystery about that," remarked one of the two. His smile was at once sad and wry. "Her husband just left her for a twenty-five-year-old."

LOVE AND DYNASTY, passion and family. It was around this time that Alistair's story got into full swing. (Names, of course, and some details of the story have been changed.) I was his confidant. We played squash together twice a week, and over beers afterward he would tell me all about it. As he spoke, his voice was full of laughter and his face burned with excitement. "You've blown your marriage," I warned him. He laughed out loud and used sports terminology: playing away, scoring in extra time, next week's game plan. "The logistics can be so complicated," he said, chuckling. He even giggled. And you could see what an enormous sense of release he felt in this first affair after eight years of marriage. Alistair was a very sober, solid, reliable man, but now the great dam of vows and virtue was crumbling beneath a tidal wave of Dionysiac excitement.

We worked together at the university, and in the corridor I showed him a passage from a book I was translating, Roberto Calasso's *The Marriage of Cadmus and Harmony*. "Dionysus is not a useful god who helps weave or knot things together, but a god who loosens and unties," it said. "The weavers are his enemies. Yet there comes a moment when the weavers will abandon their looms to dash off after him into the mountains. Dionysus is the river we hear flowing by in the distance, an incessant booming from far away; then one day it rises and floods everything, as if the normal above-water state of things, the sober delimitation of our existence, were but a brief parenthesis overwhelmed in an instant."

"You're possessed," I told him. Alistair nodded and laughed. He had been a weaver for so long. He had woven together family-house-career-car. But the following evening, after squash again, he described how in that family car his mistress had pulled up her skirt–they were on the turnpike from Verona to Venice–and started masturbating, then rubbed her scented hand across his face, pushed her fingers in his mouth. Since we live in Italy, and have both lived here a long time, he occasionally broke into Italian. "*Evviva le puttanelle!*" he said, and laughed again. "Long live the little whores!" He was in love with her. For those of us still safely married, it's hard not to feel a mixture of trepidation and envy on seeing a friend in this state. Clearly it is very exciting when you start destroying everything.

Alistair referred to his wife as "the Queen of Unreason" or "She Who Must Be Obeyed." She was still a weaver. They had two young children. In the way that feminism has changed everything and nothing, she was in charge at home; she felt primarily responsible for the children. Men, of course, now help in the home, and Alistair, being a reasonable and generous man, helped a great deal–more than most. But he was not in charge. His wife's conscientiousness and maternal anxiety, heightened no doubt by her decision to stay at work despite the kids, must have frequently looked like bossiness to him. Their arguments were trivial–whose turn it was to do this or that. He felt himself the butt of her imperatives, his behavior constantly under observation. Making love is difficult in these circumstances, though doubtless these two people loved each other. Or perhaps with everything now achieved it was time for something else to happen. All of us have so much potential that will never be realized within the confines necessary to weave anything together. Job and marriage are our two greatest prisons. When Alistair asked his wife what was wrong and how could he understand if she didn't tell him, she said if only he spared her a moment's attention he would understand without being told. Every intimacy is a potential hell. Alistair referred to sex with his wife as "duty-fucking."

The affair began. Chiara was a young divorcée, thirty-three, with a ten-year-old daughter and an excellent job in education administration which took her to the same conferences Alistair attended. Rather than a decision, infidelity was a question of opportunity coinciding with impulse – no, with a day when Alistair felt he deserved this escape. Sex was new again. They made love in Rome, Naples, Geneva, Marseilles. They made love in cars, trains, boats. They made love in every possible way. Anal sex, water sports, mutual masturbation: I had to listen to it all. The complicated logistics of their encounters seemed to be at least half the thrill – the advantages and disadvantages of mobile phones, the dangers of credit cards. They adored each other's bodies, inside and out. Alistair was in love with Chiara. Wasn't she beautiful? After lovemaking they had such intelligent conversations: philosophy, psychology, politics, their lives. They gave books to each other. They swapped stories. They experienced the delirium of all that information flowing back and forth – your own life retold, another life discovered. There is always something to talk about when one is falling in love. As so often there is not in the long-haul mechanics of marriage.

But how could Alistair leave his children? He loved his children. His wife, though, was becoming more and more difficult. He would interrupt his long descriptions of frantic sex to tell me self-justifying stories of his wife's unreasonableness. Why did she always object to the way he did even the most trivial things: the way he hung a picture; the way he left his toothbrush – get this – turned outward from the tooth glass, so it dripped on the floor, instead of inward, so it didn't? "Can you imagine!" he protested. Not to mention the fact that she never gave him blowjobs. But Alistair admitted that he couldn't be sure anymore whether his arguments with his wife were purely between them or had to do with his mistress. Perhaps he was deliberately stirring up these petty conflicts in order to justify his eventual departure. Perhaps they weren't arguing about a toothbrush at all. Out of nostalgia, or guilt, or just in order to see what it felt like, Alistair would try to be romantic with his wife. He would bring flowers. When the children were safely asleep, he would persuade her to make love. And immediately he would realize he didn't really want to make love to her. He felt no vigor, no zest. He wanted to be with his mistress. "I told her I'd heard the baby coughing," he said, and he laughed, sadly.

Passion, family. Was it time for Alistair to leave home? I thought so. But he said that when he and his wife sat together of an evening, playing with the children or catching a movie on TV, they were perfectly happy. Not to mention the economics involved. And perhaps the thing he had with Chiara couldn't be turned into long-term cohabitation. He lived in the ecstasy of the choice unmade, the divided mind. Convinced that he was trying to come to a decision, he relentlessly applied the logic that was so effective in his research, as if this were a technical problem that it must be possible to solve somehow. It's the Cartesian legacy that has filled the stores with self-help books: life is a problem to solve if only you know the formula. I was equally glib. "You've just got to work out which means most to you," I told him. "Perhaps it's only sex with Chiara."

"You must never put the word 'only' in front of 'sex,'" he objected. "Or not the kind we have. It's an absolute."

"So you're only staying at home for the children," I tried. "You should leave."

But then he said that you couldn't put the word "only" in front of "children," either. Passion and children were both absolutes. You couldn't weigh them against each other. In the end, Alistair managed to prolong a state of doubt and potential, of anything-can-happen precariousness, for nigh on eighteen months. Later, he would appreciate that this had been the happiest time of his life.

But now Chiara was cooling. There were limits to this feverish equilibrium. Finally, Alistair and his wife decided to take separate holidays. The months of July and August would be spent apart. "Are you sure you mean it?" I asked him. He had phoned me to say

he'd told Chiara he was leaving his wife. "After all, that's not strictly true," I said. "You only decided on separate holidays." He said
he thought he meant it. Anyway, the point was that *he felt he had
to make something happen.* The expression stayed in my mind. It
gnawed – because it was unusually honest. As I think back on the
many people I know who have divorced, or separated, or left each
other and got back together, then left each other again and got
back together again, or divorced and married someone else and
divorced again and married someone else again, it occurs to me
that while most of them talk earnestly of their search for happiness,
their dream of the perfect relationship, what really drives them
is the thirst for intensity, for some kind of destiny, which often
means disaster. It's the same endearing perversity that made Paradise so tedious that, one way or another, that apple just had to be
eaten. Man was never innocent. Marriage was never safe. "I have
to make something happen," Alistair said. In this finely managed,
career-structured world that we've worked so hard to build, with
its automatic gates and hissing lawns, its comprehensive insur-
ance policies, divorce remains one of the few catastrophes we can
reasonably expect to provoke. It calls to us like a siren, offering a
truly spectacular shipwreck. Oh, to do some really serious damage at last!

But Chiara said no. Chiara didn't want to live with Alistair.
She didn't want to risk the happy routine she had built up with her
daughter after her divorce. She didn't want to risk love again. She
didn't want to be responsible, she said, for ruining Alistair's marriage. They must stop seeing each other completely.

Alistair collapsed. The gods abandoned him. Intoxication
was gone, and he couldn't live without it. He couldn't live without joy, he said. His smoking shot up to sixty a day. He drank heavily. His wife, alarmed, became excessively kind. This infuriated
Alistair. He could barely speak to her. He could barely speak to
his children. He could barely *see* his children. Unable to sleep at
night, he dozed all day. His work went to pieces. He tortured himself with the thought that if he had asked sooner Chiara would

have said yes. His procrastination had destroyed her passion. He should have trusted his instincts. Finally, I managed to persuade him to see an analyst.

AS I SAID, we live in Italy. It's a country where people divorce significantly less than in the U. S. A. but probably have more affairs. It's a country which perhaps never fully believed that romance should be the lifeblood of marriage, or not after the children have arrived; a country where a friend of mine told me that at his wedding his grandmother advised him to try to be faithful for at least the first year. In short, it's a place where people expect a little less of each other, and of marriage. Above all, they don't expect the privilege of unmixed feelings. Hence a country where analysts give different advice.

The analyst told Alistair that only the wildest optimist would divorce in order to remarry, presuming that things would be better next time round. Why should they be? Was there anything intrinsically unsuitable about his wife, anything intrinsically right about his mistress? Alistair's problems sprang from his Anglo-Saxon puritan upbringing, from the fact that he'd never been unfaithful before. This had led him to attach undue significance to the sentimental side of his new relationship in order to justify the betrayal of values – monogamy, integrity – that would not bear examination. He had "mythicized" it. What he must do now was take a few mild tranquilizers, settle down, and have another affair at the first opportunity, being careful to attach no more sentimental importance to it than an affair was worth – some, but not much. And keep it brief. Meanwhile, he might remember that he had an ongoing project with his wife. They were old campaigners. Think of the practical side. Think of your professional life. He told Alistair that every family was also a business, or *hacienda*, as the Spanish say, a family estate, a place where people share the jobs that have to be done.

Is such advice merely cynical? Or, in a very profound way, romantic? Old campaigners. Discussing it with Alistair after he had put in a decidedly lackluster performance on the squash court, I felt it wise to agree with the analyst – at least about the ingenuousness of imagining that things would be better next time. I also told him that during the Italian referendum on divorce in 1974 one of the arguments against divorce put forward by some intellectuals was that it would change the nature of affairs. I tried to make him laugh. You'd never know if your mistress wasn't planning to become your second wife!

But visions of such consummate convenience leave little scope for myth and misery. Alistair had been *in love* with Chiara. He had given his heart. Such clichés do count for something, whatever an analyst says. Trying and failing one evening to have sex with his wife, unable to feel any stimulus at all, Alistair suddenly found himself telling her the truth. He didn't decide to tell her, as indeed he had decided nothing in this whole adventure. Everything had been done, usually after enormous resistance, under an overwhelming sense of compulsion. Perhaps this is the way with anything important. He told her the whole truth and got his catastrophe.

The wife was destroyed. Alistair had spared no details. She insisted he leave. He did, discovering as he did so what a large space home and children had played in his life. Most of this he struggled to fill with whiskey and Camel Lights in a lugubriously furnished apartment in a cheaper area of town. Legal proceedings had just begun when Chiara came back. At this point, there was a brief hiatus, since Alistair no longer felt the need to be in touch with me. He was happy, or so I heard later. He had won his dream. The hell with the analyst. The hell with squash. His wife was more than generous with access to the children; Alistair was more than generous with money. All was well – indeed, perfect. It was about three months before I got another call.

I SUPPOSE WHAT fascinates me about divorce is how tied up it is with our loss, our intelligent loss, of any sense of direction, of any supposed system of values that might be worth more than our own immediate apprehension of whether or not we are happy. We are not ignorant enough to live well, or too arrogant to let old conventions decide anything for us. For many of us, and especially for men, who do not bear children and do not breast-feed them, the only thing that is immediately felt to be sacred, the only meaningful intensity, or the last illusion, is passion. D. H. Lawrence puts this very simply in *Women in Love*. Birkin says:

> "The old ideals are dead as nails – nothing there. It seems to me there remains only this perfect union with a woman – sort of ultimate marriage – and there isn't anything else."
> "And you mean if there isn't the woman, there's nothing?" said Gerald.
> "Pretty well that – seeing there's no God."
> "Then we're hard put to it," said Gerald.

Perfect union with a woman: over beers again, depressed and tranquilized, Alistair was explaining how he thought he'd got that, until one night after lovemaking when Chiara casually asked him if he wanted to know the real reason she had refused his initial proposal that they live together. It was because she had just started an affair with another man. With Alistair being married and mostly absent, that had been inevitable. She'd wanted to see how it would work out with this man – quite well, as it turned out. "Though he wasn't at your level in bed," she said, laughing. Alistair hit her.

Alistair now became obsessed by the fact that there really had been no great love. Quite gratuitously, Chiara had exposed the illusion around which he was rebuilding his life. She went on to confess to three or four other lovers during their affair. Why should she have put all her eggs in one basket, she asked. Alistair, who had never hit anybody, hit her again. The analyst explained to him that hitting her was his way of trying to preserve some sort of myth, albeit negative, about the affair – trying to insist on its importance. Disturbingly, Chiara appeared to like being hit. She came back for more, told him more. It took them another year and two trips to the hospital to stop seeing each other. It was always Chiara who came back. Alistair told the whole story to his wife, and she commiserated. They made love. They started seeing each other more often, but without interrupting the divorce proceedings. Alistair began a long series of affairs whose main purpose seemed to be to relive the passion of the earlier affair, whose main purpose, perhaps, had been to rediscover the enthusiasm that had led him to marry in the first place.

Marriage and divorce are so tangled up with our sense of mortality. One lives such a short time, yet wishes to do everything, and then to recapture everything. Start again, the springtime says. Unfaithfulness never fails to rejuvenate. But if we start again too often nothing will be brought to completion. And happiness? That long-term monogamy is unnatural is something that every male of the species has felt. Yet where would we be without some repression? The perfect union begins again. Another intimacy beautifully galvanized by the unbridgeable distance between men and women. A radical incomprehension. The children arrive. There are disagreements. The project falters. Our biology cares little for wholesome values and domestic routine now that the reproduction is done. The sound of a river in the distance lifts your head from the loom. The sound of rushing water. Time to batten down the windows, sandbag the doors. Old campaigners will take their kids to baseball, or take up baseball themselves. Or piano. Or drawing classes. Or martial arts.

In a chaos of receding floodwater, Alistair surveys his rearranged landscape. He has the kids alternate weekends, eats regularly with them and their mother. Sometimes it's hard to tell whether they're separated or not. The analyst has become a friend, plays squash with Alistair and swaps stories of affairs over beers. His main boast is three in three days at a conference in Palermo. The divorce has come through at last. And, as divorcés will, both Alistair and his ex-wife assure me, perhaps a little too insistently, that this is the ideal solution.

Jayne Anne Phillips
Sweethearts

WE WENT TO THE MOVIES EVERY FRIDAY AND SUNDAY. On Friday nights the Colonial filled with an oily fragrance of teenagers while we hid in the back row of the balcony. An aura of light from the projection booth curved across our shoulders, round under cotton sweaters. Sacred grunts rose in black corners. The screen was far away and spilling color – big men sweating on their horses and women with powdered breasts floating under satin. Near the end the film smelled hot and twisted as boys shuddered and girls sank down in their seats. We ran to the lobby before the lights came up to stand by the big ash can and watch them walk slowly downstairs. Mouths swollen and ripe, they drifted down like a sigh of steam. The boys held their arms tense and shuffled from one foot to the other while the girls sniffed and combed their hair in the big mirror. Outside the neon lights on Main Street flashed stripes across asphalt in the rain. They tossed their heads and shivered like ponies.

On Sunday afternoons the theater was deserted, a church that smelled of something frying. Mrs. Causton stood at the door to tear tickets with her fat buttered fingers. During the movie she stood watching the traffic light change in the empty street, pushing her glasses up over her nose and squeezing a damp Kleenex. Mr. Penny was her skinny yellow father. He stood by the office door with his big push broom, smoking cigarettes and coughing.

Walking down the slanted floor to our seats we heard the swish of her thighs behind the candy counter and our shoes sliding on the worn carpet. The heavy velvet curtain moved its folds. We waited, and a cavernous dark pressed close around us, its breath pulling at our faces.

After the last blast of sound it was Sunday afternoon, and Mr. Penny stood jingling his keys by the office door while we asked to use the phone. Before he turned the key he bent over and pulled us close with his bony arms. Stained fingers kneading our chests, he wrapped us in old tobacco and called us his little girls. I felt his wrinkled heart wheeze like a dog on a leash. Sweethearts, he whispered.

Jayne Anne Phillips
Slave

SHE WANTED TO HAVE ORGASMS MORE AND MORE OFTEN.
She watched her men have orgasms with their eyes closed, sailing
on their breath, and gone. She had the pleasure of helping them
leave, and was left in possession of them until they returned. She
had memorized faces in that moment of unconsciousness. Many
times she was actually seeing that face rather than the face she
was talking to, aware that this person whose face it was had never
seen that face of himself. So the face became her secret. She herself had a tiny orgasm of fear when she saw someone she loved
after a long separation, who usually no longer loved her. Something turned over once in her. She had the same turning ache when
reading something suggestive or having a memory of arousal. She
had it when she realized she wanted someone. When she mas-
turbated she always had a brief intense orgasm, turning over ten
times, and fell asleep released. But she seldom had orgasms with
her men. She loved to make love with someone she wanted. They
soared away from her arched and paralyzed and for an instant
she had what she wanted. There was one man she liked to talk to,
whom she didn't particularly want because he was so much like
her. She already had what he had. She could get along without him,
because when he came, there was no triumph of conquering their
separation and winning him. So she told him that although she
liked men she seldom had orgasms with them but only with herself. They talked about it patiently. After that she wanted to make
love with him less because her power was exposed and solidified.

He wanted to make love with her more but was self-conscious because he was unsure of his power. She felt he was no longer like her but was less than her, and she didn't want him. The relationship cooled. One day he called her on the phone and a fight ensued in which they each cataloged what was weak about the other. She was getting the best of him so he said Go fuck yourself, since you can do more for yourself than I can anyway. She sat there listening to the dial tone. She knew that he thought her power was uppermost because she could make him come but he couldn't make her come. He had the secret of what her power was about, but she had the secret of his powerlessness over her. That made him ashamed. He felt lonely but free because he thought there had to be two people to have the question of power. She knew her power over him happened because of her power over herself. The phone began bleeping frantically. Alone, she could feel her power holding her up. But what did that make her?

Amy Hempel
In the Animal Shelter

EVERY TIME YOU SEE A BEAUTIFUL WOMAN, *SOMEONE* IS tired of her, so the men say. And I know where they go, these women, with their tired beauty that someone doesn't want – these women who must live like the high Sierra white pine, there since before the birth of Christ, fed somehow by the alpine wind.

They reach out to the animals, day after day smoothing fur inside a cage, saying, "How is Mama's baby? Is Mama's baby lonesome?"

The women leave at the end of the day, stopping to ask an attendant, "Will they go to good homes?" And come back in a day or so, stooping to examine a one-eyed cat, asking, as though they intend to adopt, "How would I introduce a new cat to my dog?"

But there is seldom an adoption; it matters that the women have someone to leave, leaving behind the lovesome creatures who would never leave them, had they once given them their hearts.

Amy Hempel
The Orphan Lamb

HE CARVED THE COAT OFF THE DEAD WINTER LAMB, wiped her blood on his pants to keep a grip, circling first the hooves and cutting straight up each leg, then punching the skin loose from muscle and bone.

He tied the skin with twine over the body of the orphaned lamb so the grieving ewe would know the scent and let the orphaned lamb nurse.

Or so he said.

This was seduction. This was the story he told, of all the farm-boy stories he might have told; he chose the one where brutality saves a life. He wanted me to feel, when he fitted his body over mine, that this was how I would go on – this was how I would be known.

5. Happiness

You have flown the nest. You are married.
Your hair is filled with rice.
Your brain is flooded with dopamine.

Linda Brewer   20/20
Amy Hempel   Weekend

Happiness

WHO KNOWS HOW TO WRITE ABOUT HAPPINESS (WHICH, according to Henry de Montherlant, "writes in white ink on a white page")? Many writers take their essentially happy, middle-class lives and pull out all the consolations. They have no wisdom, so they fake it by sounding dire.

Two stories that succeed in describing happiness are Linda Brewer's "20/20" and Amy Hempel's "Weekend."

The opening line of "20/20" – "By the time they reached Indiana, Bill realized that Ruthie, his driving companion, was incapable of theoretical debate" – leaves the story with only two doors to open: either Ruthie becomes capable of theoretical debate (yawn) or Bill's admiration of theoretical debate gets undermined (potentially much more interesting). The second sentence is told in the voice of literal-minded masculinity, a logbook prose: "she drove okay," "she went halves on gas," "etc." (Bill is interested in bills; Ruthie's name evokes her childlikeness.) Condescension is the dominant tone. Bill believes Ruthie literally doesn't know how to argue, and when he says that she "stuck to simple observation, like 'Look, cows,'" we sense him gawking not at the cows but at his companion, as if, for Bill, it's Ruthie's outlook that's positively bovine.

As we move from east to west – from the region, supposedly, of theoretical debate, to the region, supposedly, of natural wonders – we parallel, of course, Bill's emotional journey. When do a man and woman "drive into the setting sun"? At the end of a romantic comedy. The last line of the second paragraph sets up the story's ending; the romance is encrypted in the image. (While watching a TV documentary on building ships in bottles, Gordon Lish noticed that the mechanism is much the same for a story as for the model ship: once the builder gets the ship with its collapsed masts into the bottle, he pulls a string to which all the masts are attached. To erect the superstructure, the writer pulls up the lines to her "masts"–the motifs she has developed from beginning to end. This is precisely the way in which Brewer is using the "setting sun" here.) Now it's Bill who's resting and Ruthie who's speaking–a major change, and one that leads to the transformation in Bill.

Is Ruthie crazy, delusional, stupid, visionary? She's the kind of person who, on a trip, imagines she sees things out of the corner of her eye and, to make the trip more interesting, yields to the phantasm. In many ways she's the embodiment of "fancy," just as Bill is, until the very end, the embodiment of practicality.

Bigfoot, Indian paintbrush, golden eagle–none of these exist, but it takes Bill quite a while to catch on.

When Bill insists on driving again, "they changed places in the light of the evening star." This romantic language (very un-Bill-like) is another sharp pull on the line leading to the Bill + Ruthie mast erected in the final paragraph. Ruthie is now glad to be along for the ride, and he is now a serious fan of her reality-remaking vision, because she conjures up not only a white buffalo near Fargo and a UFO above Twin Falls but also a "handsome genius in the person of Bill himself."

In French, romance is sometimes referred to as a *folie à deux*, a delusion shared by two people–which is how Brewer is defining romance here as well. Bill signs on only when he also gets inserted into the snow globe. He began with perfect sight–20/20–and now has better-than-perfect sight: seeing more than what's there. The story is as precisely made as a geometry proof.

Amy Hempel has been dramatizing the *folie à deux* between men and women for thirty years. "Weekend" is one of her very, very few stories that ends happily ("Today Will Be a Quiet Day" perhaps also qualifies). "Weekend" works because of its carefully orchestrated undertone of sadness, even despair. The story is divided neatly in half: the calm and the storm-for-now-averted. The first section is an evocation of the epitome of middle-class, familial contentment and pleasure: the weekend, kids, dogs, softball, drinks. There are the faintest hints of trouble: dog tags, the leg cast, the dogs' "mutiny," but all is more or less joy.

Section break: time passes. The postprandial debates are about nothing of consequence. Adults smoke, pick ticks off sleeping dogs, repel mosquitoes, throw horseshoes (a near-ringer: this much heartbreak we can live with). We are on what feels like Long Island, and the men are readying to return to the city for work the next morning. When the men kiss the women good night – their "weekend whiskers" scratching the women's cheeks – the women want the men not to shave but to *"stay,"* which is the story's brilliant final word, conveying sweetness but also the command of a dog's owner to a dog and the strong implication that sooner rather than later the bewhiskered men will wind up like the dogs, straying, "barking, mutinous." *Here, right now – this is gorgeous; please let's keep it so.* As soon as we think this/say this, paradise is ruined.

The word *paradise* is derived from a mistranslation of an ancient Arabic word that means "a wall enclosing a garden or orchard," rather than the garden itself. Maybe in the end, though, it is in fact the walls – the boundaries, the limits – of paradise that speak most to its nature. Write your own essay or story or prose poem (no longer than 500 words), in which you persuasively evoke happiness. Perhaps the key, for a contemporary writer, when evoking happiness is to evoke a *qualified* happiness. Be happy, but worry about it. At least a little.

Linda Brewer
20/20

BY THE TIME THEY REACHED INDIANA, BILL REALIZED that Ruthie, his driving companion, was incapable of theoretical debate. She drove okay, she went halves on gas, etc., but she refused to argue. She didn't seem to know how. Bill was used to East Coast women who disputed everything he said, every step of the way. Ruthie stuck to simple observation, like "Look, cows." He chalked it up to the fact that she was from rural Ohio and thrilled to death to be anywhere else.

She didn't mind driving into the setting sun. The third evening out, Bill rested his eyes while she cruised along making the occasional announcement.

"Indian paintbrush. A golden eagle."

Miles later he frowned. There was no Indian paintbrush, that he knew of, near Chicago.

The next evening, driving, Ruthie said, "I never thought I'd see a Bigfoot in real life." Bill turned and looked at the side of the road streaming innocently out behind them. Two red spots winked back – reflectors nailed to a tree stump.

"Ruthie, I'll drive," he said. She stopped the car and they changed places in the light of the evening star.

"I'm so glad I got to come with you," Ruthie said. Her eyes were big, blue, and capable of seeing wonderful sights. A white buffalo near Fargo. A UFO above Twin Falls. A handsome genius in the person of Bill himself. This last vision came to her in Spokane and Bill decided to let it ride.

Amy Hempel
Weekend

THE GAME WAS CALLED ON ACCOUNT OF DOGS – HUNTER in the infield, Tucker in the infield, Bosco and Boone at first base. First-grader Donald sat down on second base, and Kirsten grabbed her brother's arm and wouldn't let him leave third to make his first run.

"Unfair!" her brother screamed, and the dogs, roving umpires, ran to third.

"Good power!" their uncle yelled, when Joy, in a leg cast, swung the bat and missed. "Now put some wood to it."

And when she did, Joy's designated runner, Cousin Zeke, ran to first, the ice cubes in his gin and tonic clacking like dog tags in the glass.

And when Kelly broke free from Kirsten and this time came in to make the run, members of the Kelly team made Tucker in the infield dance on his hind legs.

"It's not who wins – " their coach began, and was shouted down by one of the boys, "There's *first* and there's *forget it*."

Then Hunter retrieved a foul ball and carried it off in the direction of the river.

The other dogs followed – barking, mutinous.

DINNER WAS A simple picnic on the porch, paper plates in laps, the only conversation a debate as to which was the better grip for throwing shoes.

After dinner, the horseshoes were handed out, the post

pounded in, the rules reviewed with a new rule added due to falling-down shorts. The new rule: Have attire.

The women smoked on the porch, the smoke repelling mosquitoes, and the men and children played on even after dusk when it got so dark that a candle was rigged to balance on top of the post, and was knocked off and blown out by every single almost-ringer.

Then the children went to bed, or at least went upstairs, and the men joined the women for a cigarette on the porch, absently picking ticks engorged like grapes off the sleeping dogs. And when the men kissed the women good night, and their weekend whiskers scratched the women's cheeks, the women did not think *shave*, they thought: *stay*.

6. Decades

Time does its work. Your marriage is fraying. Your job is a drag.

Leonard Michaels	In the Fifties
Wayne Koestenbaum	My 1980s
Barry Hannah	The Wretched Seventies
S. L. Wisenberg	Brunch

Decades

THE DECADE IS, OF COURSE, AN ARTIFICIAL CONSTRUCT, journalistic shorthand, and yet it can help us to organize our thoughts, our eras. Leonard Michaels, in his brilliant story/essay, locates the intersection of narcissism and violence, then goes on to show how the interior violence of the fifties became the public violence of the sixties, but not until the final paragraph could we have any sense that was where the story was going; when it gets there, we can circle back and see the escalating hints Michaels laid for us throughout.

Wayne Koestenbaum's "My 1980s" is also something of a comic portrait of a decade – the foci here are AIDS, sex, drugs, and critical theory – but the campy, tongue-in-cheek tone only partially obscures from us the narrator's very real terror that he will not survive the AIDS epidemic. "I was not thinking about the world. I was not thinking about history. I was thinking about my body's small, precise, limited, hungry movement forward into a future that seemed at every instant on the verge of being shut down," he writes. Throughout the essay, the narrator gestures at and then buries this anxiety. In the final paragraph, when it all swells up to the surface, the ground is finally pulled out from under his feet: "When I look back at the eighties I see myself as a small boat. It is not an important, attractive, or likable boat, but it has a prow, a sail, and a modest personality. It has no consciousness of the water it moves through. Some days it resembles Rimbaud's inebriated vessel. Other, clearer days, it is sober and undemonstrative. There are few images or adjectives we could affix to the boat; there are virtually no ways to classify it. Its only business is staying afloat. Thus the boat is amoral. It has been manufactured in a certain style. Any style contains a history. The boat is not conscious of the history shaping its movements. The boat, undramatic, passive, at best pleasant, at worst slapdash, persistently attends to the work of flotation, which takes precedence over responsible navigation. As far as the boat is concerned, it is the only vessel on the body of water. How many times must I repeat the word *boat* to convince you that in the eighties I was a small boat with a minor mission and a fear of sinking? The boat did not sink."

Your assignment, if you choose to accept it, is to write your version of a decades story or essay using Koestenbaum's essay as a model. List dozens of events in very short paragraphs. Make the list *appear* to be random, arbitrary, but under the surface of this seemingly casual list, create a subtle subtext. Subtly pull through the thread of that subtext. At the very end of the story or essay, pull the lines to get the masts to go up; get the piece to rotate outward; get the metaphor to exfoliate. Do this in 1,500 words or fewer. It's probably best to do this assignment by first "shooting a lot of film"–write down everything you can possibly think of about a particular decade: probably the nineties or the so-called aughts, but it could be an earlier or much earlier decade (e.g., the 1840s) or even a future decade (2020s, anyone?). Then radically compress your list, looking for what the pattern in the carpet is. Then make sure the reader can see the pattern, but not see it clearly until the very end. It's complicated. That's why they call it art.

Alternatively, use Sandi Wisenberg's "Brunch" or Barry Hannah's "The Wretched Seventies" as your model. These are what we might call wandering-tableau stories: the writer keeps extrapolating from a single *mise-en-scène* until it yields thematic gold. You still are trying to evoke a decade by marrying the personal and the public; you still are building a thematic lattice that is not apparent until the story's end, but this is not a list story. The details circulate around a single tableau, viewed at different times of day and from different angles.

Hannah's story drives toward a beautiful and powerful merging of Ned Maxy's middle-aged exhaustion and the end of the self-indulgent 1970s (which for Maxy lasted two decades – reminiscent of the Woody Allen joke about Scott and Zelda's returning from a New Year's Eve party in April): "Some big quiet thing had fallen down and locked into place, like a whisper of some weight. Ned Maxy had been granted contact with paradise, and he could hardly believe the lack of noise. His awful seventies decade had gone past twenty years. Finally it was over." The evocation of Maxy's sybaritic pleasures gets subtly interwoven with the decade's sybaritic pleasures. A man's middle-aged, bittersweet mellowing comes to stand for the culture's newfound, post-Black Monday sobriety – but not until 1996, when the story was published and Hannah was fifty-four.

Sandi Wisenberg's "Brunch" works in a somewhat similar way. It's divided into three equal sections: in the first section, the narrator is wryly affectionate toward her friends, all of whom affirm left-wing political activism during the Reagan era as their raison d'être, thereby placing their emotional lives, especially romance, a distant second. In the middle section, the narrator is ambivalent toward this tradeoff. And in the final section we feel the psychic cost to the narrator – her serious regret, even anger – about how her friends/colleagues have organized their lives to make sure that they don't have one, or at least a conventional one with its ordinary, domestic pleasures. Wisenberg's masterstroke in the final paragraph is to convey the narrator's melancholy through several degrees of remove, avoiding any too easy sentiment and conveying how distant she and her cohort are from the affective life: "Once I was going to be [Susan's] maid of honor. She was going to marry Bruce. She bought a midcalf-length tea dress, pinky-peach, with lace. Then he decided he didn't want anything for life, though he still wanted to live with her. She left for six months, and came back for two years before leaving for good. During that six months, she went around the world. One afternoon she was on a boat in Indonesia. She turned and saw a man sitting on a bench on deck, in three-quarter profile. He looked like Michael – Michael the sculptor from her early twenties, whom she'd met on New Year's and had left by May because he was jealous of her time. The man on the bench was asleep and he slept like Michael – head thrown back, arms out. Susan cried for two hours. When she describes this to me, her voice still breaks."

Leonard Michaels
In the Fifties

IN THE FIFTIES I LEARNED TO DRIVE A CAR. I WAS FRE-
quently in love. I had more friends than now.

When Khrushchev denounced Stalin my roommate shit
blood, turned yellow, and lost most of his hair.

I attended the lectures of the excellent E. B. Burgum until
Senator McCarthy ended his tenure. I imagined NYU would burn.
Miserable students, drifting in the halls, looked at one another.

In less than a month, working day and night, I wrote a bad
novel.

I went to school – NYU, Michigan, Berkeley – much of the time.

I had witty, giddy conversation, four or five nights a week, in
a homosexual bar in Ann Arbor.

I read literary reviews the way people suck candy.

Personal relationships were more important to me than
anything else.

I had a fight with a powerful fat man who fell on my face and
was immovable.

I had personal relationships with football players, jazz musi-
cians, ass-bandits, nymphomaniacs, non-specialized degenerates,
and numerous Jewish premedical students.

I had personal relationships with thirty-five rhesus monkeys
in an experiment on monkey addiction to morphine. They knew
me as one who shot reeking crap out of cages with a hose.

With four other students I lived in the home of a chiroprac-
tor named Leo.

I met a man in Detroit who owned a submachine gun; he claimed to have hit Dutch Schultz. I saw a gangster movie that disproved his claim.

I knew two girls who had brains, talent, health, good looks, plenty to eat, and hanged themselves.

I heard of parties in Ann Arbor where everyone made it with everyone else, including the cat.

I knew card sharks and con men. I liked marginal types because they seemed original and aristocratic, living for an ideal or obliged to live it. Ordinary types seemed fundamentally unserious. These distinctions belong to a romantic fop. I didn't think that way too much.

I worked for an evil vanity publisher in Manhattan.

I worked in a fish-packing plant in Massachusetts, on the line with a sincere Jewish poet from Harvard and three lesbians; one was beautiful, one grim; both loved the other, who was intelligent. I loved her, too. I dreamed of violating her purity. They talked among themselves, in creepy whispers, always about Jung. In a dark corner, away from our line, old Portuguese men slit fish in open flaps, flicking out the bones. I could see only their eyes and knives. I'd arrive early every morning to dash in and out until the stench became bearable. After work I'd go to bed and pluck fish scales out of my skin.

I was a teaching assistant in two English departments. I graded thousands of freshman themes. One began like this: "Karl Marx, for that was his name ... " Another began like this: "In Jonathan Swift's famous letter to the Pope ... " I wrote edifying comments in the margins. Later I began to scribble "Awkward" beside everything, even spelling errors.

I got A's and F's as a graduate student. A professor of English said my attitude wasn't professional. He said that he always read a "good book" after dinner.

A girl from Indiana said this of me on a teacher-evaluation form: "It is bad enough to go to an English class at eight in the morning, but to be instructed by a shabby man is horrible."

I made enemies on the East Coast, the West Coast, and in the Middle West. All now dead, sick, or out of luck.

I was arrested, photographed, and fingerprinted. In a soundproof room two detectives lectured me on the American way of life, and I was charged with the crime of nothing. A New York cop told me that detectives were called "defectives."

I had an automobile accident. I did the mambo. I had urethritis and mononucleosis.

In Ann Arbor, a few years before the advent of Malcolm X, a lot of my friends were black. After Malcolm X, almost all my friends were white. They admired John F. Kennedy.

In the fifties I smoked marijuana, hash, and opium. Once I drank absinthe. Once I swallowed twenty glycerine caps of peyote. The social effects of "drugs," unless sexual, always seemed tedious. But I liked people who inclined the drug way. Especially if they didn't proselytize. I listened to long conversations about the phenomenological weirdness of familiar reality and the great spiritual questions this entailed – for example, "Do you think Wallace Stevens is a head?"

I witnessed an abortion.

I was godless, but I thought the fashion of intellectual religiosity more despicable. I wished that I could live in a culture rather than study life among the cultured.

I drove a Chevy Bel Air eighty-five miles per hour on a two-lane blacktop. It was nighttime. Intermittent thick white fog made the headlights feeble and diffuse. Four others in the car sat with the strict silent rectitude of catatonics. If one of them didn't admit to being frightened, we were dead. A Cadillac, doing a hundred miles per hour, passed us and was obliterated in the fog. I slowed down.

I drank Old Fashioneds in the apartment of my friend Julian. We talked about Worringer and Spengler. We gossiped about friends. Then we left to meet our dates. There was more drinking. We all climbed trees, crawled in the street, and went to a church. Julian walked into an elm, smashed his glasses, vomited on a lawn, and returned home to memorize Anglo-Saxon grammatical forms. I ended on my knees, vomiting into a toilet bowl, repeatedly flushing the water to hide my noises. Later I phoned New York so that I could listen to the voices of my parents, their Yiddish, their English, their logics.

I knew a professor of English who wrote impassioned sonnets in honor of Henry Ford.

I played freshman varsity basketball at NYU and received a dollar an hour for practice sessions and double that for games. It was called "meal money." I played badly, too psychological, too worried about not studying, too short. If pushed or elbowed during a practice game, I was ready to kill. The coach liked my attitude. In his day, he said, practice ended when there was blood on the boards. I ran back and forth, in urgent sneakers, through my freshman year. Near the end I came down with pleurisy, quit basketball, started smoking more.

I took classes in comparative anatomy and chemistry. I took classes in Old English, Middle English, and modern literature. I took classes and classes.

I fired a twelve-gauge shotgun down the hallway of a railroad flat into a couch pillow.

My roommate bought the shotgun because of his gambling debts. He expected murderous thugs to come for him. I'd wake in the middle of the night listening for a knock, a cough, a footstep, wondering how to identify myself as not him when they broke through our door.

My roommate was an expensively dressed kid from a Chicago suburb. Though very intelligent, he suffered in school. He suffered with girls though he was handsome and witty. He suffered with boys though he was heterosexual. He slept on three mattresses and used a sun lamp all winter. He bathed, oiled, and perfumed his body daily. He wanted soft, sweet joys in every part, but when some whore asked if he'd like to be beaten with a garrison belt he said yes. He suffered with food, eating from morning to night, loading his pockets with fried pumpkin seeds when he left for class, smearing caviar paste on his filet mignons, eating himself into a monumental face of eating because he was eating. Then he killed himself.

A lot of young, gifted people I knew in the fifties killed themselves. Only a few of them continue walking around.

I wrote literary essays in the turgid, tumescent manner of darkest Blackmur.

I was a waiter in a Catskill hotel. The captain of the waiters ordered us to dance with the female guests who appeared in the casino without escorts and, as much as possible, fuck them. A professional *tummler* walked the grounds. Wherever he saw a group of people merely chatting, he thrust in quickly and created a tumult.

I heard the Budapest String Quartet, Dylan Thomas, Lester Young and Billie Holiday together, and I saw Pearl Primus dance, in a Village nightclub, in a space two yards square, accompanied by an African drummer about seventy years old. His hands moved in spasms of mathematical complexity at invisible speed. People left their tables to press close to Primus and see the expression in her face, the sweat, the muscles, the way her naked feet seized and released the floor.

Eventually, I had friends in New York, Ann Arbor, Chicago, Berkeley, and Los Angeles.

I did the cha-cha, wearing a tux, at a New Year's party in Hollywood, and sat at a table with Steve McQueen. He'd become famous in a TV series about a cowboy with a rifle. He said he didn't know which he liked best, acting or driving a racing car. I thought he was a silly person and then realized he thought I was. I met a few other famous people who said something. One night, in a yellow Porsche, I circled Manhattan with Jack Kerouac. He recited passages, perfectly remembered from his book reviews, to the sky. His manner was ironical, sweet, and depressing.

I had a friend named Chicky who drove his chopped, blocked, stripped, dual-exhaust Ford convertible, while vomiting out the fly window, into a telephone pole. He survived, lit a match to see if the engine was all right, and it blew up in his face. I saw him in the hospital. Through his bandages he said that ever since high school he'd been trying to kill himself. Because his girlfriend wasn't good-looking enough. He was crying and laughing while he pleaded with me to believe that he really had been trying to kill himself because his girlfriend wasn't good-looking enough. I told him that I was going out with a certain girl and he told me that he had fucked her once but it didn't matter because I could take her away and live somewhere else. He was a Sicilian kid with a face like Caravaggio's angels of debauch. He'd been educated by priests and nuns. When his hair grew back and his face healed, his mind healed. He broke up with his girlfriend. He wasn't nearly as narcissistic as other men I knew in the fifties.

I knew one who, before picking up his dates, ironed his dollar bills and powdered his testicles. And another who referred to women as "cockless wonders" and used only their family names – for example, "I'm going to meet Goldberg, the cockless wonder." Many women thought he was extremely attractive and became his sexual slaves. Men didn't like him.

I had a friend who was dragged down a courthouse stairway, in San Francisco, by her hair. She'd wanted to attend the House Un-American hearings. The next morning I crossed the Bay Bridge to join my first protest demonstration. I felt frightened and embarrassed. I was bitter about what had happened to her and the others she'd been with. I expected to see thirty or forty people like me, carrying hysterical placards around the courthouse until the cops bludgeoned us into the pavement. About two thousand people were there. I marched beside a little kid who had a bag of marbles to throw under the hoofs of the horse cops. His mother kept saying, "Not yet, not yet." We marched all day. That was the end of the fifties.

Wayne Koestenbaum
My 1980s

Les Fleuves m'ont laissé descendre où je voulais.
– ARTHUR RIMBAUD

I MET TAMA JANOWITZ ONCE IN THE 1980S. (WAS IT 1987?)
She probably doesn't remember our encounter. She was a visiting fellow at Princeton, where I was a graduate student in English.
At a university gathering, Joyce Carol Oates complimented the
ostentatious way that Tama and I were dressed. Seeking system, I
replied, "Tama is East Village. I'm West Village."

* * *

I had little to do with art in the eighties. I saw Caravaggio in Rome,
and Carpaccio in Venice. I neglected the contemporary. For half
the decade I lived in New York City, and yet I didn't go to a single
Warhol opening. Missed opportunities? My mind was elsewhere.

* * *

My mind was on *écriture feminine* as applied to homosexuals. I was
big on the word "homosexual." I read *Homosexualities and French
Literature* (edited by George Stambolian and Elaine Marks). I read
Hélène Cixous. On a train I read *Roland Barthes by Roland Barthes*
(translated by Richard Howard); I looked out dirty windows onto
dirty New Jersey fields. I began to take autobiography seriously
as a historical practice with intellectual integrity. On an airplane
I read Michel Leiris's *Manhood* (translated by Richard Howard)
and grooved to Leiris's mention of a "bitten buttock"; I decided to
become, like Leiris, a self-ethnographer. I read André Gide's *The
Immoralist* (translated by Richard Howard) in Hollywood, Florida,

while lying on a pool deck. I read many books translated by Richard Howard. In the eighties I read *The Fantastic* by Tzvetan Todorov (translated by Richard Howard) and meditated on the relation between fantasy and autobiography. I brought Richard Howard flowers the first time I met him (1985), in his book-lined apartment. He assured me that I was a poet.

* * *

I discovered the word *essentialism* in the late eighties. I should have discovered it earlier. Sex-and-gender essentialism was a dread fate. I feared that it was my condition. In the early nineties, after I stopped worrying about my essentialism, I realized that I'd never been an essentialist after all.

* * *

Too many of these sentences begin with the first-person singular pronoun. Later I may jazz up the syntax, falsify it.

* * *

I am typing this essay on the IBM Correcting Selectric III typewriter I bought in 1981 for one thousand dollars. I borrowed the money from my older brother, a cellist. It took me several years to pay him back.

* * *

In the eighties I worked as a legal secretary, a paralegal, and a legal proofreader. I freelanced as a typist, $1.50 per page. I temped for Kelly Girl; one pleasurable assignment was a stint at the Girl Scouts headquarters. I taught seventh- through twelfth-grade English at a yeshiva. I tutored a man from Japan in English conversation. I didn't turn a single trick.

* * *

This morning I asked my boyfriend, an architect, about the 1980s. I said, "Let's make a list of salient features of our eighties." We came up with just two items: cocaine, AIDS.

* * *

In 1980, after Reagan was elected, I began, in repulsed reaction, to read the *New York Times*. Before then, I'd never read the newspaper.

* * *

I remember a specific homeless woman on the Upper West Side in the 1980s. She smelled predictably of pee or shit and hung out in an ATM parlor near the Seventy-Second Street subway stop. She seemed to rule the space. Large, she epitomized. Did I ever give her money? I blamed Reagan.

* * *

A stranger smooched me during a "Read My Lips" kiss-in near the Jefferson Market Public Library: festive politics. I stumbled on the ceremony. Traffic stopped.

* * *

A cute short blond guy named Mason used to brag about sex parties; I was jealous. I didn't go to sex parties. He ended up dying of AIDS. I'm not pushing a cause-and-effect argument.

* * *

In 1985 I read Mario Mieli's *Homosexuality and Liberation*. I bought, but did not read, an Italian periodical, hefty and intellectually substantial, called *Sodoma: Rivista Omosessuale di Cultura*. That year, I turned to Georges Bataille for bulletins on the solar anus, for lessons on smart, principled obscenity.

* * *

A handsome brunet poet came to my apartment, and I dyed his hair blond. I had a crush on him. He talked a lot about Michel Foucault. The poet and I bought the dye on Sixth Avenue in the Village.

In my kitchen he stripped to his undershorts, which had holes. His nipples were large and erect: impressive! I'd never seen such ready-to-go nipples. He leaned over the kitchen sink; I washed his hair and applied the dye. I kept my undershirt on during the session; I wasn't proud of my body (though in retrospect I respect its scrawniness). I continued to read Foucault throughout the eighties. Foucault never deeply moved me. I switched to Blanchot in the late nineties.

* * *

My boyfriend worked out downstairs. We lived above a gay gym: the Body Center, corner of Sixth and Fifteenth, now the David Barton Gym. After midnight we could hear loud music coming through our radiators: The Body Center's cleaning crew had turned up the sound system.

* * *

Geographical facts: During the 1980s, I lived in Cambridge, Baltimore, New York, New Haven. The important city was New York: 1984–1988. There, I worked out at the McBurney Y. I swam in its skanky, dank, tiny, cloudy, over-warm pool. I recall a not-handsome guy shaving off his body hair at the sink. Careful, I didn't once enter the Y's cramped sauna.

* * *

I read all of Proust in summer 1986. Proust and summer passed quickly. That same summer I reread James Schuyler's *The Morning of the Poem* and experienced an AIDS-panic-related sense of life's brevity; houseguest, I sat on an Adirondack chair in Southold, Long Island. My host, hardy in the garden, was ill with AIDS. I recall wild blueberries I picked with him, and his reticence, and mine.

* * *

In 1986 or '87 I heard Eve Kosofsky Sedgwick give a lecture on "unknowing" in Diderot's *The Nun*. I had just read her *Between Men*. Her difficult lucidity gave my stumbling concepts one warm, fruitful context.

* * *

In 1984 I took a course in feminist theory with Elaine Showalter and decided to be a male feminist. I decided not to write a dissertation about John Ashbery and W. H. Auden. Instead, I wanted to write a flaming treatise. In a seminar on the Victorian novel, Showalter showed slides of Charcot's hysterics in *arcs-en-cercle* and of fin-de-siècle faces disfigured by syphilis. I flipped out with intellectual glee. Hysteria would be my open sesame.

* * *

In the eighties I was happiest when writing "syllabic" poems. Superstitiously I discovered my existence's modicum of dignity and value by counting duration in syllables, on my fingers, while I typed, on the same Selectric I am using now.

* * *

I saw *Taxi zum Klo* and *Diva*: two films that made a dent. I went to all the gay movies. *L'homme blessé*. On TV I saw *Brideshead Revisited* and the Patrice Chéreau production of Wagner's *Ring*. I went to Charlie Chan movies (guilty pleasure) at Theater 80 St. Marks; there, my treat was buying a blue mint from the transparent vessel on the dim-lit lobby's counter. I saw *Shoah*: only the first part. I heard Leonie Rysanek sing Elisabeth in *Tannhäuser* and Ortrud in *Lohengrin* and Kundry in *Parsifal* at the Met, and Sieglinde in *Die Walküre* in San Francisco. I heard Christa Ludwig's twenty-fifth-anniversary performance at the Met: Klytämnestra in Strauss's *Elektra*, December 20, 1984.

* * *

I wore a bright red Kikit baseball jacket and red espadrilles. I decided that bright blue and red–DayGlo, neon, opalescent–were passports to private revolution. I wore a paisley tux jacket and black patent-leather cowboy boots. I didn't mind looking vulgar, slutty, off-base.

* * *

I spent a lot of the eighties thinking about Anna Moffo, soprano – her career's ups and downs, and her timbre's uncanny compromise between vulnerability and voluptuousness. I regret not buying her Debussy song album, used, at Academy Records on West Eighteenth Street: on the soft-focus cover, she wore a summer hat. The LP era ended.

* * *

I focused on my sadness as if it were an object in the room, a discrete, dense entity, impervious to alteration. I never used the word *subjectivity* in the eighties, though I was fond of *gap, blank page, masculine,* and *feminine*. I planned to call my first book of poems *Queer Street*, nineteenth-century British slang for shady circumstances, debt, bankruptcy, blackmail. I found the phrase in Robert Louis Stevenson's *The Strange Case of Dr. Jekyll and Mr. Hyde*.

* * *

In 1980 my new boyfriend gave me a 45 rpm single (blue-labeled Chrysalis) of Blondie's "Call Me" (from *American Gigolo*). We considered it our theme song. Then I stopped listening to "popular" music. Not consciously. Not programmatically. The defection happened naturally.

* * *

In 1981 I made an onion-bacon-apple casserole from *The Joy of Cooking*. I served it, as a main dish, to a schizophrenic friend. A few years later she sent me a letter, dated 1975. This significant confusion of chronology meant that she had cracked up. I began methodically to cook from Marcella Hazan. I tirelessly stirred risotto in a cheap aluminum saucepan with high sides. I made a *bombe aux trois chocolats* from Julia Child: a molded dessert, for which I used a beige Tupperware bowl.

* * *

In 1983 I served a friend a veal roast stuffed with pancetta. We agreed that the roast tasted like human baby. We blamed the pancetta.

* * *

Sometime in the mid-eighties I stopped swallowing cum. I don't miss its taste.

* * *

The first guy I knew with AIDS died at age thirty-five. His name was Metro. I've written about this death before, and I hesitate to repeat myself. I have almost no visual memory of Metro, though I recall his precision and hypercapability; we lay on a stony beach, Long Island Sound, more rock than sand. What sand there was he dusted off his body with decisive, practiced gestures.

* * *

I went to Paris for the first time in the eighties: I wore blue leather gloves purchased on Christopher Street. In a rue Jacob hotel bedroom I woke up, sweat-drenched, feverish; I observed the wallpaper's mesmerizing, dull pattern, its refusal to serve as reliable augury. On the flight back from Paris I read Marianne Moore's prose and picked up pointers from its ornery mannerism.

* * *

Despite my best efforts, I existed in history, not as agent but as frightened, introspective observer. I began to fine-tune my sentences – a fastidiousness I learned from Moore's prose. Precise sentences were my ideals, though in practice I was slipshod and sentimental. I began to seek a balance between improvisation and revision. I revised by endlessly retyping.

* * *

I read Freud in the eighties. He was always describing me, my likenesses, my forebears. Anna O. became my touchstone. I decided that psychoanalysis was the hysterical child born from Freud's anus.

* * *

In 1981 I read Susan Sontag's *On Photography*. In 1982 I read her *Under the Sign of Saturn*. I swore allegiance to the aphorism. But I didn't read Walter Benjamin until the nineties.

* * *

In 1981 I published for the first time: a story, "In the White Forest," in a small periodical, *Pale Fire Review*. In 1982 I stopped writing fiction. The last story I wrote, "Liberty Baths," autobiographically reported my San Francisco bathhouse experiences of summer 1979. A guy I met at the baths took me to his loft. A commercial photographer, he shot a whole roll of me nude, from the rear. I was insulted that he didn't photograph me frontally. I should have been grateful that he found one angle comely.

* * *

I spent the summer of 1983 writing fifty sonnets. My stylistic model was Auden's sequence *In Time of War*: I loved his phrase "Anxiety / Receives them like a grand hotel." I put together a manuscript called, unadventurously, "Fifty Sonnets." It never got published as a book. In one of the sonnets, I rhymed "Callas" and "callous."

* * *

The world was doing its best to ignore the fact that I was a writer. In search of fragile legitimacy, I obsessively submitted work to periodicals. Rejection slips arrived, sometimes with a beckoning "Thanks!" or "Sorry!" or "Send more?" I always sent more, immediately, with a treacly letter, informing the hapless editor how much the invitation to send more had meant to me.

* * *

I was not thinking about the world. I was not thinking about history. I was thinking about my body's small, precise, limited, hungry movement forward into a future that seemed at every instant on the verge of being shut down.

* * *

I didn't take the HIV test until the nineties. I spent most of the eighties worried about being HIV-positive, only discovering, in the nineties, that I was negative. My attitude in the eighties was: wait and see. Wait for symptoms. When a friend suggested I get tested, I broke off the friendship. It wasn't much of a friendship. She wanted us to write a collaborative book on Verdi's Oedipus complex. A semi-invalid, she sent me on errands to buy dollhouse furniture – her hobby.

* * *

I heard Leontyne Price sing a recital at the Met on March 24, 1985. I still remember the sensation of her voice in my body. I think she gave "Chi il bel sogno di Doretta" from *La Rondine* as an encore.

* * *

I read Derrida's *Spurs* (translated by Barbara Harlow). I wondered why he didn't use male testicles – instead of vaginas and veils – as metaphors. Invaginate, indeed! In the 1980s I made snap judgments.

* * *

Poems I published in the eighties, in small periodicals, but never collected into a book: "Where I Lived, And What I Lived For"; "*Carmen* in Digital for a Deaf Woman"; "Teachers of Obscure Subjects"; "The Babysitter in the Ham Radio." I published my first full-length essay in 1987: Its polite subtitle was "Oblique Confession in the Early Work of John Ashbery."

* * *

In the eighties I wrote book reviews for the *New York Native*, a now-defunct gay newspaper. Among my subjects: James Schuyler's *A Few Days*, John Ashbery's *April Galleons*, Sylvère Lotringer's *Overexposed: Treating Sexual Perversion in America*.

* * *

Does any of this information matter? I am not responsible for what matters and what doesn't matter. Offbeat definition of materialism: a worldview in which every detail matters, in which every factual statement is material.

* * *

I bought soft-core porn magazines – *Mandate, Honcho*, others – from a newsstand on Fourteenth Street. I felt guilty about my insatiably scopophilic core; culpable, it could never get its fill of images. Over the years I began to notice changes in porn bodies: the men were growing younger. Now, when I look back at those magazines (I've saved many), the men seem like old friends, guys I went to school with. Max Archer. Chad Douglas. Jesus.

* * *

I have always had a rather limited circle of friends; although I am superficially gregarious, most human contact makes me, eventually, uncomfortable. I didn't realize this fact in the eighties. During those years, I was intensely ill at ease.

* * *

I stopped using drugs (pot, cocaine) when I began to take AIDS seriously. Health suddenly mattered: I wanted always to feel tip-top, without chemical enhancement.

* * *

If my eighties don't match yours, chalk up the mismatch to the fact

that I am profoundly out of touch with my time. I never chose to
nominate myself as historical witness.

* * *

Notice, please, my absence of nostalgia.

* * *

I started dyeing my hair in 1984: reddish highlights. I stopped in
1988. I returned to nature.

* * *

My mission in the eighties was to develop my aestheticism. My
mission in the nineties was to justify my aestheticism.

* * *

In 1988 I started teaching at Yale. I decided to wear bow ties. I had
several: red polka-dot; blue polka-dot; amber with black triangles;
neon yellow. The first semester, I taught a required core course
on Chaucer, Spenser, and Donne. I also taught my first elective: a
seminar decorously titled "Literature and Sexuality: Countertra-
ditions." I was hyperconscious of authorities. In 1989, I published
my first book, *Double Talk: The Erotics of Male Literary Collaboration*.
When the published book first arrived in my apartment, I admired
its cover – George Platt Lynes's photograph *The Second Birth of Dionysus* – but wished the book were a novel instead: same cover, different contents.

* * *

In New Haven, outside my apartment, 1989, I was mugged. A guy
said, "Give me your wallet or I'll blow your brains out."

* * *

In 1989 I developed a sustaining, mood-brightening crush on
the UPS man. Hundreds – thousands – of men and women in New
Haven must have had a crush on that same UPS man. The first time

he appeared at my doorstep with a package, I thought that a *Candid Camera* porn movie had just begun. If you want me to describe him, I will.

* * *

When I look back at the eighties I see myself as a small boat. It is not an important, attractive, or likable boat, but it has a prow, a sail, and a modest personality. It has no consciousness of the water it moves through. Some days it resembles Rimbaud's inebriated vessel. Other, clearer days, it is sober and undemonstrative. There are few images or adjectives we could affix to the boat; there are virtually no ways to classify it. Its only business is staying afloat. Thus the boat is amoral. It has been manufactured in a certain style. Any style contains a history. The boat is not conscious of the history shaping its movements. The boat, undramatic, passive, at best pleasant, at worst slapdash, persistently attends to the work of flotation, which takes precedence over responsible navigation. As far as the boat is concerned, it is the only vessel on the body of water. How many times must I repeat the word *boat* to convince you that in the eighties I was a small boat with a minor mission and a fear of sinking? The boat did not sink.

Barry Hannah
The Wretched Seventies

MANY, TOO MANY, DAYS, NED MAXY HAD STARED OUT A window weeping, fasting, and praying, in his way. In character of both the drunkard and the penitent, he had watched life across the street. Now, in a healthier time, arising to his work at early hours, he labored at his front-window table, peering out on occasion at a world that spoke back to him. Not loudly and not a lot, but some.

Over the white board fence he'd just painted, and through the leaping wide leaves of his muscadine arbor, he spied shyly like a stranger in town. The satisfaction of this almost frightened him.

The woman in a uniform who left every morning at a quarter to eight was a paramedic. In the awful seventies Maxy had sworn to hundreds in saloons that he wanted most of all to be a paramedic. This was a bogus piety to support his drinking. But here was the real thing. Maxy did not know the paramedic woman but he watched her through a pair of opera glasses he had bought at a Hot Springs pawnshop from a man who had also been broken in the seventies and who now sat with his crutches beside him and lit up unfiltered Luckies that made him retch.

In his late forties the lifetime monster of lust had released him, first time since he was eleven, just as the monster of drink had released him four years ago. He still did not know precisely what accounted for it, but it was a deep lucky thing, now that he was able to see the woman paramedic across the street leaving for work and comprehend that she could be happy without him. He looked on in high admiration, good will, and with no panic. She was engaged to a wide man with a crewcut who came out with her to the doorway on his big white legs, in Bermuda shorts, and embraced her, seeing his love off in the cool of the morning. Maxy applauded their love. He had been in love this way twice in his life. He recalled the stupid rapture and had no advice for them at all.

He had spoken to the woman only once, told her she looked good in her uniform – all ready to fly away in a helicopter in her high-top black leather sneakers. She had the voice of a country girl, the kind of girl who had soothed his old man dying in the hospital at age eighty-seven. The old fellow had got rich in the city but loved the country much better, and the nurse was a sweet comfort at the last. Maxy liked that this country girl had the moxie to fly in a machine that would have terrified many hillbillies, and he told her so. Even from a hundred yards he could see her go shy, having an unexpected compliment sail out to her from a man who didn't need anything, here in the late cool of a summer morning, her head of blond hair lowered to look at her own eminent bosom of which he was no longer required to dream in impossible lechery.

She answered some way he couldn't make out, in a whisper, a country whisper of thanks, good beyond form. This whole exchange would not have been possible even three months ago, when in his mind he would have been teaching her the needs of his famished world, her body a naked whirlwind of willing orifices, as he smiled at her all the while like the prince of liars.

The whisper had fetched back for him his old mighty friend Drum, lately a suicide. Drum was a practicing Christian, one of maybe four selfless men Ned Maxy had known in life, brought low by pain and anxiety after a heart attack. He was cut off from good work and high spirits and could not go on, they said. Drum was the only whispering drunkard Maxy knew. Through all the thundering seventies he had never raised his voice.

He killed himself in the bathroom of a double-wide mobile home he rented from a preacher who lamented to the police: Now poor Drum can't ever go to Heaven. But he had been tidy, there in the bathtub with the large-calibre pistol, much appreciated.

His drinking buddy Drum's whispers of encouragement, his pleading to Maxy that he was a man who must respect himself, that he must work hard, that he must not waste the precious days or the gifts poured on him by nature – Ned Maxy would take that whisper with him until his own heart stopped, too, and he knew this.

The whisper of the paramedic country girl was there for him now. He did not want to make too much out of it. Thousands must have been given this gift. He didn't want to be only another kind of fool, a sort of Peeping Tom of charity.

But he was a new fool. Some big quiet thing had fallen down and locked into place, like a whisper of some weight. Ned Maxy had been granted contact with paradise, and he could hardly believe the lack of noise. His awful seventies decade had gone past twenty years. Finally it was over.

The next day, Maxy, in a daze, got his rushed suit out of the cleaners and attended the wedding of the woman paramedic at a country church down between Water Valley and Coffeeville. He shook hands with the bride and groom, then stood out of the pounding heat under the shade of a tall brothering sycamore.

Nobody ever figured out quite who he was. Their faces were full of baffled felicity, as if each one was whispering, Well, howdy, stranger, I guess.

S. L. Wisenberg
Brunch

WHEN BRUCE HAS BRUNCH, HE MAKES TWO TRIPS TO the deli, then sits at his beat-up table and tells me, "There are no happy couples, Leah, only people who haven't broken up yet." Then he jumps up to check the Nicaraguan drip-grind decaf and runs back to the deli and thinks up puns about lox. When Bruce makes brunch, he could invite Jerry, but he can't invite Jerry if he invites me, because since we broke up I won't see Jerry. And Bruce has to give me first dibs on all invitations, because I've known him since before we knew anybody else. Bruce and I met at O'Hare, first day in town for both of us. So he doesn't even ask if he can invite Jerry. He knows. And if he did ask I'd turn around and say, "If I had a brunch, could I invite Susan?" Only it's not the same, because since March Susan's been living in D.C.

Now Bruce is planning a brunch and I ask if Sam is going. Bruce says no, that Sam's got that conference in Carolina on religion and the left, and he'll be back Monday. Bruce doesn't know about Sam and me. If Sam came to brunch I wouldn't leave, but we'd probably try to ignore each other at first, then talk a little too loud and laugh a little too hard and lecture a little too much, and finally have a tight, whispered conversation in the kitchen. We'd tell people we were talking strategy.

Most of us met through coalitions. Bruce knows Jerry from the fight against Contra aid. Bruce was a liaison to the Quakers; Jerry was a liaison from the Quakers. The first time Jerry said he loved me was at a conference on the Sanctuary Movement. When we broke off, I said, "You take the Religious Task Force, I'll take Fellowship of Reconciliation." When Bruce and Susan broke up, they were both working on Harold Washington's reelection, out of the North Side. Susan moved down to the South Side headquarters. She refused to help out at the training session for deputy voter registrars, because she knew Bruce and his friends would be running it. She voted absentee so she wouldn't see anybody she knew at the poll.

With each breakup, our territories get smaller and smaller. I do solidarity work with Central American labor unions, but lately only the ones in Guatemala and Honduras. When Jerry and I broke up, he refused to give up El Salvador. He writes to the F. D. R. leaders in Spanish. In his Spanish for Progressives class he met Brenda. She runs a Third World trading outfit and used to live with Ben. They met during Washington's first campaign for mayor. They believe that monogamy is bourgeois. I think she and Jerry sleep together occasionally. I don't think they remove their woven friendship bracelets for the disappeared in Guatemala. I don't take mine off when I sleep. No one was wearing them back when I first met Bruce. The disappeared weren't disappeared yet, or we didn't know about them yet, word hadn't filtered back up to us. Susan used to wear hers even when we went swimming. Jill, my ex-roommate, doesn't have one. Jerry had his before I met him. I think some Buddhists gave it to him when he protested at the U.N.

In the middle of the old days, Jerry and I would have brunch and invite Bruce, Susan, Brenda, Ben, Alan, Jill, Art, Crista, Mark, Esther, Liz, Frank. We didn't hang out with Sam. Now Crista and Art are divorced, Liz and Frank are engaged, Brenda and Ben are occasional. The rest aren't speaking. Jerry has my skis and skates and we discuss his returning them on the phone, in exchange for his socks and second-best tennis racquet. He gets mad because I won't talk about this with him in person.

So I don't make brunch.

ONCE THERE WAS a time when I didn't know all of them, but I hardly remember it. I get calls from that time – from Ajax, who's out in California making bookcases. I wait for him to want me back. He tells me about his kids. I know you can't erase kids. Jerry doesn't want me back. Bruce doesn't want Susan back. Crista doesn't want Art back. Jill doesn't want Alan back. Mark wants Esther back but is too proud to say so. Brenda and Ben still talk free love. On weekends I see Crista and Alan and Tom or Art and Jan and Esther, but never Crista and Art or Jan and Alan. We can't go to anyone's old favorite restaurants, so we go to new places no one likes all that much. Before fund-raisers, we make extensive calls to determine who'll be there.

Riding on the El, I think: I'll run into someone I know. Or: That man over there will fall for me. I know that Jerry sees Sam on the El. They talk baseball and nerve-gas legislation.

On weekends, Jerry goes camping in Michigan. He doesn't take anyone to his fund-raising dinners, doesn't mention my name anymore at work, doesn't have anyone to call "my little June Bug." I don't know why he started calling me that. He'd write it in letters, say it into my answering machine, buy me bugs made of licorice or chocolate. He'd send me cards showing sweet domestic scenes in color on the front, and inside, on the blank part, he'd write, "To my one, my only, Bed Bug."

On weekends, I call Susan in Washington or she calls me. We talk about Bruce. I don't tell her about Sam and me. It's been three weeks. Three Saturday nights ago, after the benefit at the Heartland Café for Nicaraguan medical aid. Weather a bit warmer than tonight, even. We were sitting on Sam's porch. I said, "It's nice out here." Sam said, "You're pretty." He said, "You fascinate me." He twirled the curls at the back of my neck. He frightened me. Fascination, I thought. Awe. I can't live with awe. But I did. I hung in. Two weeks later, he said, "I bit off too much, I confess. I hadn't expected ... " He said, "It's not the right time."

I am not the right person at the right time. I was not the right person for Sam, Jerry, or Jill. Tom and Ajax were not the right people for me. Susan was not the right person for Bruce. I am thirty-two. Jill is twenty-eight. Bruce is thirty-two and has worked in three Presidential campaigns. Susan is twenty-eight. Jerry is thirty. Sam is thirty-five. Art is forty. Tom is thirty-five. Michael the sculptor is a month and a day younger than Susan. Ajax is thirty-eight. Bebe, his new girlfriend, is twenty.

BACK WHEN MY sister and I were little, before either of us had ever had a boyfriend, we would ask each other, "If you had to marry somebody now, who would it be?"

Who would it be? Would it be Bruce, Sam, or Jerry? Or Ajax? Or Tom? Maybe Sam, because it would be a challenge to make him grow to love me, the way he said he did three Saturday nights ago. It's the challenge that people accept when they adopt a dog from the S.P.C.A. that's said to have "a discipline problem," and they think: Not with me – I'll be the one who tames him. Would it be Jerry? No, because he would grow abrupt again. He would be impatient and refuse counseling.

Bruce knew Jerry first, but it was Susan who'd introduced me to him. She'd met Jerry through Michael the sculptor, whom she'd met at a New Year's Eve party put on by Artists Against Racism. When she came back from Washington to visit this summer, she showed me the house where the party had been. Or so she thought – she wasn't sure. She'd been drunk and it was nine years ago. Every time we passed a yellow Rabbit, she said, "I wonder if that's the car I sold when I left here."

Once I was going to be her maid of honor. She was going to marry Bruce. She bought a midcalf-length tea dress, pinky-peach, with lace. Then he decided he didn't want anything for life, though he still wanted to live with her. She left for six months, and came back for two years before leaving for good. During that six months, she went around the world. One afternoon she was on a boat in Indonesia. She turned and saw a man sitting on a bench on deck, in three-quarter profile. He looked like Michael – Michael the sculptor from her early twenties, whom she'd met on New Year's and had left by May because he was jealous of her time. The man on the bench was asleep and he slept like Michael – head thrown back, arms out. Susan cried for two hours. When she describes this to me, her voice still breaks.

7. Collage

A molecular chain reaction causes your skin to lose its elasticity, resulting in wrinkles. Life splinters.

Dinty W. Moore	Son of Mr. Green Jeans
Elizabeth Cooperman	Creation

Collage

COLLAGE GETS RID OF THE "SLOW BURN" CHARACTERISTIC of the classic, epiphany-based short story. Its thematic investigation is manifest, although encrypted, from the beginning. As with action painting, Language poetry, New Music, and self-reflexive documentary film, collage teaches the reader to understand that the movements of the writer's mind are intricately intertwined with the work's meaning. Forget "intricately intertwined with the work's meaning" – *are* the work's meaning.

A traditional story depends upon the elaboration of plot; collage depends upon the orchestration of variegated materials – separated by white space and unconnected by plot – into theme.

Collage: tiny paragraph-units working together to project a linear motion. The traditional novel is a freeway with very distinct signage. Collage is surface street to surface street – with many more road signs, and each one is *seemingly* more open to interpretation, giving the traveler just a suggestion or a hint. One reader might think he's going through the desert; the next, that she's driving to the North Pole. The conventional novel tells the reader pretty much where he's going; he's a passenger, looking at the pretty sights along the way. Collage demands that the reader figure out for herself where she is and where she's going (hint: she's going somewhere quite specific, guided all along by the subterranean collagist).

Said another way: When plot shapes a narrative, it's equivalent to knitting a scarf. You have a long piece of string and many choices about how to knit, but we understand a sequence is involved, a beginning and an end, with one part of the weave very logically and sequentially connected to the next. You can figure out where the beginning is and where the last stitch is cast off. Webs look orderly, too, but unless you watch the spider weaving, you'll never know where it started. It could be attached to branches or table legs or eaves in six or eight places. You won't know the sequence in which the different cells were spun and attached to each other. You have to decide for yourself how to read its patterning, but if you pluck it at any point, the entire web will vibrate.

Orchestration of theme rather than elaboration of plot: collage is not a refuge for the compositionally disabled. It's an evolution beyond narrative.

In 1,500 words or fewer, compose your own collage. Use any materials you want–fiction, nonfiction, diary entry, email, photo, tweet, text, family album, newspaper caption, dirty joke, etc., etc. The key thing is to organize the material in such a way that the reader, slowly but surely, gets what connects all the materials and gets what you are saying about the material. Picasso: "A great painting comes together, just barely." That's exactly what you want your collage to do–come together, but just barely.

Dinty W. Moore's collage-essay "Son of Mr. Green Jeans," which appeared in *Harper's* as a slightly redacted reprint from its earlier incarnation in *Crazyhorse*, is better in its later incarnation. In its original form, it feels slightly too long; edited down a bit, it's exactly the right length. Collage is very much about getting the music right, getting the rhythm right, getting just enough material in just the right juxtaposition that the reader gets how all the pieces come together, but then not belaboring the point.

Moore's collage is about a classic ambivalence: a husband's wariness/reluctance about becoming a father. There are many ways to write about such material: as a traditional essay exploring one's own ambivalence; as a short story perhaps rendered as a series of conversations/debates/arguments between husband and wife. Moore chooses to explore his ambivalence or chart his ambivalence, and he works with remarkable concision, precision, and power.

"Son of Mr. Green Jeans" is pseudo-alphabetized to give us a semi-handrail to hold onto. The title hints that the essay is going to perhaps be about fathers and sons, but as we read the first two sections, we couldn't possibly know where the essay is headed – is it about Tim Allen? TV? Pop culture? We haven't a clue. "Carp," "Divorce," and "Emperor Penguins" should help us some, at least in retrospect. The bricolage seems to be a sort of boxing match between how horrifically humans take care of their young, and how devoted other members of the animal kingdom are to theirs.

With "Father Knows Best" and then "Hugh Beaumont," we get a new thread in the tapestry. The new thread is another strand from pop culture, TV shows from the fifties. We are struck over and over by the discrepancy between how happy characters are on the show and how miserable they seem to be off-set. This leads to "Inheritance," which is, of course, the most crucial and the longest section in the collage, and it comes at exactly the right time – exactly in the middle – neither too early, when it would seem unearned, nor too late, when it would seem sentimental. It's just here as data: Moore's own father lost his mother at age three, stuttered severely, and could find surcease from the stutter only when drunk, which he was every evening. As a boy, Dinty "coped with the family's embarrassment by staying glued to the television. I desperately wanted someone like Hugh Beaumont to be my father, or maybe Robert Young."

The pieces of the jigsaw puzzle are now starting to fit into place: TV, pop culture, paternity, unhappy families. We still don't know what it's about yet, though. The boxing match between adorable animals and ghastly humans continues. We seem to see more examples of bad human behavior than admirable animal behavior, but the score is close – 7–5, say. The first example of a human sounding semi-happy occurs in "Religion." Lauren Chapin, "the troubled actress who played Kitten [on *Father Knows Best*], had a religious conversion. She credits her belief in Jesus with saving her life. After his television career ended, Methodist minister Hugh Beaumont became a Christmas-tree farmer." The essay is not in any way religious in its vision, but these actors finding their footings seem to presage Dinty finding his footing immediately after. "Xenogenesis: the supposed generation of offspring completely and permanently different from the parent." Dinty believes in xenogenesis and changes his mind about having children after he earlier rejected his wife's first suggestion of the idea.

Now we know what the essay has been about all along: Moore is afraid he'll be as bad a father to his child as his father was to him. He hopes he'll be as devoted a father as the characters on the shows are, but he knows how different the actors are in real life. He clings to the admirable parental behavior that he sees animals display, and he finds final refuge/affirmation in his hope that he and his wife will have a girl, because he's afraid a boy would inherit his own characteristics. This is sad, convincing, and beautiful.

Cooperman's collage also examines the theme of birth, riffing on the story of the creation of the world in the Book of Genesis. It was intended to serve as the opening section for a long essay about creative crises and blocks.

The reader's first thought: what *is* this? A drawing? Cartoon? Diagram? Flowchart? Turning the pages, we begin to study the networks of words, supplied sparingly at first, engulfed in white space. That white space gives us an opportunity to contemplate each term – "father," "engender," "procreate," "mother." Save for simple lines and bubbles, there is little to no explanation about how the pieces and parts connect. Therefore, the reader has to do a great deal of work; she has to translate the cartoon into a new language. In this way, "Creation" serves as a sort of Platonic form of how collage works, asking us to proceed with faith and creativity and intuition across gaps in a text and to track and trust the movements of the writer's mind. Either you figure out how to read a collage or you put it down.

This collage, as we eventually learn, motions beyond Genesis to our personal geneses. In the repetition of "mother" and "father" there's an allusion not only to the creation of the world but also to childbirth. By the third and fourth pages, the womblike central chamber has sprouted limbs, as if the piece itself is becoming a body. By page six we are meant to understand the horror of giving birth: "horror vacui." This is a crucial turn. People assume that creation is inherently about abundance but the essay suggests that the urge comes from a darker place – that the creative instinct is a psychological crux related to our fear of emptiness, loneliness, waste, poverty, void, and that to create too much can even be vulgar, monstrous (see: "creeping creatures"). Perhaps the essay's author wants to exist within the world's vacuum more quietly and watchfully, and to depict through fragment and proto-expression a kind of non-expression. Who am I, the author seems to be saying; I am not God.

Dinty W. Moore

Son of Mr. Green Jeans

Allen, Tim

Best known as the father on ABC's *Home Improvement*, the popular comedian was born Timothy Allen Dick on June 13, 1953. When Allen was eleven years old, his father, Gerald Dick, was killed by a drunk driver while driving home from a University of Colorado football game.

Bees

"A man, after impregnating the woman, could drop dead," Camille Paglia suggested to Tim Allen in a 1995 *Esquire* interview. "That is how peripheral he is to the whole thing."

"I'm a drone," Allen responded. "Like those bees."

"You are a drone," Paglia agreed. "That's exactly right."

Carp

After the female Japanese carp gives birth to hundreds of tiny babies, the father carp remains nearby. When he senses approaching danger, he sucks the helpless babies into his mouth and holds them there until the coast is clear.

Divorce

University of Arizona psychologist Sanford Braver tells the story of a woman who felt threatened by her husband's close bond with their young son. The husband had a flexible work schedule, but the wife did not, so the boy spent the bulk of his time with the father. The mother became so jealous of the tight father-son relationship that she filed for divorce and successfully fought for sole custody. The result was that instead of being in the care of his father while the mother worked, the boy was now left in day care.

Emperor Penguins

Once a male emperor penguin has completed mating, he remains by the female's side for the next month to determine if the act has been successful. When he sees a single greenish-white egg emerge from his mate's egg pouch, he begins to sing. Scientists have characterized his song as "ecstatic."

Father Knows Best

In 1949, Robert Young began *Father Knows Best* as a radio show. Young played Jim Anderson, an average father in an average family. The show later moved to television, where it was a major hit, but Young's successful life was troubled by alcohol and depression.

At age eighty-three, Young attempted suicide by running a hose from his car's exhaust pipe to the interior of the vehicle. The attempt failed because the battery was dead and the car wouldn't start.

Hugh Beaumont

The actor who portrayed the benevolent father on the popular TV show *Leave It to Beaver* was a Methodist minister. Tony Dow, who played older brother Wally, reports that Beaumont actually hated kids. "Hugh wanted out of the show after the second season," Dow told the *Toronto Sun*. "He thought he should be doing films and things."

Inheritance

My father was a skinny, asthmatic, and eager-to-please little boy, not the tough guy his hard-living Irish father had wanted. My dad lost his mother at age three and later developed a severe stuttering problem, perhaps as a result of his father's disapproval. My father's adult vocabulary was outstanding, due to his need for alternate words when faltering over difficult consonants like B or D.

The stuttering grew worse over the years, with one exception: after downing a few whiskeys, my father could sing like an angel. His Irish tenor became legendary in local taverns, and by the time I entered the scene my father was spending every evening visiting the bars. Most nights he would stumble back drunk around midnight; some nights he was so drunk he would stumble through a neighbor's back door, thinking he was home.

As a boy, I coped with the family's embarrassment by staying glued to the television. I desperately wanted someone like Hugh Beaumont to be my father, or maybe Robert Young.

Hugh Brannum, though, would have been my first choice. Brannum played Mr. Green Jeans on *Captain Kangaroo*, and I remember him as being kind, funny, and extremely reliable.

Lauren Chapin

Kitten, the youngest daughter on *Father Knows Best*, was played by Lauren Chapin. Chapin's father molested her, and her mother was a severe alcoholic. After the show ended in 1960, Chapin's life came apart. At age sixteen, she married an auto mechanic. At age eighteen, she became addicted to heroin and began working as a prostitute.

Male Breadwinners

Wolf fathers spend the daylight hours away from the home hunting but return every evening. The wolf cubs, five or six to a litter, rush out of the den when they hear their father approaching and fling themselves at him, leaping up to his face. The father backs up a few feet and disgorges food for them, in small, separate piles.

Penguins, Again

The female emperor penguin "catches the egg with her wings before it touches the ice," Jeffrey Moussaieff Masson writes in his book *The Emperor's Embrace*. She then places it on her feet, to keep it from contact with the frozen ground.

At this point, both penguins will sing in unison, staring at the egg. Eventually, the male penguin will use his beak to lift the egg onto the surface of his own feet, where it remains until hatching.

Not only does the male penguin endure the inconvenience of walking around with an egg balanced on his feet for months but he also will not eat for the duration.

Religion

In 1979, Lauren Chapin, the troubled actress who played Kitten, had a religious conversion. She credits her belief in Jesus with saving her life. After his television career ended, Methodist minister Hugh Beaumont became a Christmas-tree farmer.

Ward's Father

In an episode titled "Beaver's Freckles," the Beaver says that Ward had "a hittin' father," but little else is ever revealed about Ward's fictional family. Despite Wally's constant warning – "Boy, Beav, when Dad finds out, he's gonna clobber ya!" – Ward does not follow his own father's example and never hits his sons on the show. This is an excellent example of xenogenesis.

Xenogenesis

(zen'*u*-jen'*u*-sis), n. *Biol.* 1. heterogenesis 2. the supposed generation of offspring completely and permanently different from the parent.

Believing in xenogenesis, I changed my mind about having children about four years after rejecting my wife's first suggestion of the idea.

Y Chromosomes

The Y chromosome of the father determines a child's gender, and is unique, because its genetic code remains relatively unchanged as it passes from father to son. The DNA in other chromosomes, however, is more likely to get mixed between generations, in a process called recombination. What this means, apparently, is that boys have a higher likelihood of inheriting their ancestral traits.

Zappa

Internet chatrooms and discussion lists repeatedly recycle the news that the actor who played Mr. Green Jeans was the father of musician Frank Zappa. But, in fact, Hugh Brannum had only one son, and he was neither Frank Zappa nor this author.

Sometimes, though, I still wonder what it might have been like.

Elizabeth Cooperman
Creation

Creation:

TO father bring forth multiply beget breed
enact coin hatch yield originate actualize
evoke produce through effort make cause
bubble smelt arouse stir draw forth style
bring into being engender procreate render
realize give rise to work substantiate
clear a path by removing objects for conjure
sire confect paint intertwine turn out give
tack together components develop mother

Night

TO father bring forth multiply beget breed
enact coin hatch yield originate actualize
evoke produce through effort make cause
bubble smelt arouse stir draw forth style
bring into being engender procreate render
realize give rise to work substantiate
clear a path by removing objects for conjure
sire confect paint intertwine turn out give
tack together components develop mother

Day

Sky

Night

TO father bring forth multiply beget breed enact coin hatch yield originate actualize evoke produce through effort make cause bubble smelt arouse stir draw forth style bring into being engender procreate render realize give rise to work substantiate clear a path by removing objects for conjure sire confect paint intertwine turn out give tack together components develop mother

Day

Water

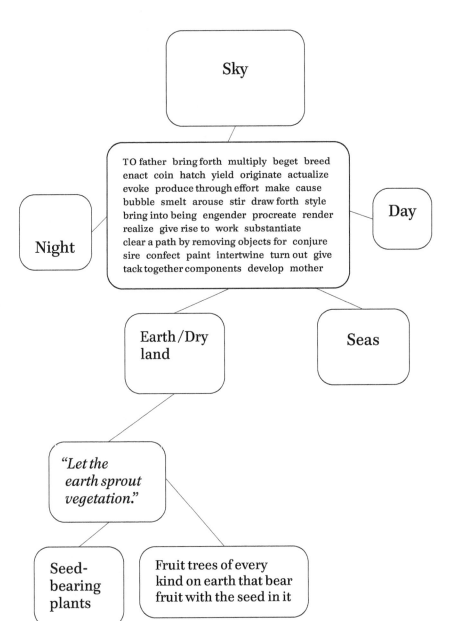

Sky

TO father bring forth multiply beget breed enact coin hatch yield originate actualize evoke produce through effort make cause bubble smelt arouse stir draw forth style bring into being engender procreate render realize give rise to work substantiate clear a path by removing objects for conjure sire confect paint intertwine turn out give tack together components develop mother

Night

Day

Earth/Dry land

Seas

"Let the earth sprout vegetation."

Seed-bearing plants

Fruit trees of every kind on earth that bear fruit with the seed in it

.

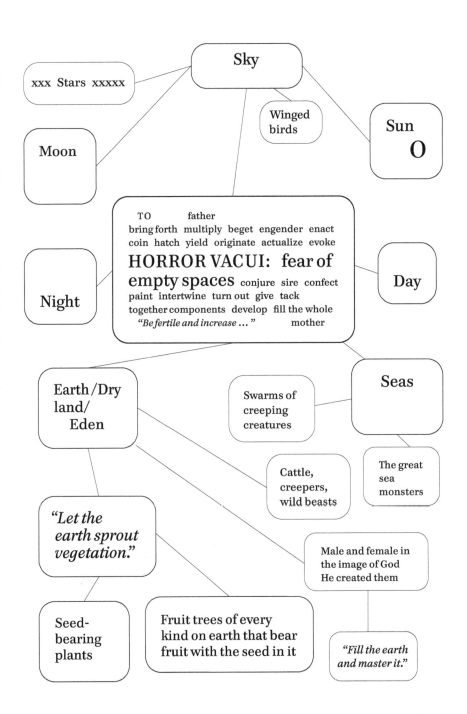

Sky

xxx Stars xxxxx

Winged birds

Sun
O

Moon

TO   father
bring forth multiply beget engender enact
coin hatch yield originate actualize evoke
HORROR VACUI: fear of
empty spaces conjure sire confect
paint intertwine turn out give tack
together components develop fill the whole
"Be fertile and increase ... "   mother

Day

Night

Seas

Earth/Dry
land/
Eden

Swarms of
creeping
creatures

The great
sea
monsters

Cattle,
creepers,
wild beasts

*"Let the
earth sprout
vegetation."*

Male and female in
the image of God
He created them

Seed-
bearing
plants

Fruit trees of every
kind on earth that bear
fruit with the seed in it

*"Fill the earth
and master it."*

father   engender beget multiply
work   play tack together

"Be fertile and increase
. . . *"*

sire intertwine yield hatch
fill the whole   coin   mother

Earth / Dry land /
Eden

Male and female
in the image of
God He created
them

"God is really only
another artist. He
invented the giraffe, the
elephant and the cat. He
has no real style, He just
goes on trying other
things."

Les Demoiselles
d'Avignon

*"Fill the
earth and
master it."*

Nature
morte au
compotier

Tête d'homme

Pablo
Picasso

Paysage

"Coleridge conceives God's
creation to be a continuing
process, which has an analogy
in the creative perception
(*'primary imagination'*) of all
human minds."

Femme nue

Artist

Copulation /
Couples

8. Trick Story

The world is no longer speaking to you.
It's high time you got tricky,
wily, clever – in order to deal with life.

Rick Moody	Primary Sources
Barry Lopez	Class Notes
Gregory Burnham	Subtotals
David Shields	Life Story
Paul Theroux	Acknowledgments

Trick Story

IN THE EXTREMELY BUREAUCRATIZED CULTURE IN which almost all of us now live, we're inundated by documents: itineraries, instruction manuals, lectures, permit forms, advertisements, primers, catalogues, comment cards, letters of complaint, end-of-year reports, accidentally forwarded email, traffic updates, alumni-magazine class notes, etc., etc. The five fraudulent artifacts collected here exact/enact giddy, witty, imaginative revenge on the received forms that dominate and define our lives. These counterfeit texts capture the barely suppressed frustration and feeling and yearning that percolate about 1/16th of an inch below most official documents.

These elegant forgeries appeal to those of us bored by the conventions of traditional fiction. Or those of us who, out of similar boredom with the conventions, turn to genre-bending and genre-defying work to reanimate their literary passions. Such stories are a detour around the dead ends of traditional realism, modernism, and postmodernism; for every soul trapped in bureaucratic hell who would give his or her eyeteeth to take that latest interoffice memo and turn it into a whoopee cushion – ditto, here is your form or anti-form. In 1,000 words, create a fraudulent artifact; choose a documentary gesture you're interested in, build in a theme and/or plot, and work to pull the thematic and/or narrative line through the story. Just as in a traditional story, the narrative and thematic threads need to get pulled forward under the surface of the pseudo-document.

This section's five examples of the form/anti-form manage – in their different ways, but all within a very small space – to tell the story of someone's life.

Rick Moody, "Primary Sources": ostensibly a list of Moody's favorite works of art while growing up, but really a devastating meditation on how, in the absence of his father, "I was looking elsewhere for the secrets of ethics and home." Moody's booklist establishes the upper-middle-class milieu in which he grew up and subtly suggests a coming-of-age narrative: prep school, college career, alcoholism, first office job, mental hospital stint. As Dinty W. Moore does in "Son of Mr. Green Jeans," Moody holds his trump card until the end, revealing his father as the most primary of sources; the whole story/works cited page explodes as metaphor.

Barry Lopez, "Class Notes": on one level an *Onion*-style parody of alumni-magazine class notes; on another level, an anthropology of Reagan-era unfettered capitalism; and on still a deeper level a chart of the transition over the course of a man's life from hyper-aggression to inevitable loss to the bliss that comes from the knowledge that "what thou lovest well remains; the rest is dross." The final sentence enacts the entirety of the story – from testosterone to loss to salvation: "ROGER BOLTON, who played professional baseball for nine years, lost his family in flooding outside New Orleans and has entered a Benedictine monastery."

Gregory Burnham, "Subtotals": seemingly a pointless data sheet of the number of times the narrator has climbed stairs, sent a postcard, received a kiss, etc. It isn't that at all; it is a beautiful ode – if we're lucky – not to finding God or winning a Purple Heart but to averting calamity and muddling through in the middle. Burnham conveys in the most elegant shorthand that everything is significant and nothing is meaningful.

David Shields, "Life Story": hundreds of bumper stickers that take a man from adolescence to senility, lost the entire time in American-fed fantasy. David says, "For years, I had been amassing a huge, seemingly useless file of catchy bumper stickers, swerving in and out of traffic to jot them down. The essay came to fruition one Valentine's Day when I heard a poet read a love/hate poem made out of twelve bumper sticker slogans. The poem had a small emotional arc. After hearing the poem, I realized that I could arrange my own collection chronologically from birth to old age, composing a sad portrait of someone who had bought into the logic of late market capitalism."

Paul Theroux's "Acknowledgments" parodies the acknowledgments in the back of a scholarly book, suggesting an awful lot of scholars are just pushing a wheelbarrow down the road of life, not doing anything at all. This is a brutal commentary on the vampiric nature of the well-funded critic (getting fat on the bones of the obscure poet). So much of writing – in this chapter and beyond – is about the difference between the official and actual versions of people's lives.

Rick Moody
Primary Sources[1]

Abbé, William Parker.[2] *A Diary of Sketches*. Concord, N.H.: St. Paul's School, 1976.

Bangs, Lester.[3] *Psychotic Reactions and Carburetor Dung*. Edited by Greil Marcus. New York: Knopf, 1987.

Barnes, Djuna. *Interviews*. Washington, D.C.: Sun & Moon, 1985.

Barrett, Syd.[4] "Golden Hair." On *The Madcap Laughs*. EMI Cassette C4-46607, 1990 (reissue).

1   Born 10.18.61 in NYC. Childhood pretty uneventful. We moved to the suburbs. I always read a lot. I did some kid stuff, but mostly I read. So this sketchy and selective bibliography – this list of some of the books I have around the house now – is really an autobiography.

2   Art instructor at St. Paul's School when I was there (1975-79). Abbé was an older, forgetful guy when I met him. He was in his late sixties, probably. He lived alone in an apartment above the infirmary at S.P.S. His studio had burned down years before, taking a lot of his paintings, and I believe this accounted for the halo of sadness around him. He could be infectiously happy, though. His house was full of jukeboxes, dolls, and electrical toys. Games of every kind.
     One time I showed him my *Sgt. Pepper's* picture disk – remember those collector's gimmicks which revolutionized the LP for a few minutes in the seventies? The famous jacket art was printed on the vinyl. Abbé laughed for a good long time over that. He sat in the old armchair in my room, the one with the stuffing coming out of it, and laughed. He loved that kind of thing. He had a lot of Elvis on his jukeboxes.

3   Lester's last published piece, in the *Voice*, appeared in my senior year of college. I moved back to NYC a little later, after six months in California, where it was too relaxed. By the time I got to New York, the East Village galleries were already disappearing. Lester was dead. The Gap had moved in on the northwest corner of St. Mark's and Second Avenue.

4   In 1978, back at S.P.S., I took six hits of "blotter" acid and had a pretty wrenching bad trip. Eternal damnation, shame, humiliation, and an endless line of men in clown costumes chanting my name and laughing. That kind of thing. I turned myself in, confessed to a master I liked, the Reverend Alden B. Flanders. Somewhere in the middle of the five or six hours it took to talk me down, I asked him if he thought I would remember this moment for the rest of my life.

Barthes, Roland. *A Lover's Discourse*.[5] Translated by Richard Howard. New York: Hill & Wang, 1978.

Bernhard, Thomas. *The Lime Works*. Chicago: Univ. of Chicago Press, 1986 (reprint of New York: Knopf, 1973).

Book of Common Prayer and Administration of the Sacraments and Other Rites and Ceremonies of the Church, According to the Use of the Protestant Episcopal Church[6] in the United States of America, The. New York: Harper & Brothers, 1944.

Borges, Jorge Luis. *Labyrinths*.[7] Edited by Donald A. Yates and James E. Irby. New York: New Directions, 1964.

Breton, André. *Manifestoes of Surrealism*.[8] Ann Arbor, Mich.: Univ. of Michigan Press (Ann Arbor Paperbacks), 1969.

Carroll, Lewis. *The Annotated Alice*. Edited with an introduction and notes by Martin Gardner.[9] New York: Clarkson N. Potter (Bramhall House), 1960.

Carter, Angela.[10] *The Bloody Chamber and Other Adult Tales*. New York: Harper & Row, 1979.

5   "The necessity for this book is to be found in the following consideration: that the lover's discourse is today of *an extreme solitude* ... Once a discourse is thus ... exiled from all gregarity, it has no recourse but to become the site, however exiguous, of an *affirmation*."

6   I didn't get baptized until I was fifteen. The minister, who had buried my grandparents and my uncle and performed my mother's remarriage, couldn't remember my name. Right then, the church seemed like the only thing that would get me through adolescence. I was going to get confirmed later, too, but instead I started drinking.

7   Cf. "Eco, Umberto," and also n. 9, below.

8   The band I played in, in college, was called Forty-five Houses. We got our name from the first Surrealist manifesto: "Q. 'What is your name?' A. 'Forty-five houses.' (*Ganser syndrome, or beside-the-point replies*.)" Our drummer, Kristen, preferred women to men, but I sort of fell in love with her anyway. After we graduated, she gave me a ride on her motorcycle. It was the first time I ever rode one. I held tight around her waist.

9   See n. 20, below.

10   The first day of Angela's workshop in college, a guy asked her what her work was like. She said, "My work cuts like a steel blade at the base of a man's penis." Second semester, there was a science-fiction writer in our class who sometimes slept through the proceedings—and there were only eight or nine of us there. One day I brought a copy of *Light in August* to Angela's office hours and she said, "I wish I were reading *that* [Faulkner], instead of *this*" [pointing to a stack of student work].

Cheever, John. *The Journals of John Cheever.*[11] New York: Knopf, 1991.

———. *The Wapshot Chronicle.* New York: Harper & Brothers, 1957.

Coover, Robert. *In Bed One Night & Other Brief Encounters.* Providence, R.I.: Burning Deck, 1983.

Daniels, Les. *Marvel: Five Fabulous Decades of the World's Greatest Comics.*[12] With an introduction by Stan Lee. New York: Abrams, 1991.

Danto, Arthur C. *Encounters & Reflections: Art in the Historical Present.* New York: FSG, 1990.

"Darmok."[13] *Star Trek: The Next Generation.* Paramount Home Video, 1991, 48 minutes.

Davis, Lydia. *Break It Down.* New York: FSG, 1986.

De Montaigne, Michel. *The Complete Essays of Montaigne.* Translated by Donald M. Frame. Stanford, Calif.: Stanford Univ. Press, 1958.

Derrida, Jacques. *Of Grammatology.*[14] Translated by Gayatri Chakravorty Spivak. Baltimore, Md.: Johns Hopkins Press, 1976 (originally published as *De la grammatologie* [Paris: Editions de Minuit, 1967]).

---

11   As a gift for graduating from boarding school, my dad gave me a short trip to Europe. Two weeks. I was a little bit afraid of travel, though, as I still am, and in London I spent much of the time in Hyde Park, in a chair I rented for 15p a day. The sticker that served as my lease still adorns my copy of *The Stories of John Cheever*, also given to me by my dad. I haven't been back to the U.K. since.

12   We moved a lot when I was a kid. In eighth grade I had a calendar on which I marked off the days until I'd be leaving Connecticut forever. My attachments weren't too deep. I spent a lot of time with Iron Man, the Incredible Hulk, and the Avengers. I also liked self-help books and Elton John records.

13   Picard and the crew of the *Enterprise* attempt to make contact with a race of aliens, the Children of Tama, who speak entirely in an allegorical language. Picard doesn't figure out the language until the captain of the Tamarians is already dead. A big episode for those who realize how hard communicating really is.

14   One guy I knew in college actually threw this book out a window. Here are some excerpts from my own marginalia: "Function of art is supplementalism though devalorization of weighted side of oppositions"; "Attendance as performance: more absence creates more real presence." I'm not sure what I meant, but I loved Derrida's overheated analogies: "Writing in the common sense is the dead letter, it is the carrier of death. It exhausts life. On the other hand, on the other face of the same proposition, writing in the metaphoric sense, natural, divine, and living writing, is venerated" (page 17).

Elkin, Stanley. *The Franchiser*. Boston: Godine (Nonpareil Books), 1980 (reprint of New York: FSG, 1976).

"Erospri." In *The Whole Earth 'Lectronic Link*,[15] modem: (415) 332-6106, Sausalito, Calif., 1985–.

Feelies, The. *The Good Earth*.[16] Coyote TTC 8673, 1986.

Fitzgerald, F. Scott, *The Crack-Up*. New York: New Directions, 1945.

Foucault, Michel. *Discipline and Punish: The Birth of the Prison*. New York: Vintage, 1979 (reprint of New York: Random House, 1977; originally published as *Surveiller et punir* [Paris: Gallimard, 1975]).

Gaddis, William. *The Recognitions*.[17] New York: Penguin, 1986 (reprint of New York: Harcourt, Brace, 1955).

Genet, Jean. *The Thief's Journal*. Translated by Bernard Frechtman. New York: Bantam, 1965 (reprint of New York: Grove, 1964; originally published as *Journal du voleur* [Paris: Gallimard, 1949]).

Gyatso, Tenzin, the 14th Dalai Lama. *Freedom in Exile*. New York: HarperCollins, 1990.

---

15   The WELL – as it is abbreviated – has a really good "Star Trek" conference, too. This private conference is about sex. I started messing with computers in junior high, when my grades got me out of study hall. Which was good because people used to threaten me if I didn't let them copy my homework. It was on the WELL that I learned both the address for a mail-order catalogue called Leather Toys and how to affix clothespins.

16   My drinking got really bad in graduate school. In the mid-eighties, I was in love with a woman who was living in Paris, and I took the opportunity to get mixed up at the same time with a friend in New York. Kate, the second of these women, first played this record for me. The snap of the snare drum that begins *The Good Earth* has a real tenderness to it, for me. I was playing this record when I was really ashamed of myself and also afterward, when I was hoping for forgiveness.

17   At the end of my drinking, when I was first living in Hoboken, I started writing my first novel, *Garden State*. Later, through a chain of kindnesses, someone managed to slip a copy of it to William Gaddis, the writer I most admired, then and now. Much later, long after all this, I came to know Gaddis's son Matthew a little bit, and he said that the book had probably got covered up with papers, because that's the way his dad's desk is. But maybe there was one afternoon when it was on top of a stack.

197 LIFE IS SHORT – ART IS SHORTER

Hawkes, John.[18] *Second Skin*. New York: New Directions, 1964.

Hawthorne, Nathaniel. *Hawthorne: Short Stories*.[19] Edited with an introduction by Newton Arvin. New York: Knopf, 1946.

Hogg, James. *The Private Memoirs and Confessions of a Justified Sinner*. New York: Penguin, 1989.

Johnson, Denis. *Angels*. New York: Vintage, 1989 (reprint of New York: Knopf, 1983).

Joyce, James. *Ulysses*. New York: Vintage, 1961.

Jung, C. G. "Individual Dream Symbolism in Relation to Alchemy." In *Collected Works*, Vol. 12, Part II. Translated by R. F. C. Hull. Princeton, N.J.: Princeton Univ. Press (Bollingen Series), 1968.

Kapuściński, Ryszard. *The Emperor*. Translated by William R. Brand and Katarzyna Mroczkowska-Brand. New York: Vintage, 1989 (reprint of New York: HBJ, 1983).

Lewis, James. "Index."[20] *Chicago Review* 35 (I [autumn 1985]): 33–35.

Marcus, Greil. *Lipstick Traces: A Secret History of the Twentieth Century*.[21] Cambridge, Mass.: Harvard Univ. Press, 1989.

---

18 The last day of class with Jack Hawkes we were standing out on one of those Victorian porches in Providence – a bunch of us, because there was always a crowd of people trying to get into Jack's classes (and they were usually really talented) – firing corks from champagne bottles out into the street. We got a couple that made it halfway across. Hawkes was mumbling something about how sad it was that so many writers were so afflicted by drink. In less than a week, I was going to graduate.

19 "Another clergyman in New England, Mr. Joseph Moody, of York, Maine, who died about eighty years since, made himself remarkable by the same eccentricity that is here related of the Reverend Mr. Hooper. In his case, however, the symbol had a different import. In early life he had accidentally killed a beloved friend; and from that day till the hour of his own death, he hid his face from men."

20 See n. 7, above.

21 During the period when I was finishing my first novel, I had an office job in publishing, from which I was later fired. I judged everything against the books I loved when I was a teen-ager: *The Crying of Lot 49*, Beckett's *Murphy*, *One Hundred Years of Solitude*, etc. Besides Lester Bangs (see above), Marcus's *Lipstick Traces* was one of the few recently published books I liked. Another was *Responses: On Paul de Man's Wartime Journalism* (Univ. of Nebraska Press).

Marx, Groucho. *The Groucho Letters: Letters from and to Groucho Marx*.[22] New York: Fireside, 1987.

Mitchell, Stephen. *The Gospel According to Jesus*. New York: Harper-Collins, 1991.

Pagels, Elaine. *The Gnostic Gospels*.[23] New York: Vintage, 1989 (reprint of New York: Random House, 1979).

Paley, Grace. *Enormous Changes at the Last Minute*. New York: FSG, 1974.

Pärt, Arvo. *Tabula Rasa*.[24] ECM new series 817 (1984).

Peacock, Thomas Love. *Headlong Hall and Gryll Grange*. Oxford: Oxford Univ. Press (The World's Classics), 1987.

Plato. *Great Dialogues of Plato*. Edited and translated by W. H. D. Rouse. New York: Mentor, 1956.

"Polysexuality." *Semiotext(e)*[25] 4 (I [1981]).

Sacks, Oliver. *Awakenings*. 3rd ed. New York: Summit, 1987.

Schulz, Bruno. *Sanatorium Under the Sign of the Hourglass*.[26] Translated by Celina Wieniewska. New York: Penguin, 1979.

Sebadoh. *Sebadoh III*.[27] Homestead HMS 168-4, 1991.

Thomas à Kempis. *The Imitation of Christ*. New York: Penguin, 1952.

---

22   In 1987, I institutionalized myself. At that moment, Thurber and Groucho Marx and anthologies of low comedy seemed like the best that literature had to offer. I thought I was going to abandon writing – something had to give – but I didn't. I felt better later.

23   "The accusation that the gnostics invented what they wrote contains some truth: certain gnostics openly acknowledged that they derived their *gnosis* from their own experience. ... The gnostic Christians ... assumed that they had gone far beyond the apostles' original teaching."

24   And Cage's book, *Silence*; and *Music for Airports*; and La Monte Young's "The Second Dream of the High-Tension Line Stepdown Transformer from the Four Dreams of China"; and Ezra Pound after St. Elizabeth's, and *Be Here Now* and Mark Rothko.

25   The back cover of this issue consists of a newspaper photo of a man in a wedding gown slumped over on a toilet, his skin ribbed with gigantic blisters. He's really destroyed, this guy. The photo, supposedly, was from the *Daily News*. And since my grandfather worked for the *News* the luridness of this horror struck close. This, I learned, was an act of *pleasure*.

26   Angela Carter assigned this book to us in sophomore year. I was taking a lot of quaaludes that spring. One night I stayed up all night on quaaludes and wrote a story, cribbed from Bruno Schulz, about a guy who lives in a house that *is actually his grandmother*. Later, when I told Angela that I'd written the story high, she said, "Quaaludes, the aardvark of the drug world."

27   "All these empty urges must be satisfied."

W., Bill. "Step Seven." In *Twelve Steps and Twelve Traditions*.[28] New York: Alcoholics Anonymous World Service, 1986.

Williams, William Carlos. *The Collected Poems of William Carlos Williams*.[29] Volume II: 1939–1962.

Zappa, Frank, Captain Beefheart and the Mothers of Invention. *Bongo Fury*.[30] Barking Pumpkin D4-74220, 1975, 1989.

---

28   "The chief activator of our defects has been self-centered fear – primarily fear that we would lose something we already possessed or would fail to get something we demanded."

29   "Sick as I am / confused in the head / I mean I have / endured this April / so far / visiting friends" (p. 428). *Garden State* was published in spring 1992. I was already pretty far into my second book, *The Ice Storm*. I left Hoboken for good.

30   There was a time when I was an adolescent when I didn't feel like I had a dad, even though he didn't live that far away, and I saw him on Sundays. This is an admission that won't please him or the rest of my family. The way I see it, though, there has never been a problem between me and my *actual* dad. But dads make the same tentative decisions we sons make. Once, my father said to me, "I wonder if you kids would have turned out differently if I had been around to kick some ass." This was during one of those long car rides full of silences. The question didn't even apply to me, I didn't think. He might have been there, he might not have. Didn't matter. I was looking elsewhere for the secrets of ethics and home.

Barry Lopez
Class Notes

TED MECHAM MAY BE THE FIRST MEMBER OF THE CLASS
of '77 to retire. I met him and his beautiful wife Kathy at a Bucca-
neers game in Tampa Bay in October. His investments in sugar
refining and South American cattle have paid off handsomely. Any
secret? "Yes," says Ted. "In and out, that's the key." Also in Florida,
I saw JIM HASLEK and BILL STEBBINS. They left their families
behind in Columbus and Decatur, respectively, to tune up a 1300-
h.p. open-class, ocean racing boat, Miss Ohio, for trial runs near
Miami. The racing season is set to open there in December, and
Jim and Bill (famous for their Indy 500 pilgrimages) are among
the favorites. JOHN PESKIN writes to say, sad to relay, that he has
been sued by BILL TESKER. Bill, general manager at the Dayton
office of TelDyne Industries, claims he gave John the idea for a sit-
com episode that John subsequently sold to NBC. It all took place
16 years ago and is more than I can believe. RALPH FENTIL, han-
dling the case for Bill, made it clearer. Ralph is director of Penalty,
Inc., a franchised California paralegal service, which helps clients
develop lawsuits. "This is a growing and legitimate consumer-
interest area. We encourage people to come in, we go over their
past. It's a potential source of income for the client. We let the
courts decide what's right and wrong." Hmmm. RICHARD END-
ERGELL phoned a few weeks ago from Houston, under arrest for
possession of cocaine – third time since 1974. Richard thinks this
is it. Unless a miracle happens he is looking at 15 years or more for
dealing in a controlled substance. STANFORD CRIBBS, mangled

practically beyond recognition in an automobile accident in 1979, took his own life on March 19, according to a clipping from the Kansas City *Star*. His former roommate, BRISTOL LANSFORD, has fared no better. Bristol was shot in the head by his wife's lover at the Lansfords' vacation home outside Traverse City. ROBERT DARKO of Palo Alto (where else?) sends word he is moving up very quickly at Mastuchi Electronics, and to thank DAVID WHITMAN. David, of Shoremann, Polcher & Edders, Los Angeles, specializes in celebrity and personality contracts. Bob Darko is the sixth middle-management executive hired in David's Free Corporate Agent draft. "Corporate loyalty is something from the fifties," says David. "I want to market people on a competitively-bid, short-term contract basis, with incentive and bonus clauses." Tell that to STEVEN PARKMAN. He has been living on unemployment benefits and his wife's income from a hairdressing concern since April of last year – with four kids. FRANK VESTA is certainly glad his job (in aerospace planning with General Dynamics of St. Louis) is holding up – he and his wife Shirley had their ninth – a boy – in July. GREG OUTKIRK has grim news – daughter Michelle rode her thoroughbred Arabian, Botell III, off the boat dock in front of their Waukegan home in an effort to make the animal swim. It drowned almost immediately. DENNIS MITFORD, owner of a well-known Nevada wh———house (no class discounts, he jokes), reports an unruly customer was shot on the premises in October by his bodyguard, LAWRENCE ADENSON. Larry, who served in Vietnam, says the publicity is awful. He may go back to New York – after Denny officially fires him for the violence. Violence is no stranger to BILL NAST. His wife turned up in terrible shape at Detroit General Hospital two months ago, the victim of Bill's hot temper. Fifth time in memory. Four hours in surgery? JACK ZIMMERMAN's second wife and two children by his first wife visited over Easter. SUE ZIMMERMAN was a 1978 Penthouse Pet. Jack is managing her modeling career, his entertainment career, *and* raising the kids. Kudos, Jack. TIM GRAYBULL is dead (of alcohol abuse) in Vermillion, South Dakota, where he taught English at the university.

(Please let the editor of *Alumnus* know you want to see Tim's poems in a future issue.) ALEX ROBINSON won't say what films he distributes, but hints broadly that "beauty is in the eye of the beholder," even in *that* area. The profit margin, he claims, is not to be believed. I'm reminded of KEVIN MITCHELL, who embezzled $3.2 million from Sperry Tool in 1971. He periodically calls from I-know-not-where. Kevin was home free in 1982, with the expiration of the case. DONALD OVERBROOK – more bad news – is in trouble with the police again for unrequited interest in young ladies, this time in Seattle. JAMES COLEMAN called to say so. Jim and his wife Nancy are quitting their jobs to sail around the world in their 32′ ferroconcrete boat. Nancy's parents died and left them well-off. "We were smart *not* to have kids," Jim commented. HAROLD DECKER writes from Arkansas that he is angry about Alumni Association fund-raising letters that follow him everywhere he goes. "I haven't got s---, and wouldn't give it if I did." Wow. NORMAN BELLOWS has been named managing editor of *Attitude*. He says the magazine's 380,000 readers will see a different magazine under his tutelage – "aimed at aggressive, professional people. No tedious essays." Norm's erstwhile literary companion in New York, GEORGE PHILMAN (Betsy BELLOWS and George are living together, sorely testing that close friendship from *Spectator* days) reports *Pounce* is doing very well. George's "funny but vicious" anecdotes about celebrities appear bi-weekly in the fledgling, nationally-syndicated column. "At first the humor went right by everyone," says George, feigning disbelief. "George is an a—h---," was GLEN GREEN's observation when I phoned. Glen opens a five-week show in Reno in January (and *he* will see to it that you get a free drink *and* best seats in the house). Another class celebrity, actor BOYD DAVIDSON, has entered Mt. Sinai, Los Angeles, for treatment of cocaine and Percodan addiction. Dr. CARNEY OLIN, who broke a morphine habit at Mt. Sinai in 1979, thinks it's the best program in the country. Carney says he's fully recovered and back in surgery in the Phoenix area. THOMAS GREENVILLE's business brochure arrived in the mail last week. He has opened his fifteenth *Total Review* salon. Tom combines a revitalizing physical fitness program with various types of modern therapy, like est, to provide clients with brand-new life-paths. Some sort of survival prize should go to DEAN FRANCIS. MBA Harvard 1968. Stanford Law 1970. Elected to the California State Assembly in 1974, after managing Sen. Edward Eaton's successful '72 election campaign. In 1978, elected to Congress from California's 43rd District. It all but collapsed like a house of cards last fall. A jealous brother-in-law, and heir to the Greer fortune, instigated a series of nasty suits, publicly denounced Dean as a fraud, and allegedly paid a woman to sexually embarrass him. Dean won re-election, but the word is his marriage is over – and Phyllis Greer FRANCIS will go to court to recover damages from her brother. A sadder story came to light when I met DOUGLAS BRAND for drinks after the Oklahoma game last fall. Doug's wife Linda went berserk in August and killed their three children. She's in prison. Doug said he used to bait her to a fury with tales of his adulteries and feels great remorse. BENJAMIN TROPPE has been named vice-president for marketing for Temple Industries of Philadelphia. BERNARD HANNA II is new corporate counsel in Conrad Communications, Atlantic City. HENRY CHURCH was killed by police in Newark for unspecified reasons. Well-known painter DAVID WHITCOMB moved to Guatemala and left no forwarding address (Dave?). FREDERICK MANDELL weeps uncontrollably in his crowded apartment in Miami Beach. JOEL REEDE lives in self-destructive hatred in Rye, New York. JAY LOGAN has joined insurgency forces in Angola. ADRIAN BYRD travels to the Netherlands in the spring to cover proceedings against the Federal Government at The Hague for *Dispatch*. GORDON HASKINS has quit the priesthood in Serape, a violent New Mexican border town, to seek political office. ANTHONY CREST succeeds father Luther (Class of '36) as chairman of Fabré. DANIEL REDDLEMAN continues to compose classical music for the cello in Hesterman, Tennessee. ODELL MASTERS cries out in his dreams for love of his wife and children. PAUL GREEN, who never married, farms 1200 acres in eastern Oregon with his father.

ROGER BOLTON, who played professional baseball for nine years, lost his family in flooding outside New Orleans and has entered a Benedictine monastery. (Paul Jeffries, 1340 North Michigan, Chicago, IL 60602.)

Gregory Burnham

Subtotals

NUMBER OF REFRIGERATORS I'VE LIVED WITH: 18. NUMBER of rotten eggs I've thrown: 1. Number of finger rings I've owned: 3. Number of broken bones: 0. Number of Purple Hearts: 0. Number of times unfaithful to wife: 2. Number of holes in one, big golf: 0; miniature golf: 3. Number of consecutive push-ups, maximum: 25. Number of waist size: 32. Number of gray hairs: 4. Number of children: 4. Number of suits, business: 2; swimming: 22. Number of cigarettes smoked: 83. Number of times I've kicked a dog: 6. Number of times caught in the act, any act: 64. Number of postcards sent: 831; received: 416. Number of spider plants that died while under my care: 34. Number of blind dates: 2. Number of jumping jacks: 982,316. Number of headaches: 184. Number of kisses, given: 21,602; received: 20,041. Number of belts: 21. Number of fuckups, bad: 6; not so bad: 1,500. Number of times swore under breath at parents: 838. Number of weeks at church camp: 1. Number of houses owned: 0. Number of houses rented: 12. Number of hunches played: 1,091. Number of compliments, given: 4,051; accepted: 2,249. Number of embarrassing moments: 2,258. Number of states visited: 38. Number of traffic tickets: 3. Number of girlfriends: 4. Number of times fallen off playground equipment, swings: 3; monkey bars: 2; teeter-totter: 1. Number of times flown in dreams: 28. Number of times fallen down stairs: 9. Number of dogs: 1. Number of cats: 7. Number of miracles witnessed: 0. Number of insults, given: 10,038; received: 8,963. Number of wrong telephone numbers dialed: 73. Number of times speechless: 33.

Number of times stuck key into electrical socket: 1. Number of birds killed with rocks: 1. Number of times had the wind knocked out of me: 12. Number of times patted on the back: 181. Number of times wished I was dead: 2. Number of times unsure of footing: 458. Number of times fallen asleep reading a book: 513. Number of times born again: 0. Number of times seen double: 28. Number of déjà vu experiences: 43. Number of emotional breakdowns: 1. Number of times choked on bones, chicken: 4; fish: 6; other: 3. Number of times didn't believe parents: 23,978. Number of lawnmowing miles: 3,575. Number of light bulbs changed: 273. Number of childhood home telephone: 312-879-7442. Number of brothers: 3½. Number of passes at women: 5. Number of stairs walked, up: 745,821; down: 743,609. Number of hats lost: 9. Number of magazine subscriptions: 41. Number of times seasick: 1. Number of bloody noses: 16. Number of times had sexual intercourse: 4,013. Number of fish caught: 1. Number of times heard "The Star-Spangled Banner": 2,410. Number of babies held in arms: 9. Number of times I forgot what I was going to say: 631.

David Shields

Life Story

FIRST THINGS FIRST.
You're only young once, but you can be immature forever. I may grow old, but I'll never grow up. Too fast to love, too young to die. Life's a beach.

Not all men are fools – some are single. 100% Single. I'm not playing hard to get – I am hard to get. I love being exactly who I am. Heaven doesn't want me and Hell's afraid I'll take over. I'm the person your mother warned you about. Ex-girlfriend in trunk. Don't laugh – your girlfriend might be in here.

Girls wanted, all positions, will train. Playgirl on board. Party girl on board. Sexy blonde on board. Not all dumbs are blonde. Never underestimate the power of redheads. Yes, I am a movie star. 2QT4U. A4NQT. No ugly chicks. No fat chicks. I may be fat, but you're ugly and I can diet. Nobody is ugly after 2 a.m.

Party on board. Mass confusion on board. I brake for bong water. Jerk off and smoke up. Elvis died for your sins. Screw guilt. I'm Elvis – kiss me.

Ten and a half inches on board. Built to last. You can't take it with you, but I'll let you hold it for a while.

Be kind to animals – kiss a rugby player. Ballroom dancers do it with rhythm. Railroaders love to couple up. Roofers are always on top. Pilots slip it in.

Love sucks and then you die. Gravity's a lie – life sucks. Life's a bitch; you marry one, then you die. Life's a bitch and so am I. Beyond bitch.

Down on your knees, bitch. Sex is only dirty when you do it right. Liquor up front – poker in the rear. Smile – it's the second-best thing you can do with your lips. I haven't had sex for so long I forget who gets tied up. I'm looking for love but will settle for sex. Bad boys have bad toys. Sticks and stones may break my bones, but whips and chains excite me. Live fast – love hard – die with your mask on.

So many men, so little time. Expensive but worth it. If you're rich, I'm single. Richer is better. Shopaholic on board. Born to shop. I'd rather be shopping at Nordstrom. Born to be pampered. A woman's place is the mall. When the going gets tough, the tough go shopping. Consume and die. He who dies with the most toys wins. She who dies with the most jewels wins. Die, yuppie scum.

This vehicle not purchased with drug money. Hugs are better than drugs.

You are loved.

Expectant mother on board. Baby on board. Family on board. I love my kids. Precious cargo on board. Are we having fun yet? Baby on fire. No child in car. Grandchild in back.

I fight poverty; I work. I owe, I owe, it's off to work I go. It sure makes the day long when you get to work on time. Money talks; mine only knows how to say goodbye. What do you mean I can't pay off my Visa with my MasterCard?

How's my driving? Call 1-800-545-8601. If this vehicle is being driven recklessly, please call 1-800-EAT-SHIT. Don't drink and drive – you might hit a bump and spill your drink.

My other car is a horse. Thoroughbreds always get there first. Horse lovers are stable people. My other car is a boat. My other car is a Rolls-Royce. My Mercedes is in the shop today. Unemployed? Hungry? Eat your foreign car. My other car is a 747. My ex-wife's car is a broom. I think my car has PMS. My other car is a piece of shit, too. Do not wash – this car is undergoing a scientific dirt test. Don't laugh – it's paid for. If this car were a horse, I'd have to shoot it. If I go any faster, I'll burn out my hamsters. I may be slow, but I'm ahead of you. I also drive a Titleist. Pedal downhill.

Shit happens. I love your wife. Megashit happens. I'm single again. Wife and dog missing – reward for dog. The more people I meet, the more I like my cat. Nobody on board. Sober 'n' crazy. Do it sober. Drive smart – drive sober.

No more Mr. Nice Guy. Lost your cat? Try looking under my tires. I love my German shepherd. Never mind the dog – beware of owner. Don't fence me in. Don't tell me what kind of day to have. Don't tailgate or I'll flush. Eat shit and die. My kid beat up your honor student. Abort your inner child. I don't care who you are, what you're driving, who's on board, who you love, where you'd rather be, or what you'd rather be doing.

Not so close – I hardly know you. Watch my rear end, not hers. You hit it – you buy it. Hands off. No radio. No Condo / No MBA/No BMW. You toucha my car – I breaka your face. Protected by Smith & Wesson. Warning: This car is protected by a large sheet of cardboard.

LUV2HNT. Gun control is being able to hit your target. Hunters make better lovers: they go deeper into the bush – they shoot more often – and they eat what they shoot.

Yes, as a matter of fact, I do own the whole damn road. Get in, sit down, shut up, and hold on. I don't drive fast – I just fly low. If you don't like the way I drive, stay off the sidewalk. I'm polluting the atmosphere. Can't do 55.

I may be growing old, but I refuse to grow up. Get even: Live long enough to become a problem to your kids. We're out spending our children's inheritance.

Life is pretty dry without a boat. I'd rather be sailing. A man's place is on his boat. Everyone must believe in something; I believe I'll go canoeing. Who cares!

Eat dessert first – life is uncertain. Why be normal?

Don't follow me; I'm lost, too. Wherever you are, be there. No matter where you go, there you are. Bloom where you are planted.

Easy does it. Keep it simple, stupid. I'm 4 Clean Air. Go fly a kite. No matter – never mind. UFOs are real. Of all the things I've lost, I miss my mind the most. I brake for unicorns.

Choose death.

Paul Theroux
Acknowledgments

THANKS ARE DUE TO DR. MILTON RUMBELLOW, CHAIRMAN of the Department of Comparative Literature, Yourgrau College (Wyola Campus), for generously allowing me first a small course load and then an indefinite leave of absence from my duties; to Mrs. Edith Rumbellow for many kindnesses, not the least of which was her interceding on my behalf; to the trustees of Yourgrau College for a grant-in-aid, to the John Simon Guggenheim Memorial Foundation for extending my fellowship to two years, and to the National Endowment for the Arts, without whose help this book could not have been written; to Miss Sally-Ann Fletcher, of Wyolatours, for ably ticketing and cross-checking a varied itinerary, and to Miss Denise Humpherson, of the British Tourist Authority, who provided me with a map of the cycling paths in the areas of England lived in by Matthew Casket; to Mrs. Mabel Nittish for arranging the sublet of my Wyola apartment and providing me with a folding bike.

As with many other biographers of minor West Country dialect poets, Casket's output was so small that he could feed himself only by securing remunerative employment in unrelated fields. I am grateful for the cooperation of his former employers – in particular to Bewlence & Sons (Solid Fuels), Ltd., Western Feeds, Yeovil Rubber Goods, and Raybold & Squarey (Drugs Division), Ltd., for allowing me access to their in-house files and providing me with hospitality over a period of weeks; and especially to Mrs. Ronald Bewlence for endlessly informative chats and helping me dispose of a bike, and Mrs. Margaret Squarey, F.P.S., for placing herself entirely at my disposal and sharing with me her wide knowledge of poisons and toxic weeds.

At a crucial stage in my ongoing research, I was privileged to meet Mrs. Daphne Casket Hebblewhite, who, at sixty-two, still remembered her father's run of bad luck. For three months of hospitality at "Limpets" and many hours of tirelessly answering my questions, I must express my thanks and, with them, my sorrow that the late Mrs. Hebblewhite was not alive to read this memorial to her father, which she and I both felt was scandalously overdue. It was Mrs. Hebblewhite who, by willing them to me, gave me access to what few Casket papers exist, and who graciously provided me with introductions to Casket's surviving relations – Miss Fiona Slaughter, Miss Gloria Wyngard, and Miss Tracy Champneys; I am happy to record here my debt for their warmth and openness to a stranger to their shores. Miss Slaughter acceded to all my requests, as well as taking on some extensive chauffeuring; Miss Wyngard unearthed for me a second copy of Casket's only book, but annotated in his own hand, enabling me to speculate on what he might have attempted in revised form had he had the means to do so, and allowing me the treasured memento of another warm friendship and our weeks in Swanage; Miss Champneys made herself available to me in many ways, giving me her constant attention, and it is to her efforts, as well as those of Ruck & Grutchfield, Barristers-at-Law, that I owe the speedy end of what could have been a piece of protracted litigation. To Señorita Luisa Alfardo Lizardi, who kept Mrs. Hebblewhite's house open to me after her late mistress's tragic passing and was on call twenty-four hours a day, I am more grateful than I can sufficiently express here.

Special thanks must go to the staff of Broomhill Hospital, Old Sarum, and particularly to Miss Francine Kelversedge, S.R.N., for encouraging me in my project during a needed rest from exhausting weeks of research. Colonel and Mrs. Hapgood Chalke came to my rescue at a turning point in my Broomhill sojourn; to them I owe more than I can adequately convey, and to their dear daughter, Tamsin, my keenest thanks for guiding my hand and for her resourcefulness in providing explanations when they were in short supply. To Dr. Winifred Sparrow, Director of Broomhill, I can only state my gratitude for waiving payment for my five months of convalescence; and to Stones & Sons, Tobacconists, Worsfold's Wine Merchants, and Hine's Distilleries, all of Old Sarum, my deepest thanks for understanding, prompt delivery, and good will in circumstances that would have had lesser tradesmen seeking legal redress.

I am grateful for the hospitality I received during the weeks I spent at the homes of Mr. and Mrs. Warner Ditchley, Mrs. R. B. Ollenshaw, Dr. and Mrs. F. G. Cockburn, Major and Mrs. B. P. Birdsmoor, and the late Mrs. J. R. W. Gatacre, all of Devizes, as well as for the timely intervention of Miss Helena Binchey, of Devizes, who, on short notice, placed a car at my disposal in order that I could visit the distant places Casket had known as a child. The Rev. John Punnel, of St. Alban's Primary School, Nether Wallop, provided me with safe harbor as well as a detailed record of Casket's meagre education; he kindly returned Miss Binchey's car to Devizes, and it was Mrs. Dorothy Punnel who took me on a delightfully informal tour of the attic bedroom in the dorm, which cannot be very different today from what it was in 1892, when, just prior to his expulsion on an unproved charge of lewdness, Casket was a boarder.

I feel lucky in being able to record my appreciation to Pamela, Lady Grapethorpe, of Nether Wallop Manor, for admitting a footsore traveller and allowing him unlimited use of her house; for her introducing him to the Nether Wallop Flying Club and Aerodrome and to Miss Florence Fettering, who expertly piloted him to Nettlebed, in West Dorset, and accompanied him through his visit in the village where Casket was employed as a twister and ropeworker at the Gundry. I am obliged also to Miss Vanessa Liphook, of The Bull Inn, Nettlebed, for very kindly spiriting me from Nettlebed to Compton Valence, where Casket, then a lay brother, worked as a crofter at the friary after the failure of his book. It is thanks to the good offices of Miss Liphook, and her indefatigable

Riley, that I was able to tour the South Coast resorts where Casket, in his eighties and down on his luck, found seasonal employment as a scullion and kitchen hand; for their faith in my project and their sumptuous hospitality, I am indebted to the proprietors of The Frog and Nightgown, Bognor Regis; The Raven, Weymouth; The Kings Arms, Bridport; Sprackling House, Eype; and The Grand Hotel, Charmouth. To Miss Josephine Slape, of Charmouth, where Casket died of consumption, I owe the deepest of bows for the loan of a bicycle when it was desperately needed; and to the staff of the Goods Shed, Axminster, I am grateful for their speeding the bicycle back to its owner.

To Mrs. Annabel Frampton, of the British Rail ticket office, Axminster, my sincere thanks for being so generous with a temporarily embarrassed researcher; and to Dame Marina Pensel-Cripps, casually met on the 10:24 to London, but fondly remembered, I am grateful for an introduction to the late Sir Ronald and to Lady Mary Bassetlaw, of Bassetlaw Castle, at which the greater part of this book was written over an eventful period of months as tragic as they were blissful. It is impossible for me adequately to describe the many ways in which Lady Mary aided me in the preparation of this work; she met every need, overcame every obstacle, and replied to every question, the last of which replies, and by far the hardest, was her affirmative when I asked her to be my wife. So, to my dear Mary, the profoundest of thank yous: this book should have been a sonnet.

Lastly, to Miss Ramona Slupski, Miss Heidi Lim Choo Tan, Miss Piper Vathek, and Miss Joylene Aguilar Garcia Rosario, all of the Graduate Section of British Studies, Yourgrau College, my thanks for collating material and answering swiftly my transatlantic letters and demands; to Miss Gudrun Naismith, for immaculately typing many drafts of this work and deciphering my nearly illegible and at times tormented handwriting, my deepest thanks. And to all my former colleagues at Yourgrau (Wyola Campus), who, by urging me forward in my work, reversed my fortunes, my grateful thanks for assisting me in this undertaking.

9. Criticism as Autobiography

Looking in the mirror, you can still see a young self behind the mask of age. You are also well aware that you don't have all the answers. You are a grouch.

Wayne Koestenbaum	Of Jackie Onassis and the Stargazer in Every Heart
Lee Siegel	Angles in America

219 | LIFE IS SHORT – ART IS SHORTER

Criticism as Autobiography

MANY, PERHAPS MOST, REVIEWERS USE CRITICISM AS a way to brandish what they pretend is their own more evolved morality, psyche, humanity, but this flies in the face of what is an essential assumption of the compact between writer and reader – namely, that we're all Bozos on this bus. No one here gets out alive. Let he who is without sin etc.

In "Of Jackie Onassis and the Stargazer in Every Heart," Wayne Koestenbaum, who has himself written a wonderfully wayward and complicit book about Jackie Onassis, writes (concerning the play *Jackie: An American Life*), "I don't recommend that we Belasco theatergoers piously declare, 'Why must these artists take advantage of the late First Lady?' Nor do I suggest that we ignorantly exclaim, 'Why is contemporary art so detrimentally addicted to famous people?' I hope that we ask more intimate and demanding questions of ourselves: 'I wonder what my relation to Jackie is or was. Enjoying a simulacral Jackie, am I prurient, déclassé, trivial, morbid? Perhaps other activities" – now, watch Koestenbaum's great, self-reflexive move here – "in my life – moviegoing, praying, reading, child-rearing – are forms of stargazing. I wonder whether we go to a play to experience our own desire or to police someone else's. I will certainly try, when I talk about Jackie Onassis in the future, if I do talk about her, to be sure" – now watch as he clinches it – "I know the extent to which I am also talking about myself.'"

Koestenbaum provides the perfect template for your assign-

220 Criticism as Autobiography

ment. Write a review of a book, play, movie, TV show, painting, stand-up routine, YouTube video, or artwork of any kind. Convey the essence of the work, but don't stand back from the text as if you, too, aren't human, subjective, flawed, needy. Implicate yourself and your drives and passions. You can do this directly, as Terry Castle does in her brilliant essay "My Heroin Christmas" (not included here, since it is quite long), or somewhat more obliquely, as Lee Siegel does in his evisceration of Tony Kushner's play-become-film *Angels in America*. The key thing here is to place yourself in harm's way. Make the arrow point in both directions: outward toward the work and inward toward yourself. And do all this in 1,500 words or fewer. Piece of cake.

Love is good, but hate is good, too. Hate is interesting, especially hating hard. What you hate is at least as telling as what you love. Siegel writes, *"Angels in America* is a second-rate play written by a second-rate playwright who happens to be gay, and because he has written a play about being gay, and about AIDS, no one – and I mean no one – is going to call *Angels in America* the overwrought, coarse, posturing, formulaic mess that it is." One of the definitions of good writing is that it undermines the conventional wisdom. Waging war against received opinion, Siegel discusses another play of Kushner's, *Caroline, or Change*, which is about a black maid working for a Jewish family in Louisiana in 1963. "Again, we get the fearless dialectic: Jews and blacks, the victims of prejudice, are shown to have their own prejudices against each other. Imagine! ... A truly engaging play would enact the confrontation between a Jewish playwright mindlessly exploiting the black experience and, say, an accomplished black writer who returns enraged from the former's play to contend with far less transparent modes of racism, and passive-aggressive projection, and condescension." You may or may not agree with Siegel's assessment of Kushner. That doesn't matter. What matters is writing about a work of art with so much love or hate or even ambivalence that you are revealed along with the work in question.

Wayne Koestenbaum

Of Jackie Onassis and the Stargazer in Every Heart

SOME KILLJOYS MAY SAY, "LET JACKIE REST IN PEACE." But that is not the way desire works. No one wants to put away a good toy.

The next stage of Jacqueline Kennedy Onassis's afterlife has begun. She is coming to Broadway.

Jackie: An American Life opens tomorrow at Belasco Theater. Written and directed by Gip Hoppe, the comedy stars Margaret Colin in the title role, supported by nine actors who assume more than 100 parts, often with the aid of puppets and cardboard cutouts on sets designed by David Gallo. The author calls the play a "loving satire."

The country has secretly known for a long time that Jackie and her several clans were hilarious (as well as noble, sad, inspiring, photogenic); now, perhaps, it is considered proper to laugh about the Bouvier/Kennedy/Onassis carnival in public, especially if the laughter is complicated by tears.

When we looked at Jackie, while she was alive, we were doing something wicked. She knew it, and so did we. She sued Ron Galella for invading her privacy; anyone who gazed with curiosity or pleasure at a photograph of Jackie participated in the abject art of Jackie-watching. The paparazzo, in turn, was a sort of metaphorical killer.

The circumstances of Princess Diana's death have strengthened the symbolic connection between photography and assassination. Jackie responded to photographers as if they were potential assassins of whom she had good reason to be afraid, while Diana's paparazzi – at least in the public mind – were "actual" slayers.

Paradoxically, Diana's death has made it easier to look, without shame, at Jackie's image. We need no longer fear that our attentions desecrate or vandalize poor Jackie, who survived our gaze in a way that Diana, it seemed, did not.

The Jackie and Diana phenomena pose this question: Is it sinful to look at stars? Nothing is easier than to condemn stargazers. We can call the behavior degrading, depressing or dangerous. We can feel sorry for the hounded star, victimized by the public. And yet we rarely admit that looking at stars is one of those practices that defines us as modern. The fact that stargazing may be morally compromised does not mean that it should be treated as a sociopathological tendency to be routed out by columnists and politicians. We are all fans, and we are all photographers.

The arrival of this play gives us a chance to refresh our store of Jackie memories, and to examine our own attitudes toward unfettered desire.

I don't recommend that we Belasco theatergoers piously declare, "Why must these artists take advantage of the late First Lady?" Nor do I suggest that we ignorantly exclaim, "Why is contemporary art so detrimentally addicted to famous people?"

I hope that we ask more intimate and demanding questions of ourselves: "I wonder what my relation to Jackie is or was. Enjoying a simulacral Jackie, am I prurient, déclassé, trivial, morbid? Perhaps other activities in my life – moviegoing, praying, reading, child-rearing – are forms of stargazing.

"I wonder whether we go to a play to experience our own desire or to police someone else's. I will certainly try, when I talk about Jackie Onassis in the future, if I do talk about her, to be sure I know the extent to which I am also talking about myself."

To mention Jackie, then or now, is never an innocent or meaningless act. It behooves us to admit the swirl of feelings (identification, ecstasy, envy, violence, pity, coldness, indifference) that a glossy personage like Jackie evokes.

Posthumous Jackie's most searing star turn is performed not in the theater but in the dance hall of the dreaming mind.

Lee Siegel
Angles in America

"MADE FOR TELEVISION." THE DESIGNATION MADE MY heart sink when I was a boy: it amounted to a disclaimer of quality. The stops were definitely not going to be pulled out. Big frights would be cast as little scares; the violence would be not cathartic but exasperatingly phony; complex psychologies would be flattened into caricature. Not to mention the fact that a movie made for television had television stars, not movie stars. You were going to get the gifted but life-sized Darren McGavin and Marlo Thomas.

All this has changed, obviously. Thanks in large part to HBO, the little screen can barely contain the edgy artistic and production values of films made strictly for television. (It is no coincidence that the television screen is itself growing larger and larger every year.) As war, crime, and civil unrest wracked the country in the 1970s, the evening news expanded the frontiers of what was permitted on television, to the point where media-history came full circle and numerous movies, from *Natural Born Killers* to *15 Minutes*, now portray the six o'clock news as a laboratory for turning real violence into thrilling entertainment. Indeed, starting with Peter Finch in *Network* screaming that he was mad as hell and not going to take it anymore, Hollywood has become increasingly obsessed with television. More and more producers and directors realize that there is a good chance their films will be seen for the first time not in the theater, but as rented videos or DVDs on television's small screen.

So just about all the dimensions of dramatic entertainment

are either made for television or suited to television, whether it is the script, the style of directing, or the method of acting. And filling the small screen to bursting with the big screen's super-sophisticated techniques can sometimes hide the smallness of what actually is appearing. Such is certainly the case with *Angels in America*: Tony Kushner's play was not so much made for television as made to be rescued by television. The rescue consists in turning it into an "event." Sleekly directed by a celebrity, Mike Nichols, the contemporaneity artist who perfected the skill of making movies into "events," and peopled by celebrities—Al Pacino, Meryl Streep, Emma Thompson—HBO's *Angels* hits the screen with such glamour and noise that Nichols and company almost succeed in burying the play's essential mediocrity in this production's illusion of significance. In the *New Yorker*, Nancy Franklin actually called these six hours of chic "fearless," as if the film had defied the censors of a police state. Others, who never question why the likes of Paris Hilton have their own reality shows, have hailed the show as something on television finally "to argue about." But the only thing worth arguing about with regard to *Angels in America* is why anyone would think *Angels in America* is worth arguing about.

 Angels in America is a second-rate play written by a second-rate playwright who happens to be gay, and because he has written a play about being gay, and about AIDS, no one—and I mean no one—is going to call *Angels in America* the overwrought, coarse, posturing, formulaic mess that it is. And the Bandwagon Plays On. Nichols knows this trick well: before directing the film of this play about AIDS, he directed the film of *Wit*, a play about a woman dying of cancer. When, in *Angels*, Roy Cohn says that America "is just no country for the infirm," he might have added that America is, however, a great place for novels and movies that find a profitable use for illness and the infirm.

 Centering a work of art on the experience of marginality and suffering is like waterproofing your shoes. It repels criticism. You make the work seamless with its subject, so that anyone who criticizes the work seems callous about the subject. (Do you think that

The Pianist was tedious and familiar, and that Adrien Brody simply walked through a critic-proof role? Then you hate the Jews and ride with the Cossacks.) And once you join in the praise of a protected work such as *Angels in America*, you reap the benefit of demonstrating your own virtue by celebrating the play. This confers on you the added halo of not appearing as a snob who presumes to know the difference between artistic success and artistic failure. After all, not everyone can judge the illusions of art, but everyone can project the illusion of goodness.

There is no doubt that Kushner possesses a gift for creating illusion in the theater. In fact in Portland, Maine, I once saw his production of *The Illusion*, an obscure play by Corneille, and I remember the actors moving across the stage in thrall to a mesmerizing moon suspended above it, as if the play's own spirit were casting a spell over the play's own world. The angel that descends sensationally toward the stage in *Angels in America* had a similar effect. But all of Kushner's plays are adaptations, whether they adapt another play or not. They give no evidence of an original experience offered to an audience to do with it what it will; instead they consist of a preconceived set of ideas adapted for the stage in the form of characters who constantly speak about who they are and what they are doing, rather than allowing their identities and their actions to speak for themselves. Kushner's people develop point by point. In the case of *Angels in America*, Kushner made his ideas theatrical ideas. Its appeal on stage was that, at the height of the AIDS epidemic, when that disease was decimating the gay community and particularly the theater community, the play celebrated both the gay element in American theater and the theatrical element of being gay.

The angel appears to Prior, a gay man stricken with AIDS. She announces that he has been chosen to be a prophet of the new age, and invites him to ascend with her to heaven, where presumably he will occupy an honored position; he refuses and clings to life. Now the device of the angel is wonderfully campy, akin to the wild farces of Charles Ludlam's Ridiculous Theatre Co. But

Kushner's angel, flying around the stage on visible wires, is also a descendant of the ancient *deus ex machina*, literally a god swung down from the heavens by means of a machine onto the stage at the last minute to radically change the outcome of events. And the angel's grandiose declarations, and Prior's earthy undercutting replies, and the frenetic, almost hysterical struggle between them, is pure opera buffa. The angel is also a woman – with eight vaginas, we are told: the vagina dialogues! – who, in some sense, is tempting Prior to reject his love of men and live a "normal" life, free from the curse of death; that is, the curse of being gay, that is, the curse of being mortal. And so in one deft, ingenious stroke Kushner makes the theater synonymous with being gay; and homosexuality synonymous with the free, antic, wise spirit of the theater; and the survival of gay men and the theater synonymous with the continuation of decency and humanity.

The San Francisco theatergoers who applauded the play's first full production in 1991 were also applauding their own still-beating hearts, and the American theater's resilience. To write a play about hope was, after all, why Kushner and San Francisco's Eureka Theater had gotten a grant in the first place. And the play was so affirmative, so much more broadly appealing than, say, Larry Kramer's polemics. It was acclaimed from San Francisco to London. For many people, it was not so much a piece for theater as proof that theater still existed. It really didn't matter that Kushner's play had almost no artistic merit. The play did not produce a catharsis through art. It was a catharsis, and thus could dispense with the complicated business of trying to make art.

Angels in America's dramatic guts were as trite and tame as its theatricality was gratifyingly overblown. Its principal antagonist was Roy Cohn, whose self-deceit about his own homosexuality Kushner laboriously links to Reagan's economic policies, to Reagan's indifference to the AIDS epidemic, and to human untruth in general. The play's several subplots involve a closeted Mormon husband named Joe Pitt, who is lying to himself about his identity and thus pursuing the same destructive right-wing politics as

Cohn; Harper, his anguished wife; Mother Pitt, Joe's devoutly Mormon mother; the black Belize, the hip, cool, wise, ironic, cynical, vitriolic, saintly former drag queen and now male nurse; and Louis, the Kushner persona, Prior's cerebral, head-in-the-clouds lover, who callously and spinelessly leaves Prior when Louis discovers that he is sick with AIDS, and whose callousness and spinelessness are presented as Kushner's sensitivity and courage about his own condition and life's universal complexity. The only element that all these garrulous subplots have in common is their histrionic intensity.

Cohn, the bad guy with AIDS, dies; Prior, the good guy with AIDS, lives – but since Cohn is the only actor with a hint of complexity, and wit, and candor, and since Prior echoes the litigious Cohn at play's end by saying about an indifferent-seeming God, "Sue Him," you begin to suspect that Kushner has not fully resolved his attraction to Cohn. Mother Pitt, for all her upset when she discovers her son's homosexuality, ends up caring for Prior. Harper snaps out of her Valium addiction and heads for a happy new life sans Joe; Joe comes to terms with his gayness. Belize holds everyone together, just like the stock wisdom-figure of the drag queen in countless gay plays since at least the 1970s, but he is more Wilder than wild since he serves precisely the same function as the all-seeing narrator in *Our Town*. Louis, who alternates between feeling guilty that he didn't see his grandmother often enough before she died – Orestes, meet Chaim Potok – and feeling guilty that he abandoned Prior, gets roundly scolded and disapproved of before being taken back into everybody's affections. The play ends less like a drama by Kushner's hero Brecht than a musical by Rodgers and Hammerstein, with everyone teamed up together in the end, in harmony and love. How comforting. If an anti-depressant went to sleep and dreamed that it was a play, it would dream that it was this play.

The worst part of all this, especially for a politically engaged Brechtian such as Kushner, is that *Angels*, with its incessant raging references to Reagan, was already dated when its first curtain rose. In 1991, Reagan had been out of office for three years, and the country was on the brink of a Democratic government whose immediate priority was integrating gays into the military, and whose vision of Kushner-like diversity co-existed very comfortably with Reaganite ideas about dismantling welfare and government entitlements. And insofar as *Angels* is an explicit brief for the multi-cultural movement that surged in the late '80s and '90s, it undermines its "message" because of the dead-end dynamic of its argument. In order to make the case for diversity, Kushner has to emphasize everyone's sexual, ethnic, and racial identity, which has the effect of making his vision of tolerance at the end look as much like fantasy as the airborne angel. But Kushner, who actually has his angel recite a version of Walter Benjamin's remark about the angel of history, to the effect that material progress is really spiritual regress, is as mushy-headed as Reagan ever was. His devotion to Brecht and Benjamin has about it a college freshman's starry-eyed susceptibility to the first difficult ideas that he encounters. And the characters wear the dialectical technique like a straitjacket: Louis will attack Reagan's heartlessness, and then Belize will expose Louis's own insensitivity while deriding Louis's ineffectual intellectualizing. Kushner thinks that by contradicting his pieties, he is moving beyond them, but he has really just found a way to hide his pieties behind the veneer of "complexity."

It boggles a tender mind that this quaint film of *Angels* should draw so much praise in late 2003. Here are Kushner's characters pleading for the acceptance of gay rights even as the Supreme Court declares a ban on sodomy unconstitutional and the Massachusetts Supreme Court declares gay marriage legal. This movie has exactly nothing to do with political reality. If there is one thing it does not do, it is clarify our moment. Even looking back, *Angels in America* really bears no more connection to its Reaganite subject than *Waiting for Lefty* did to the Depression. Like Odets's play, its appeal lies solely in its facile, upbeat vision of human survival in the midst of crisis, any crisis.

But sentimental, historical carpet-bagging is Kushner's

trademark. On stage now at the Public Theater, you can see a superb group of actors wasting their gifts in *Caroline, or Change*, Kushner's "politically engaged" musical centered on the travails of a black maid working for a Jewish family in Louisiana in 1963. Again, we get the fearless dialectic: Jews and blacks, the victims of prejudice, are shown to have their own prejudices against each other. Imagine! Never mind that in 2003 the situation of blacks cannot be reduced to the situation of a black maid in a small Louisiana town, much less to a black maid whose central conflict is with a spoiled Jewish boy named Noah, another of Kushner's courageously complex self-portraits.

A truly engaging play would enact the confrontation between a Jewish playwright mindlessly exploiting the black experience and, say, an accomplished black writer who returns enraged from the former's play to contend with far less transparent modes of racism, and passive-aggressive projection, and condescension. There is not a single black character in *Caroline* who is not a mammy, a pickaninny, a shvartze, or an entertainer with lots of rhythm. And deyz all workin' fer a nice, socially conscious Jewish family. Black artists and intellectuals were once angered by Paul Robeson's return, in the midst of the Harlem Renaissance, to the spirituals sung by slaves, but about *Caroline, or Change*, not a peep. Instead we get John Lahr in the *New Yorker* – in the same issue with Nancy Franklin's "fearless" – declaring about Kushner's musical that "There are moments in the history of theater when stagecraft takes a new turn." The worlds of Noah, the nine-year-old Jewish boy, Lahr solemnly informs us, and Caroline, the middle-aged black maid, are "negotiable, Kushner makes clear, [but] not bridgeable. *Caroline, or Change* gives the inconsolable a mature song. … " A white British mandarin condescending to a cuddly Jewish playwright condescending to black people at a time when American consciousness of race has been pushed off the political agenda and onto media obsession with the likes of Kobe Bryant and Michael Jackson: now that's theater.

Mike Nichols's ultra-slick production is a study in television's fascinating alchemy. A crowded theater, in which one is immediately aware of other people, of other experiences, automatically provides the indispensable first step for the appreciation of a work of art, which is to get out of oneself. Television, since you watch it in your environment, usually alone, keeps you comfortably close to your own experience, which is the relaxing value of entertainment. That is why sitcoms are about everyday problems; and why even great television, like *The Sopranos*, or innovative television, like *Sex and the City* or *Six Feet Under*, keeps the viewer close to the personal, the local, the ordinary experience. And that is why television drama is nearly always tied to an issue fresh out of the news.

You know that Nichols is highly conscious of topicality because midway through his film of Kushner's play, he gives us a stunningly mendacious scene in which Joe and Harper are talking against a backdrop of the World Trade Center. Throughout the play, Kushner makes a connection between the impending millennium and the AIDS-beleaguered gay community; so naturally, after September 11, 2001, an apocalyptic day if ever there was one, many viewers are going to marvel, for all the horror and devastation of that plague-period, at Kushner's parochial perspective on history's capacity for surprise. To avert this, Nichols expertly juxtaposes a bit of end-of-days patter against the twin towers: speaking of the deteriorating ozone layer, Harper foresees a cataclysm in which "the end of the world is at hand." The unsuspecting viewer might get the impression that Kushner has, with astonishing clairvoyance, envisioned the world-ending destruction of the towers. But the film was made long after 9/11, and the towers were digitally inserted so as to make the play itself fulfill the play's own pose of prophecy.

Nichols's smooth, very nearly flawless camerawork has the shine of a campaign commercial. Like a campaign commercial, its purpose is to spin a negative into a positive – in this case to turn a failed play into effective television drama. With *Angels in America*, Nichols has managed to halt all the advances that HBO has made in films for television over the past decade or so and returned to the tired old made-for-television category. He has made a big film about a little play, in which Kushner's caricatures are worked away at by the camera until all you see are the faces of the big stars, which are meant to hide the rounded-out and flattened motivations of the characters they play. But, then, star-strickenness is Nichols's aesthetic. On stage, the angel of theatricality tried to save Kushner's play from its shallow grasp of life; on screen, the camera tries to perform the rescue-work of the angel by attempting to suppress the play altogether under the aura of glossy production. Angles in America.

Nichols turns the theatricality into special effects – poor Emma Thompson, swinging around on wires as the angel, looks like she is about to throw up. And just as those old made-for-television movies appealed to audiences by their treatment of edifying and familiar issues, Nichols rivets the camera on the most superficial references to emotion or psychology. Consider this typical exchange: "You are amazingly unhappy." "Oh big deal. You meet a valium addict, you figure out she's unhappy. That doesn't count." There is nothing psychologically original, or verbally interesting, or emotionally true, about those words. Kushner doesn't write dialogue; he makes the characters declaim Brechtish notations on what should be dialogue. The characters speak lines that are really what a director would say to an actor before a scene: "OK. You suspect that your husband's gay. You're angry and helpless and confused. You are amazingly unhappy." And then the actor would have to go and express unhappiness. Or a director might say: "You don't really have emotional problems. You're in a bad marriage that is playing havoc with your emotions." But here is Harper saying to Joe: "I do not have emotional problems, and if I do have emotional problems, it's from living with you." These bulletins are mind-numbing. It's like being on a date with a newspaper.

Whenever we get one of these segments of the Evening Emotional News, Nichols handles the camera with such seriousness and urgency that you feel insentient for thinking that nothing serious or urgent is going on. The camera is so close to the actors that it endows them with that living-room dimension that makes television drama seem profound when it is really just cozy. Nichols has seized on Kushner's directorial dialogue and used it to direct the audience's attention right past the dialogue to the heart-rending music, and to the tricky camera, and to the legendary stars. This buffed manipulativeness has to be why Nichols chose Pacino and Streep (Thompson doesn't perform her characters, she endures them), because the two of them are so miscast there cannot be any other reason.

Always more studied than intuitive, the usually miraculous Streep cannot think her way into such vaguenesses as Mother Pitt and the ghost of Ethel Rosenberg, both of whom she plays, so she intellectualizes the simplicity and humility of both, and thus ends up with a parody of simplicity and humility, a famous actor performing the facial expressions of the un-famous. (Did you know that the latter smile with eyes downward in near-embarrassment?) And Pacino is even more star-corrupted. On Broadway, Ron Leibman animated his Roy Cohn with clenched red-faced rage and self-conflict, but Pacino never loses control. There is an uncanny moment in *The Godfather, Part II* when Michael Corleone, seething with rage as his wife tells him that she aborted their child, suddenly springs at her and slaps her face; Pacino's genius was to have Michael explode while elegantly retaining his cigarette between the fingers of his other hand. The detached self-possession in the midst of near-murderous rage, as if his left side and his right side were two different people in two different worlds, was breathtaking. But now Pacino's villains, even when they are torn and tormented like Cohn, are all self-possession. They have the arrogance of a star.

Brando and De Niro re-invented themselves late in their careers as self-ironizing comic actors, but the extraordinary Pacino has become humorless, solipsistic, the last self-conscious upholder of the Method. He doesn't act; he does master classes for *Inside the Actors' Studio*. He is unforgettable not as Roy Cohn but as Pacino playing Roy Cohn. James Woods's performance as Roy Cohn in HBO's *Citizen Cohn* eleven years ago, though more modest and scaled down, was simply unforgettable. Indeed, five minutes of that movie, for all of its faithfulness to the real transcripts and history books and biographies, was worth all six hours of Nichols's *Angels*. "The messenger has arrived," proclaim the ads for *Angels*. And the messenger brings nothing but messages.

10. Complicity

When a friend asks, "What's the matter with the world?" you reply, "I am."

George Orwell	Shooting an Elephant
Lauren Slater	One Nation, Under the Weather

Complicity

CENTRAL TO THE PERSONAL ESSAY IS WHAT THEODOR Adorno calls "immanence." Immanence, or complicity, allows the writer to be a kind of shock absorber of the culture, to reflect back its "whatness," refracted through the sensibility of his or her consciousness. Often this leads the essayist to sound somewhat abject or debased, given how abject or debased the culture is likely to be at any given point. Or as the photographer Robert Capa said, "If your picture isn't any good, you're not standing close enough." William Gass: "I know of nothing more difficult than knowing who you are and having the courage to share the reasons for the catastrophe of your character with the world." Phillip Lopate: "The spectacle of baring the naked soul is meant to awaken the sympathy of the reader, who is apt to forgive the essayist's self-absorption in return for the warmth of his or her candor." Wendy Lesser: "The crucial art of the essay lies in its perpetrator's masterful control over his own self-exposure. We may at times be embarrassed *by* him, but we should never feel embarrassed *for* him. He must be the ringmaster of his self-display. He may choose to bare more than he can bear (that is where the terror comes in), but *he* must do the choosing, and we must feel that he is doing it." Montaigne: "Every man contains within himself the entire human condition."

The essayist is not really interested in himself per se but in himself as a symbolic persona, as theme-carrier, as host for a specific cultural conflict or larger human dilemma. Write a 1,500-word personal essay in which you place yourself in harm's way. Explore your own character in all its contradictions and complexity, but try to make your flawedness subtly representative of a contemporary and/or timeless angst.

Adorno says a successful work "is not one that resolves objective contradictions in a spurious harmony, but one that expresses the idea of harmony negatively by embodying the contradictions, pure and uncompromised, in its innermost structure." This is what George Orwell does so precisely and vividly in "Shooting an Elephant." He doesn't pretend to be any less ambivalent than he is. He owns up to considerable confusion and prejudice: "I was stuck between my hatred of the empire I served and my rage against the evil-spirited little beasts who tried to make my job impossible. With one part of my mind I thought of the British Raj as an unbreakable tyranny, as something clamped down, *in saecula saeculorum,* upon the will of prostrate peoples; with another part I thought that the greatest joy in the world would be to drive a bayonet into a Buddhist priest's guts." Later, "Here was I, the white man with his gun, standing in front of the unarmed native crowd – seemingly the leading actor of the piece; but in reality I was only an absurd puppet pushed to and fro by the will of those yellow faces behind. I perceived in this moment that when the white man turns tyrant it is his own freedom that he destroys. He becomes a sort of hollow, posing dummy, the conventionalized figure of a sahib. For it is the condition of his rule that he shall spend his life in trying to impress the 'natives,' and so in every crisis he has got to do what the 'natives' expect of him. He wears a mask, and his face grows to fit it. I had got to shoot the elephant ... My whole life, every white man's life in the East, was one long struggle not to be laughed at." After shooting the elephant, Orwell concludes, "I often wondered whether any of the others grasped that I had done it solely to avoid looking a fool." In little more than 3,000 words, Orwell tells us more about the sources, psychology, and consequences of racism, empire, and colonialism than any book-length treatise could; all of the power of "Shooting an Elephant" derives from his willingness to locate an astonishing mix of rage and guilt within himself. We don't judge him; we are him.

Many writers pretend they don't read reviews of their books and that in particular life is too short to subject themselves to reading bad reviews. Kingsley Amis said that a bad review may spoil breakfast but you shouldn't allow it to spoil lunch. Jean Cocteau suggested, "Listen carefully to first criticisms of your work. Note carefully just what it is about your work that the critics don't like, then cultivate it. That's the part of your work that's individual and worth keeping." Sane advice; Lauren Slater, in "One Nation, Under the Weather," doesn't follow it. Receiving a bad review from Janet Maslin in the *New York Times* of her genre-troubling book *Lying*, Slater does that thing you're not supposed to do: she dwells on it, in public.

Accused of being narcissistic, exhibitionist, self-absorbed, neurasthenic, whiney, derivative, she agrees, revels in her very human frailty, and dares the reader to disagree with her when she writes, "The fact is, or my fact is, disease is everywhere. How anyone could ever write about themselves or their fictional characters as not diseased is a bit beyond me. We live in a world and are creatures of a culture that is spinning out more and more medicines that correspond to more and more diseases at an alarming pace. Even beyond that, though, I believe we exist in our God-given natures as diseased beings. We do not fall into illness. We fall from illness into temporary states of health. We are briefly blessed, but always, always those small cells are dividing and will become cancer, if they haven't already; our eyes are crossed, we cannot see. Nearsighted, farsighted, noses spurting bright blood, brains awack with crazy dreams, lassitude and little fears nibbling like mice at the fringes of our flesh, we are never well." Slater's essay is a beautiful demonstration of the truth of E. M. Cioran's observation, "Whatever his merits, a man in good health is always disappointing. As long as he remains there, he is like the objects around him; once torn from it, he opens himself to everything, knows everything: the omniscience of terror."

George Orwell
Shooting an Elephant

IN MOULMEIN, IN LOWER BURMA, I WAS HATED BY LARGE numbers of people – the only time in my life that I have been important enough for this to happen to me. I was sub-divisional police officer of the town, and in an aimless, petty kind of way anti-European feeling was very bitter. No one had the guts to raise a riot, but if a European woman went through the bazaars alone somebody would probably spit betel juice over her dress. As a police officer I was an obvious target and was baited whenever it seemed safe to do so. When a nimble Burman tripped me up on the football field and the referee (another Burman) looked the other way, the crowd yelled with hideous laughter. This happened more than once. In the end the sneering yellow faces of young men that met me everywhere, the insults hooted after me when I was at a safe distance, got badly on my nerves. The young Buddhist priests were the worst of all. There were several thousands of them in the town and none of them seemed to have anything to do except stand on street corners and jeer at Europeans.

All this was perplexing and upsetting. For at that time I had already made up my mind that imperialism was an evil thing and the sooner I chucked up my job and got out of it the better. Theoretically – and secretly, of course – I was all for the Burmese and all against their oppressors, the British. As for the job I was doing, I hated it more bitterly than I can perhaps make clear. In a job like that you see the dirty work of Empire at close quarters. The wretched prisoners huddling in the stinking cages of the lock-ups, the grey, cowed faces of the long-term convicts, the scarred buttocks of the men who had been flogged with bamboos – all these oppressed me with an intolerable sense of guilt. But I could get nothing into perspective. I was young and ill-educated and I had had to think out my problems in the utter silence that is imposed on every Englishman in the East. I did not even know that the British Empire is dying, still less did I know that it is a great deal better than the younger empires that are going to supplant it. All I knew was that I was stuck between my hatred of the empire I served and my rage against the evil-spirited little beasts who tried to make my job impossible. With one part of my mind I thought of the British Raj as an unbreakable tyranny, as something clamped down, *in saecula saeculorum*, upon the will of prostrate peoples; with another part I thought that the greatest joy in the world would be to drive a bayonet into a Buddhist priest's guts. Feelings like these are the normal by-products of imperialism; ask any Anglo-Indian official, if you can catch him off duty.

One day something happened which in a roundabout way was enlightening. It was a tiny incident in itself, but it gave me a better glimpse than I had had before of the real nature of imperialism – the real motives for which despotic governments act. Early one morning the sub-inspector at a police station the other end of the town rang me up on the 'phone and said that an elephant was ravaging the bazaar. Would I please come and do something about it? I did not know what I could do, but I wanted to see what was happening and I got on to a pony and started out. I took my rifle, an old .44 Winchester and much too small to kill an elephant, but I thought the noise might be useful *in terrorem*. Various Burmans stopped me on the way and told me about the elephant's doings. It was not, of course, a wild elephant, but a tame one which had gone "must." It had been chained up, as tame elephants always are when their attack of "must" is due, but on the previous night it had broken its chain and escaped. Its mahout, the only person who could manage it when it was in that state, had set out in pursuit, but had taken the wrong direction and was now twelve hours' journey away, and in the morning the elephant had suddenly reappeared in the town. The Burmese population had no weapons and were quite helpless against it. It had already destroyed somebody's bamboo hut, killed a cow and raided some fruit-stalls and devoured the stock; also it had met the municipal rubbish van and, when the driver jumped out and took to his heels, had turned the van over and inflicted violences upon it.

The Burmese sub-inspector and some Indian constables were waiting for me in the quarter where the elephant had been seen. It was a very poor quarter, a labyrinth of squalid bamboo huts, thatched with palm-leaf, winding all over a steep hillside. I remember that it was a cloudy, stuffy morning at the beginning of the rains. We began questioning the people as to where the elephant had gone and, as usual, failed to get any definite information. That is invariably the case in the East; a story always sounds clear enough at a distance, but the nearer you get to the scene of events the vaguer it becomes. Some of the people said that the elephant had gone in one direction, some said that he had gone in another, some professed not even to have heard of any elephant. I had almost made up my mind that the whole story was a pack of lies, when we heard yells a little distance away. There was a loud, scandalized cry of "Go away, child! Go away this instant!" and an old woman with a switch in her hand came round the corner of a hut, violently shooing away a crowd of naked children. Some more women followed, clicking their tongues and exclaiming; evidently there was something that the children ought not to have seen. I rounded the hut and saw a man's dead body sprawling in the mud. He was an Indian, a black Dravidian coolie, almost naked, and he could not have been dead many minutes. The people said that the elephant had come suddenly upon him round the corner of the hut, caught him with its trunk, put its foot on his back and ground him into the earth. This was the rainy season and the ground was soft, and his face had scored a trench a foot deep and a couple of yards long. He was lying on his belly with arms crucified and head sharply twisted to one side. His face was coated with mud, the eyes wide open, the teeth bared and grinning with an expression of unendurable agony. (Never tell me, by the way, that the dead look peaceful. Most of the corpses I have seen looked devilish.) The friction of the great beast's foot had stripped the skin from his back as neatly as one skins a rabbit. As soon as I saw the dead man I sent an orderly to a friend's house nearby to borrow an elephant rifle. I had already sent back the pony, not wanting it to go mad with fright and throw me if it smelt the elephant.

The orderly came back in a few minutes with a rifle and five cartridges, and meanwhile some Burmans had arrived and told us that the elephant was in the paddy fields below, only a few hundred yards away. As I started forward practically the whole population of the quarter flocked out of the houses and followed me. They had seen the rifle and were all shouting excitedly that I was going to shoot the elephant. They had not shown much interest in the elephant when he was merely ravaging their homes, but it was different now that he was going to be shot. It was a bit of fun to them, as it would be to an English crowd; besides they wanted the meat. It made me vaguely uneasy. I had no intention of shooting the elephant – I had merely sent for the rifle to defend myself if necessary – and it is always unnerving to have a crowd following you. I marched down the hill, looking and feeling a fool, with the rifle over my shoulder and an ever-growing army of people jostling at my heels. At the bottom, when you got away from the huts, there was a metalled road and beyond that a miry waste of paddy fields a thousand yards across, not yet ploughed but soggy from the first rains and dotted with coarse grass. The elephant was standing eight yards from the road, his left side towards us. He took not the slightest notice of the crowd's approach. He was tearing up bunches of grass, beating them against his knees to clean them and stuffing them into his mouth.

I had halted on the road. As soon as I saw the elephant I knew with perfect certainty that I ought not to shoot him. It is a serious matter to shoot a working elephant – it is comparable to destroying a huge and costly piece of machinery – and obviously one ought not to do it if it can possibly be avoided. And at that distance, peacefully eating, the elephant looked no more dangerous than a cow. I thought then and I think now that his attack of "must" was already passing off; in which case he would merely wander harmlessly about until the mahout came back and caught him. Moreover, I did not in the least want to shoot him. I decided that I would watch him for a little while to make sure that he did not turn savage again, and then go home.

But at that moment I glanced round at the crowd that had followed me. It was an immense crowd, two thousand at the least and growing every minute. It blocked the road for a long distance on either side. I looked at the sea of yellow faces above the garish clothes – faces all happy and excited over this bit of fun, all certain that the elephant was going to be shot. They were watching me as they would watch a conjurer about to perform a trick. They did not like me, but with the magical rifle in my hands I was momentarily worth watching. And suddenly I realized that I should have to shoot the elephant after all. The people expected it of me and I had got to do it; I could feel their two thousand wills pressing me forward, irresistibly. And it was at this moment, as I stood there with the rifle in my hands, that I first grasped the hollowness, the futility of the white man's dominion in the East. Here was I, the white man with his gun, standing in front of the unarmed native crowd – seemingly the leading actor of the piece; but in reality I was only an absurd puppet pushed to and fro by the will of those yellow faces behind. I perceived in this moment that when the white man turns tyrant it is his own freedom that he destroys. He becomes a sort of hollow, posing dummy, the conventionalized figure of a sahib. For it is the condition of his rule that he shall spend his life in trying to impress the "natives," and so in every crisis he has got to do what the "natives" expect of him. He wears a mask, and his face grows to fit it. I had got to shoot the elephant. I had committed myself to doing it when I sent for the rifle. A sahib has got to act like a sahib; he has got to appear resolute, to know his own mind and do definite things. To come all that way, rifle in hand, with two thousand people marching at my heels, and then to trail feebly away, having done nothing – no, that was impossible. The crowd would laugh at me. And my whole life, every white man's life in the East, was one long struggle not to be laughed at.

But I did not want to shoot the elephant. I watched him beating his bunch of grass against his knees, with that preoccupied grandmotherly air that elephants have. It seemed to me that it would be murder to shoot him. At that age I was not squeamish about killing animals, but I had never shot an elephant and never wanted to. (Somehow it always seems worse to kill a *large* animal.) Besides, there was the beast's owner to be considered. Alive, the elephant was worth at least a hundred pounds; dead, he would only be worth the value of his tusks, five pounds, possibly. But I had got to act quickly. I turned to some experienced-looking Burmans who had been there when we arrived, and asked them how the elephant had been behaving. They all said the same thing: he took no notice of you if you left him alone, but he might charge if you went too close to him.

It was perfectly clear to me what I ought to do. I ought to walk up to within, say, twenty-five yards of the elephant and test his behavior. If he charged, I could shoot; if he took no notice of me, it would be safe to leave him until the mahout came back. But also I knew that I was going to do no such thing. I was a poor shot with a rifle and the ground was soft mud into which one would sink at every step. If the elephant charged and I missed him, I should have about as much chance as a toad under a steam-roller. But even then I was not thinking particularly of my own skin, only of the watchful yellow faces behind. For at that moment, with the crowd watching me, I was not afraid in the ordinary sense, as I would have been if I had been alone. A white man mustn't be frightened in front of "natives"; and so, in general, he isn't frightened. The sole thought in my mind was that if anything went wrong those two thousand Burmans would see me pursued, caught, trampled on and reduced to a grinning corpse like that Indian up the hill. And if that happened it was quite probable that some of them would laugh. That would never do. There was only one alternative. I shoved the cartridges into the magazine and lay down on the road to get a better aim.

The crowd grew very still, and a deep, low, happy sigh, as of people who see the theatre curtain go up at last, breathed from innumerable throats. They were going to have their bit of fun after all. The rifle was a beautiful German thing with cross-hair sights. I did not then know that in shooting an elephant one would shoot to cut an imaginary bar running from ear-hole to ear-hole. I ought, therefore, as the elephant was sideways on, to have aimed straight at his ear-hole; actually I aimed several inches in front of this, thinking the brain would be further forward.

When I pulled the trigger I did not hear the bang or feel the kick – one never does when a shot goes home – but I heard the devilish roar of glee that went up from the crowd. In that instant, in too short a time, one would have thought, even for the bullet to get there, a mysterious, terrible change had come over the elephant. He neither stirred nor fell, but every line of his body had altered. He looked suddenly stricken, shrunken, immensely old, as though the frightful impact of the bullet had paralysed him without knocking him down. At last, after what seemed a long time – it might have been five seconds, I dare say – he sagged flabbily to his knees. His mouth slobbered. An enormous senility seemed to have settled upon him. One could have imagined him thousands of years old. I fired again into the same spot. At the second shot he did not collapse but climbed with desperate slowness to his feet and stood weakly upright, with legs sagging and head drooping. I fired a third time. That was the shot that did for him. You could see the agony of it jolt his whole body and knock the last remnant of strength from his legs. But in falling he seemed for a moment to rise, for as his hind legs collapsed beneath him he seemed to tower upward like a huge rock toppling, his trunk reaching skyward like a tree. He trumpeted, for the first and only time. And then down he came, his belly towards me, with a crash that seemed to shake the ground even where I lay.

I got up. The Burmans were already racing past me across the mud. It was obvious that the elephant would never rise again, but he was not dead. He was breathing very rhythmically with long rattling gasps, his great mound of a side painfully rising and falling. His mouth was wide open – I could see far down into caverns of pale pink throat. I waited a long time for him to die, but his breathing did not weaken. Finally I fired my two remaining shots into the spot where I thought his heart must be. The thick blood welled out of him like red velvet, but still he did not die. His body did not even jerk when the shots hit him, the tortured breathing continued without a pause. He was dying, very slowly and in great agony, but in some world remote from me where not even a bullet could damage him further. I felt that I had got to put an end to that dreadful noise. It seemed dreadful to see the great beast lying there, powerless to move and yet powerless to die, and not even to be able to finish him. I sent back for my small rifle and poured shot after shot into his heart and down his throat. They seemed to make no impression. The tortured gasps continued as steadily as the ticking of a clock.

In the end I could not stand it any longer and went away. I heard later that it took him half an hour to die. Burmans were bringing dahs and baskets even before I left, and I was told they had stripped his body almost to the bones by the afternoon.

Afterwards, of course, there were endless discussions about the shooting of the elephant. The owner was furious, but he was only an Indian and could do nothing. Besides, legally I had done the right thing, for a mad elephant has to be killed, like a mad dog, if its owner fails to control it. Among the Europeans opinion was divided. The older men said I was right, the younger men said it was a damn shame to shoot an elephant for killing a coolie, because an elephant was worth more than any damn Coringhee coolie. And afterwards I was very glad that the coolie had been killed; it put me legally in the right and it gave me a sufficient pretext for shooting the elephant. I often wondered whether any of the others grasped that I had done it solely to avoid looking a fool.

Lauren Slater
One Nation,
Under the Weather

I AM SELF-CENTERED. I AM AN EXHIBITIONIST. I POSE whenever possible in public places. I have a billy club (Watch out!) and it would not be beyond me to flog you on your tender head, just to get my point across, my point across, my point across. Immature and whiny, constantly ill, a voluble bellyacher, not to mention derivative in all pursuits artistic, I still, at the ripe old age of 36, blame my mother for it all.

It is Thursday, June something, and this is what I wake to, the points above, written, alas, in a huge newspaper, the *New York Times*, a newspaper as wide as the world, with print as black as an old bruise. My new book – the book I love best of all my books, my baby – has been panned by a woman named Maslin, named Janet. She hates it. She hates me. Her dislike seems to seep from the spaces between the words, and my first response, after reading it twice – "*Lying* flogs these important things to the point where they cease being important ... though she has already cataloged a full litany of complaints including depression, anorexia and self-mutilation, Ms. Slater now locates a whole new vein of illness to mine ... " – after reading the review twice, no, three times, I do what any good illness memoirist would do. I reach for the shelf and take my meds.

I take, to be specific, two Valium, which I keep on hand for emergencies such as these. The drug is fast-acting and sweet, and soon I am calm enough to eat a corn muffin. I sit at my kitchen table and think. How could she say I'm so self-absorbed? Me? ME?

Self-absorbed? I'm so nice that the mice I catch in sticky traps I later free in the woods, five miles from my home. I don't eat meat. I don't eat chicken. I personally palpate my dog's anal sacs because he's so afraid of the vet. Me? ME? Self-absorbed? I love animals and people, and to top it off I'm a psychotherapist, goddamit, I'm in the helping profession; I don't whine, I listen to other people whine, me? ME? ME?

I call my husband at work. "I got a terrible review in the *Times*," I say.

"I'm sorry," he says.

"The reviewer basically accuses me of being narcissistic, solipsistic and writing too much about illness. That's not true," I say. "Don't you think?"

He doesn't say anything.

"Listen sweetie," I say, "today is not the day I want your honest response. Lie to me."

"Honestly," he says, "you do write a lot about yourself, and yourself as ill, but I like your books."

"I don't believe you," I say.

"Really," he says.

"I'm going to call her," I say.

"Call who?" he says.

"The reviewer," I say, "Janet Maslin."

"I don't think that's a good idea," he says. "Why don't you calm down first?"

But I am calm. And it suddenly occurs to me, or the me-on-Valium, that this is exactly what I need to do. I need to call Ms. Maslin up on the phone and have a heart-to-heart.

Exactly what my heart will say to her heart is not clear to me, but the urge to hear her voice is. I feel, I suppose, a little like a jilted lover. A very powerful person has rejected me, and there is nothing like rejection to stir that little crimson clementine in our chests. I am stirred. I hang up with my husband. I imagine Ms. Maslin as very tall, with handsome hair and a freshly sharpened pencil tucked behind a compact ear. I imagine her briefcase, well-worn and Coach; her Manhattan apartment, where a cat curls on top of a sleek black stereo set. She is impeccable, powerful and beautiful, with a brain like a blade. I must redeem myself in her eyes. I must reason with her. I must persuade her to write another review, I must make her feel guilty. I call her.

I'm surprised by how easy it is to find her. All you have to do is call information and get the main number for the *New York Times*. Then you tell the gum-snapping operator on the other end of the phone that you'd like to speak with Janet Maslin. It's as though they've been waiting for my call. Not a second's hesitation, the operator ferrets me through.

I hear Janet's phone ring once, twice. I imagine her desk, with my book on it, the margins marked up. Click click. "Your call is being answered by Audix," I hear, and then a pregnant pause, and then what I know is Ms. Maslin's voice saying, "Janet Maslin is busy right now." I am taken aback by Janet's voice. I am surprised by its sound, soft, tentative in its tone, a voice without the vim and vigor of her muscular writing style. She must be short. I am shocked to think that Janet Maslin might be short, and that she has such a human sound. Suddenly, her deeply critical review of me is much harder to dismiss. Maybe I am self-centered. And why do I write so ceaselessly about being ill? I replace the phone. There is sweat on the receiver where my hand has been. Damn hand. Ugly hand. Derivative hand. Ms. Maslin has it right. I am a part of, alas, the once-fashionable, now-fading brat pack of illness memoirists, and we can be a tiring bunch to read.

So there. As a memoirist I am very good at making confessions. I concede Ms. Maslin her points. I now have three, count them three, books on the market in which psychiatric illness figures significantly. To make matters worse, I have a fourth on the way. This is an embarrassment.

Illness as an artistic or narrative device is cheap, easy to sensationalize, obvious in its plot. Illness is not subtle, and so the illness memoirist need not grapple with the problems of how to render those fleeting poignant moments of being, those Woolfian wisps that disappear in mid-formation, the quarks of emotion or perception, like how she touched her forefinger to her lip, or how the couple, rendered omnisciently, argued at the restaurant without ever saying a word. The illness memoirist need not struggle with all the possibilities of point of view – first person, close third person, alternate voices – because her tale is relentlessly singular. And how much easier it is to dramatize the syringe or the psychosis than it is to conjure up the haunting emptiness of Don DeLillo suburbia or the poverty of Jean Toomer's inner city.

Most disturbing of all, perhaps, is how the illness memoir can be reductive in its approach to the hugeness of human problems. At its worst, by framing everything as a syndrome, as diagnosis, the illness memoir underscores medicine's dangerous but alluring stranglehold on our understanding; existentialism, love, spirituality, even nihilism fade away as explanatory models, and we are left with only this: ourselves, myself, sick, staring at the singular wound, endlessly penning it bright, penning it black as an old bruise.

The day is bad. I speak to my agent. She says, "Well a review like this won't kill the book," which leads me to believe that, although the book will still be breathing, it will need some serious life support. My illness memoir has now become ill itself. It needs to be in the hospital, and I long to find a very special bed for it. My friend Lisa, who is very savvy about the publishing world, says, "I hate to say this, but other reviewers take their cues from the *New York Times*."

There is, of course, nothing I can do. Except think. And I am a reasonably good thinker, even on Valium. I think about all the problems with the illness memoir as a genre, its tendency toward artistic cheapness, its obsession with syndromes, its brass Oprahness. I think about whether or not I really *am* an illness memoirist or if I have just capitulated to the market forces that have shaped the image of work. After all, although my first book, *Welcome to My Country*, was promoted as a book about me, it was actually a series of portraits of six schizophrenic men whom I treated as a psychologist. I think about the time I went on *Roseanne*, when my second book, *Prozac Diary*, was published.

I tried to write a nuanced book about the complexities of the Prozac cure, but, ultimately, I wound up on *Roseanne*, my face caked with makeup, my hands gesturing wildly, hopefully (I saw a tape of it later), as I admitted, on air, to having this and that mental problem, and the audience clapped, and my Amazon.com number rose oh so briefly into the 80s. I will never forget Roseanne. She herself was nice, and plump and very feminist, and she seemed to feel secure enough in what she was doing.

But I will never forget myself on *Roseanne*, the six-minute segment when my writing sank to its lowest point as I allowed myself to be seen as simply sick and cured, sick and cured, trotting out on TV and showing off my war wounds – for what? For fame? Of course not for fame. I am not so naïve as to think a six-minute segment on a faltering talk show would bring fame. No. I did it simply to stay in print. I did it because, if you write about illness, there seems to be no other way of marketing it except to sensationalize it, or to let it be sensationalized by certain celebrity readers. You can't go on a talk show and discuss nuance. You have to bray, or say nothing and sell no books and lose your publishing house and your editor, who is very important to me, my editor is. In a way I even love her.

So I think about Roseanne, and whoring, on this bad day. And because even on a bad day I am a reasonably good thinker, I muse also on why the hell I keep writing these whorish books. Am I simply a whore? Is the illness memoir as a form just a crooked cheap shot by writers who can't conjure up a novel? This is what I think: Sometimes yes. But sometimes no.

As a psychologist, one of my favorite theorists to read is Irvin Yalom. He writes beautifully about existential psychotherapy and group psychotherapy, and he's one of the few in the field who has really been able to articulate what the healing principles of group therapy might be. Yalom claims that universality is a core healing component of the group therapy process. In other words, patients in group therapy learn that they are not the only ones who feel this way, that they are not aberrant, or perverse, and this in itself is deeply healing.

The best of the illness memoirs, especially those dealing with psychiatric illnesses such as depression, are offerings in this spirit. They were written, I believe, not for the purpose of a peacock display, but to offer solace, to forge connection in times of trouble. I, for one, expect that my readers will be troubled; I envision my readers as troubled, as depressed, as guilty, mourning, maybe, a medication that failed them. I write to say, you are not the only one.

I write with the full faith that the reader I envision is hungry for my tale. I know it, because, having suffered psychiatric illness myself, I am always hungry for tales from the trenches, stories in which I can see myself, stories that might help me map my way. We must consider the illness memoir not only as, or solely as, an *Oprah* bid, but also as this: a gift from me to you. A folk cure, a hand held out. I look into my heart and I see a whore there. But I also see something else. I can, if you are hurting, keep you company.

Perhaps, however, the purpose of literature is not social, or therapeutic. That may be, in which case, I suppose we should house these memoirs, my own included, on the self-help shelf. But that seems a little too easy. The illness memoir, after all, is not a prescription but a description, offered not to cure but to accompany.

Furthermore, shelving the whole lot of us in the self-help section would remove us from public discourse, and, if anything, the illness memoir as a social phenomenon is worthy of public discourse. Why are there so many? What might they mean, not only about their singular authors, but about the collective culture in which we all live? Remember this. No author authors alone. Every text is a joint construction of meaning. Every illness memoir came from the world that you and I co-created, and thus we all, together, Janet Maslin included, write and continue to write this long story of sickness. For what?

Let me begin by saying that in every age there has been a prevailing explanatory grid that the myriad writers of that time have used to frame or explain their lives. The 17th-century spiritual autobiography is a perfect example of this. So is the 1960s political memoir or the 1970s feminist memoir. Beneath these grids, however, the same essential story prevails; the grid is merely the conduit through which the tale flows. From Augustine's *Confessions* to *The Autobiography of Malcolm X* to Nancy Mairs's *Remembering the Bone House*, the tale, if it is done well, is always the classic heroic journey, the Dantean descent into the hell of sin, or oppression, or sickness, the long night of the soul, the gradual redemption, partial or complete. This is the story we, as humans, tell ourselves over and over again, and an illness memoir, if it is done deeply, will put its own signature on this transcendent tale, and will be, thus, transcendent.

It is a mistake, therefore, to dismiss illness memoirs out of hand. The worst of them are showy and whiny. The best of them are tussling with the great human themes in an utterly contemporary context; here, modern diagnosis and the ever-present pill are just jazzed up versions of polytheistic gods teasing with mere mortals, the aching Achilles' heel, Sodom, Gomorrah, burning, cities and salt.

And yet. Are there not other ways of getting at these great themes than through the relentless use of disease? So the critic argues. So might Ms. Maslin say. I say no. Not for me. Not for now. This might be my great limitation as a writer, or this might mean I'm onto something the crazy optimists just can't see.

The fact is, or my fact is, disease is everywhere. How anyone could ever write about themselves or their fictional characters as not diseased is a bit beyond me. We live in a world and are creatures of a culture that is spinning out more and more medicines that correspond to more and more diseases at an alarming pace.

Even beyond that, though, I believe we exist in our God-given natures as diseased beings. We do not fall into illness. We fall from illness into temporary states of health. We are briefly blessed, but always, always those small cells are dividing and will become cancer, if they haven't already; our eyes are crossed, we cannot see. Nearsighted, farsighted, noses spurting bright blood, brains awack with crazy dreams, lassitude and little fears nibbling like mice at the fringes of our flesh, we are never well.

Science proves me right, the great laws of the universe, the inevitability of entropy. So there. The illness memoir is so many things, a kindly attempt to keep company; a product of our culture's love of pathology, or of our sometimes whorish selves; a story of human suffering and the attempts to make meaning within it; and finally, a reflection on this awful and absurd and somehow very funny truth, that we are rotting, rotting, even as we write. *Salud.*

II. Guilty Elegy

Your parents are dead.
Your friends and colleagues are keeling over.
Death is real.

Guilty Elegy

ASSIGNMENT: WRITE YOUR OWN GUILTY ELEGY: "BURY someone"; watch someone die; tell the reader about someone who died. This can be either an essay or a story (1,000 words or fewer). But as they say about a funeral, it's not for the dead. It's for the living. So, too, this assignment uses the person who has died to cast light upon the relationship between the bereaved and the dead and especially on the bereaved. The key here is to avoid simple sentiment or mere loss. That is a given. Your composition must get to something more surprising than that.

Amy Hempel's "In the Cemetery Where Al Jolson Is Buried" is a particularly good example of this. Ostensibly, it's simply an account of the narrator – the Hempel figure – chronicling her friend's death at a terribly young age. But Hempel builds in four tracks: pop culture, the nameless narrator's thanatophobia, the friend's dying, and the narrator's surprising reluctance to visit the hospital and in particular to stay in the room overnight. All four tracks come together in the final image of the story, but really the accomplishment of the story lies in its willingness to excavate the narrator's failure. All of us have failed our friends in various and awful ways, and this story is about the narrator's terrible failure of nerve. The narrator's jokey thanatophobia becomes serious when the phobia turns into a real failure; the story turns on its head and the smiling, joking narrator panics: "I was supposed to offer something. The Best Friend," she says, now resigned to leaving her friend's bedside. "I could not even offer to come back. I felt weak and small and failed. Also exhilarated." Leaving the hospital in this state, she plans to drive her convertible, top-down, to a bar on the side of the road and indulge in food, beverage, lust, yet she cannot fully escape; this experience is entangled with other ever-present fears (fear of earthquakes, of flying, etc.). "In the Cemetery Where Al Jolson is Buried" is the first story Hempel ever wrote – and her most well known – and it was written specifically in response to a creative writing workshop prompt from her teacher Gordon Lish: "We were told to write up our worst secret," says Hempel, "the thing that would dismantle my sense of myself, as he put it." Lish: "Don't glorify yourself; convict yourself. Don't write about what you haven't paid for. And through the nose." On this particular day of the workshop, after Lish's students divulged their deepest, darkest confessions in round-robin fashion, Lish added, almost devilishly, "Did I say … that this secret doesn't have to be true?"

Leonard Michaels's story isn't entirely dissimilar; Michaels is writing about what might be an unspeakable memory. The virtuosity of "Murderers" lies in the violation of unities of time, place, and action at the end of the story. The story moves away from NYC to camp and we have no idea where it's going. It's going away from plot, deeper into theme: the narrator, Phillip Liebowitz, who bragged at the beginning about wanting to be closer to darkness, has gotten his wish. The boys, who thought they were angels, "derealized in brilliance," turn out to be made of shit, along with everyone else. They, too, are mortal – "I'd never before heard that sound, the sound of darkness, blooming, opening inside you like a mouth." They thought sex and death weren't a part of them, and weren't connected, but the boys, especially the narrator, learn that the darkness is within them, too. They, too, are murderers of sorts.

Jonathan Safran Foer is as haunted by the Holocaust as the Michaels story collection *I Would Have Saved Them If I Could* (in which "Murderers" appears). Foer's essay is an investigation of how his relatives suffered in concentration camps and how this has rendered the entire family incapable of loving anyone but the members of the family. Foer devises "A Primer for the Punctuation of Heart Disease" using software that allows us to put stock symbols into our writing; he tries and fails to adopt a jocular tone: he suffers from the family curse. Try though he might, he, too, can't love anyone outside of the family, and he can converse and converse, but he can't really say anything, either. He's capable of endless verbiage, but he can't communicate. Your family, every family, has its secrets, its way of talking. T. S. Eliot: "There's no vocabulary / For love within a family, love that's lived in / But not looked at, love within the light of which / All else is seen, the love within which / All other love finds speech. / This love is silent."

Jerome Stern's essay is an elegy for himself; Stern died not long after this short work of prose was published. What is remarkable about it is the way in which it takes what feels like a journal entry and transforms it into a meditation on a rational man who cannot countenance his own death and who, at the end, by saying "God damn store," finally, suddenly implies all the anger, self-pity, and fury that he has been refusing to acknowledge all along. That is the key to all of these stories and essays – they all "use death" to get at something surprising and discomfiting in the narrator: Stern's refusal to access his own anger, Foer's reluctance to admit the legacy he has inherited from his family, Michaels's evocation of his narrator's realization that he is neither pure nor immortal, and Hempel's willingness to explore her own quite serious failure of nerve.

Amy Hempel

In the Cemetery Where Al Jolson Is Buried

"TELL ME THINGS I WON'T MIND FORGETTING," SHE SAID. "Make it useless stuff or skip it."

I began. I told her insects fly through rain, missing every drop, never getting wet. I told her no one in America owned a tape recorder before Bing Crosby did. I told her the shape of the moon is like a banana—you see it looking full, you're seeing it end-on.

The camera made me self-conscious and I stopped. It was trained on us from a ceiling mount—the kind of camera banks use to photograph robbers. It played us to the nurses down the hall in Intensive Care.

"Go on, girl," she said. "You get used to it."

I had my audience. I went on. Did she know that Tammy Wynette had changed her tune? Really. That now she sings "Stand by Your *Friends*"? That Paul Anka did it too, I said. Does "You're Having *Our* Baby." That he got sick of all that feminist bitching.

"What else?" she said. "Have you got something else?"

Oh, yes.

For her I would always have something else.

"Did you know that when they taught the first chimp to talk, it lied? That when they asked her who did it on the desk, she signed back the name of the janitor. And that when they pressed her, she said she was sorry, that it was really the project director. But she was a mother, so I guess she had her reasons."

"Oh, that's good," she said. "A parable."

"There's more about the chimp," I said. "But it will break your heart."

"No, thanks," she says, and scratches at her mask.

WE LOOK LIKE good-guy outlaws. Good or bad, I am not used to the mask yet. I keep touching the warm spot where my breath, thank God, comes out. She is used to hers. She only ties the strings on top. The other ones – a pro by now – she lets hang loose.

We call this place the Marcus Welby Hospital. It's the white one with the palm trees under the opening credits of all those shows. A Hollywood hospital, though in fact it is several miles west. Off camera, there is a beach across the street.

SHE INTRODUCES ME to a nurse as the Best Friend. The impersonal article is more intimate. It tells me that *they* are intimate, the nurse and my friend.

"I was telling her we used to drink Canada Dry ginger ale and pretend we were in Canada."

"That's how dumb we were," I say.

"You could be sisters," the nurse says.

So how come, I'll bet they are wondering, it took me so long to get to such a glamorous place? But do they ask?

They do not ask.

Two months, and how long is the drive?

The best I can explain it is this – I have a friend who worked one summer in a mortuary. He used to tell me stories. The one that really got to me was not the grisliest, but it's the one that did. A man wrecked his car on 101 going south. He did not lose consciousness. But his arm was taken down to the wet bone – and when he looked at it – it scared him to death.

I mean, he died.

So I hadn't dared to look any closer. But now I'm doing it – and hoping that I will live through it.

SHE SHAKES OUT a summer-weight blanket, showing a leg you did not want to see. Except for that, you look at her and understand the law that requires two people to be with the body at all times. "I thought of something," she says. "I thought of it last night. I think there is a real and present need here. You know," she says, "like for someone to do it for you when you can't do it yourself. You call them up whenever you want – like when push comes to shove."

She grabs the bedside phone and loops the cord around her neck.

"Hey," she says, "the end o' the line."

She keeps on, giddy with something. But I don't know with what.

"I can't remember," she says. "What does Kübler-Ross say comes after Denial?"

It seems to me Anger must be next. Then Bargaining, Depression, and so on and so forth. But I keep my guesses to myself.

"The only thing is," she says, "is where's Resurrection? God knows, I want to do it by the book. But she left out Resurrection."

SHE LAUGHS, AND I cling to the sound the way someone dangling above a ravine holds fast to the thrown rope.

"Tell me," she says, "about that chimp with the talking hands. What do they do when the thing ends and the chimp says, 'I don't want to go back to the zoo'?"

When I don't say anything, she says, "Okay – then tell me another animal story. I like animal stories. But not a sick one – I don't want to know about all the seeing-eye dogs going blind."

No, I would not tell her a sick one.

"How about the hearing-ear dogs?" I say. "They're not going deaf, but they are getting very judgmental. For instance, there's this golden retriever in New Jersey, he wakes up the deaf mother and drags her into the daughter's room because the kid has got a flashlight and is reading under the covers."

"Oh, you're killing me," she says. "Yes, you're definitely killing me."

"They say the smart dog obeys, but the smarter dog knows when to disobey."

"Yes," she says, "the smarter anything knows when to disobey. Now, for example."

SHE IS FLIRTING with the Good Doctor, who has just appeared. Unlike the Bad Doctor, who checks the IV drip before saying good morning, the Good Doctor says things like "God didn't give epileptics a fair shake." The Good Doctor awards himself points for the cripples he could have hit in the parking lot. Because the Good Doctor is a little in love with her, he says maybe a year. He pulls a chair up to her bed and suggests I might like to spend an hour on the beach.

"Bring me something back," she says. "Anything from the beach. Or the gift shop. Taste is no object."

He draws the curtain around her bed.

"Wait!" she cries.

I look in at her.

"Anything," she says, "except a magazine subscription."

The doctor turns away.

I watch her mouth laugh.

WHAT SEEMS DANGEROUS often is not – black snakes, for example, or clear-air turbulence. While things that just lie there, like this beach, are loaded with jeopardy. A yellow dust rising from the ground, the heat that ripens melons overnight – this is earthquake weather. You can sit here braiding the fringe on your towel and the sand will all of a sudden suck down like an hourglass. The air roars. In the cheap apartments on-shore, bathtubs fill themselves and gardens roll up and over like green waves. If nothing happens, the dust will drift and the heat deepen till fear turns to desire. Nerves like that are only bought off by catastrophe.

"IT NEVER HAPPENS when you're thinking about it," she once observed. "Earthquake, earthquake, earthquake," she said.

"Earthquake, earthquake, earthquake," I said.

Like the aviaphobe who keeps the plane aloft with prayer, we kept it up until an aftershock cracked the ceiling.

That was after the big one in seventy-two. We were in college; our dormitory was five miles from the epicenter. When the ride was over and my jabbering pulse began to slow, she served five parts champagne to one part orange juice, and joked about living in Ocean View, Kansas. I offered to drive her to Hawaii on the new world psychics predicted would surface the next time, or the next.

I could not say that now – next.

Whose next? she could ask.

WAS I THE only one who noticed that the experts had stopped saying if and now spoke of *when*? Of course not; the fearful ran to thousands. We watched the traffic of Japanese beetles for deviation. Deviation might mean more natural violence.

I wanted her to be afraid with me. But she said, "I don't know. I'm just not."

She was afraid of nothing, not even of flying.

I have this dream before a flight where we buckle in and the plane moves down the runway. It takes off at thirty-five miles an hour, and then we're airborne, skimming the tree tops. Still, we arrive in New York on time.

It is so pleasant.

One night I flew to Moscow this way.

SHE FLEW WITH me once. That time she flew with me she ate macadamia nuts while the wings bounced. She knows the wing tips can bend thirty feet up and thirty feet down without coming off. She believes it. She trusts the laws of aerodynamics. My mind stampedes. I can almost accept that a battleship floats when everybody knows steel sinks.

I see fear in her now, and am not going to try to talk her out of it. She is right to be afraid.

After a quake, the six o'clock news airs a film clip of first-graders yelling at the broken playground per their teacher's instructions.

"*Bad* earth!" they shout, because anger is stronger than fear.

BUT THE BEACH is standing still today. Everyone on it is tranquilized, numb, or asleep. Teenaged girls rub coconut oil on each other's hard-to-reach places. They smell like macaroons. They pry open compacts like clam-shells; mirrors catch the sun and throw a spray of white rays across glazed shoulders. The girls arrange their wet hair with silk flowers the way they learned in *Seventeen*. They pose.

A formation of low-riders pulls over to watch with a six-pack. They get vocal when the girls check their tan lines. When the beer is gone, so are they—flexing their cars on up the boulevard.

Above this aggressive health are the twin wrought-iron terraces, painted flamingo pink, of the Palm Royale. Someone dies there every time the sheets are changed. There's an ambulance in the driveway, so the remaining residents line the balconies, rocking and not talking, one-upped.

The ocean they stare at is dangerous, and not just the undertow. You can almost see the slapping tails of sand sharks keeping cruising bodies alive.

If she looked, she could see this, some of it, from her window. She would be the first to say how little it takes to make a thing all wrong.

THERE WAS A second bed in the room when I got back to it! For two beats I didn't get it. Then it hit me like an open coffin.

She wants every minute, I thought. She wants my life.

"You missed Gussie," she said.

Gussie is her parents' three-hundred-pound narcoleptic

maid. Her attacks often come at the ironing board. The pillowcases in that family are all bordered with scorch.

"It's a hard trip for her," I said. "How is she?"

"Well, she didn't fall asleep, if that's what you mean. Gussie's great – you know what she said? She said, 'Darlin', stop this worriation. Just keep prayin', down on your knees' – me, who can't even get out of bed."

She shrugged. "What am I missing?"

"It's earthquake weather," I told her.

"The best thing to do about earthquakes," she said, "is not to live in California."

"That's useful," I said. "You sound like Reverend Ike – 'The best thing to do for the poor is not to be one of them.'"

We're crazy about Reverend Ike.

I noticed her face was bloated.

"You know," she said, "I feel like hell. I'm about to stop having fun."

"The ancients have a saying," I said. "'There are times when the wolves are silent; there are times when the moon howls.'"

"What's that, Navaho?"

"Palm Royale lobby graffiti," I said. "I bought a paper there. I'll read you something."

"Even though I care about nothing?"

I turned to the page with the trivia column. I said, "Did you know the more shrimp flamingo birds eat, the pinker their feathers get?" I said, "Did you know that Eskimos need refrigerators? Do you know *why* Eskimos need refrigerators? Did you know that Eskimos need refrigerators because how else would they keep their food from freezing?"

I turned to page three, to a UPI filler datelined Mexico City. I read her MAN ROBS BANK WITH CHICKEN, about a man who bought a barbecued chicken at a stand down the block from a bank. Passing the bank, he got the idea. He walked in and approached a teller. He pointed the brown paper bag at her and she handed over the day's receipts. It was the smell of barbecue sauce that eventually led to his capture.

THE STORY HAD made her hungry, she said – so I took the elevator down six floors to the cafeteria, and brought back all the ice cream she wanted. We lay side by side, adjustable beds cranked up for optimal TV-viewing, littering the sheets with Good Humor wrappers, picking toasted almonds out of the gauze. We were Lucy and Ethel, Mary and Rhoda in extremis. The blinds were closed to keep light off the screen.

We watched a movie starring men we used to think we wanted to sleep with. Hers was a tough cop out to stop mine, a vicious rapist who went after cocktail waitresses.

"This is a good movie," she said when snipers felled them both.

I missed her already.

A FILIPINO NURSE tiptoed in and gave her an injection. The nurse removed the pile of popsicle sticks from the nightstand – enough to splint a small animal.

The injection made us both sleepy. We slept.

I dreamed she was a decorator, come to furnish my house. She worked in secret, singing to herself. When she finished, she guided me proudly to the door. "How do you like it?" she asked, easing me inside.

Every beam and sill and shelf and knob was draped in gay bunting, with streamers of pastel crepe looped around bright mirrors.

"I HAVE TO go home," I said when she woke up.

She thought I meant home to her house in the Canyon, and I had to say No, *home* home. I twisted my hands in the time-honored fashion of people in pain. I was supposed to offer something. The Best Friend. I could not even offer to come back.

I felt weak and small and failed.

Also exhilarated.

I had a convertible in the parking lot. Once out of that room, I would drive it too fast down the Coast highway through the crab-smelling air. A stop in Malibu for sangria. The music in the place would be sexy and loud. They'd serve papaya and shrimp and watermelon ice. After dinner I would shimmer with lust, buzz with heat, life, and stay up all night.

WITHOUT A WORD, she yanked off her mask and threw it on the floor. She kicked at the blankets and moved to the door. She must have hated having to pause for breath and balance before slamming out of Isolation, and out of the second room, the one where you scrub and tie on the white masks.

A voice shouted her name in alarm, and people ran down the corridor. The Good Doctor was paged over the intercom. I opened the door and the nurses at the station stared hard, as if this flight had been my idea.

"Where is she?" I asked, and they nodded to the supply closet.

I looked in. Two nurses were kneeling beside her on the floor, talking to her in low voices. One held a mask over her nose and mouth, the other rubbed her back in slow circles. The nurses glanced up to see if I was the doctor – and when I wasn't, they went back to what they were doing.

"There, there, honey," they cooed.

ON THE MORNING she was moved to the cemetery, the one where Al Jolson is buried, I enrolled in a "Fear of Flying" class. "What is your worst fear?" the instructor asked, and I answered, "That I will finish this course and still be afraid."

I SLEEP WITH a glass of water on the nightstand so I can see by its level if the coastal earth is trembling or if the shaking is still me.

WHAT DO I remember?

I remember only the useless things I hear – that Bob Dylan's mother invented Wite-Out, that twenty-three people must be in a room before there is a fifty-fifty chance two will have the same birthday. Who cares whether or not it's true? In my head there are bath towels swaddling this stuff. Nothing else seeps through.

I review those things that will figure in the retelling: a kiss through surgical gauze, the pale hand correcting the position of the wig. I noted these gestures as they happened, not in any retrospect – though I don't know why looking back should show us more than looking *at*.

It is just possible I will say I stayed the night.

And who is there that can say that I did not?

I THINK OF the chimp, the one with the talking hands.

In the course of the experiment, that chimp had a baby. Imagine how her trainers must have thrilled when the mother, without prompting, began to sign to her newborn.

Baby, drink milk.

Baby, play ball.

And when the baby died, the mother stood over the body, her wrinkled hands moving with animal grace, forming again and again the words: Baby, come hug, Baby, come hug, fluent now in the language of grief.

For Jessica Wolfson

Leonard Michaels

Murderers

WHEN MY UNCLE MOE DROPPED DEAD OF A HEART ATTACK I became expert in the subway system. With a nickel I'd get to Queens, twist and zoom to Coney Island, twist again toward the George Washington Bridge – beyond which was darkness. I wanted proximity to darkness, strangeness. Who doesn't? The poor in spirit, the ignorant and frightened. My family came from Poland, then never went anyplace until they had heart attacks. The consummation of years in one neighborhood: a black Cadillac, corpse inside. We should have buried Uncle Moe where he shuffled away his life, in the kitchen or toilet, under the linoleum, near the coffeepot. Anyhow, they were dropping on Henry Street and Cherry Street. Blue lips. The previous winter it was cousin Charlie, forty-five years old. Moe, Charlie, Sam, Adele – family meant a punch in the chest, fire in the arm. I didn't want to wait for it. I went to Harlem, the Polo Grounds, Far Rockaway, thousands of miles on nickels, mainly underground. Tenements watched me go, day after day, fingering nickels. One afternoon I stopped to grind my heel against the curb. Melvin and Arnold Bloom appeared, then Harold Cohen. Melvin said, "You step in dog shit?" Grinding was my answer. Harold Cohen said, "The rabbi is home. I saw him on Market Street. He was walking fast." Oily Arnold, eleven years old, began to urge: "Let's go up to our roof." The decision waited for me. I considered the roof, the view of industrial Brooklyn, the Battery, ships in the river, bridges, towers, and the rabbi's apartment. "All right," I said. We didn't giggle or look to one another for moral signals. We were running.

The blinds were up and curtains pulled, giving sunlight, wind, birds to the rabbi's apartment – a magnificent metropolitan view. The rabbi and his wife never took it, but in the light and air of summer afternoons, in the eye of gull and pigeon, they were joyous. A bearded young man, and his young pink wife, sacramentally bald. Beard and Baldy, with everything to see, looked at each other. From a water tank on the opposite roof, higher than their windows, we looked at them. In psychoanalysis this is "The Primal Scene." To achieve the primal scene we crossed a ledge six inches wide. A half-inch indentation in the brick gave us fingerholds. We dragged bellies and groins against the brick face to a steel ladder. It went up the side of the building, bolted into brick, and up the side of the water tank to a slanted tin roof which caught the afternoon sun. We sat on that roof like angels, shot through with light, derealized in brilliance. Our sneakers sucked hot slanted metal. Palms and fingers pressed to bone on nailheads.

The Brooklyn Navy Yard with destroyers and aircraft carriers, the Statue of Liberty putting the sky to the torch, the dull remote skyscrapers of Wall Street, and the Empire State Building were among the wonders we dominated. Our view of the holy man and his wife, on their living-room couch and floor, on the bed in their bedroom, could not be improved. Unless we got closer. But fifty feet across the air was right. We heard their phonograph and watched them dancing. We couldn't hear the gratifications or see pimples. We smelled nothing. We didn't want to touch.

For a while I watched them. Then I gazed beyond into shimmering nullity, gray, blue, and green murmuring over rooftops and towers. I had watched them before. I could tantalize myself with this brief ocular perversion, the general cleansing nihil of a view. This was the beginning of philosophy. I indulged in ambience, in space like eons. So what if my uncle Moe was dead? I was philosophical and luxurious. I didn't even have to look at the rabbi and his wife. After all, how many times had we dissolved stickball games when the rabbi came home? How many times had we risked shameful discovery, scrambling up the ladder, exposed to their windows – if they looked. We risked life itself to achieve this emi-nence. I looked at the rabbi and his wife.

Today she was a blonde. Bald didn't mean no wigs. She had ten wigs, ten colors, fifty styles. She looked different, the same, and very good. A human theme in which nothing begat anything and was gorgeous. To me she was the world's lesson. Aryan yellow slipped through pins about her ears. An olive complexion medi-ated yellow hair and Arabic black eyes. Could one care what she really looked like? What was *really*? The minute you wondered, she looked like something else, in another wig, another style. With-out the wigs she was a baldy-bean lady. Today she was a blonde. Not blonde. *A* blonde. The phonograph blared and her deep loops flowed Tommy Dorsey, Benny Goodman, and then the thing itself, Choo-Choo Lopez. Rumba! One, two-three. One, two-three. The rabbi stepped away to delight in blond imagination. Twirling and individual, he stepped away snapping fingers, going high and light on his toes. A short bearded man, balls afling, cock shuddering like a springboard. Rumba! One, two-three. *Olé! Vaya*, Choo-Choo!

> I was on my way to spend some time in Cuba.
> Stopped off at Miami Beach, la-la.
> Oh what a rumba they teach, la-la.
> Way down in Miami Beach,
> Oh what a chroombah they teach, la-la.
> Way-down-in-Miami-Beach.

She, on the other hand, was somewhat reserved. A shift in one lush hip was total rumba. He was Mr. Life. She was dancing. He was a naked man. She was what she was in the garment of her soft, essential self. He was snapping, clapping, hopping to the beat. The beat lived in her visible music, her lovely self. Except for the wig. Also a watchband that desecrated her wrist. But it gave her a bit of the whorish. She never took it off.

Harold Cohen began a cocktail-mixer motion, masturbat-ing with two fists. Seeing him at such hard futile work, braced only by sneakers, was terrifying. But I grinned. Out of terror, I twisted an encouraging face. Melvin Bloom kept one hand on the tin. The other knuckled the rumba numbers into the back of my head. Nodding like a defective, little Arnold Bloom chewed his lip and squealed as the rabbi and his wife smacked together. The rabbi clapped her buttocks, fingers buried in the cleft. They stood only on his legs. His back arched, knees bent, thighs thick with thrust, up, up, up. Her legs wrapped his hips, ankles crossed, hooked for constriction. "Oi, oi, oi," she cried, wig flashing left, right, tossing the Brooklyn Navy Yard, the Statue of Liberty, and the Empire State Building to hell. Arnold squealed oi, squealing rubber. His sneaker heels stabbed tin to stop his slide. Melvin said, "Idiot." Arnold's ring hooked a nailhead and the ring and ring finger remained. The hand, the arm, the rest of him, were gone.

We rumbled down the ladder. "Oi, oi, oi," she yelled. In a freak of ecstasy her eyes had rolled and caught us. The rabbi drilled to her quick and she had us. "OI, OI," she yelled above congas going clop, doom-doom, clop, doom-doom on the way to Cuba. The rabbi flew to the window, a red mouth opening in his beard: "Murderers." He couldn't know what he said. Melvin Bloom was crying. My fingers were tearing, bleeding into brick. Harold Cohen, like an adding machine, gibbered the name of God. We moved down the ledge quickly as we dared. Bongos went tocka-ti-tocka, tocka-ti-tocka. The rabbi screamed, "MELVIN BLOOM, PHIL-LIP LIEBOWITZ, HAROLD COHEN, MELVIN BLOOM," as if our names, screamed this way, naming us where we hung, smashed us into brick.

Nothing was discussed.

The rabbi used his connections, arrangements were made. We were sent to a camp in New Jersey. We hiked and played volleyball. One day, apropos of nothing, Melvin came to me and said little Arnold had been made of gold and he, Melvin, of shit. I appreciated the sentiment, but to my mind they were both made of shit. Harold Cohen never again spoke to either of us. The counselors in the camp were World War II veterans, introspective men. Some carried shrapnel in their bodies. One had a metal plate in his head. Whatever you said to them they seemed to be thinking of something else, even when they answered. But step out of line and a plastic lanyard whistled burning notice across your ass.

At night, lying in the bunkhouse, I listened to owls. I'd never before heard that sound, the sound of darkness, blooming, opening inside you like a mouth.

Jonathan Safran Foer

A Primer for the Punctuation of Heart Disease

☐ THE "SILENCE MARK" SIGNIFIES AN ABSENCE OF LAN-guage, and there is at least one on every page of the story of my family life. Most often used in the conversations I have with my grandmother about her life in Europe during the war, and in conversations with my father about our family's history of heart disease – we have forty-one heart attacks between us, and count-ing – the silence mark is a staple of familial punctuation. Note the use of silence in the following brief exchange, when my father called me at college, the morning of his most recent angioplasty:

"Listen," he said, and then surrendered to a long pause, as if the pause were what I was supposed to listen to. "I'm sure every-thing's gonna be fine, but I just wanted to let you know – "

"I already know," I said.

"☐"

"☐"

"☐"

"☐"

"O.K.," he said.

"I'll talk to you tonight," I said, and I could hear, in the receiver, my own heartbeat.

He said, "Yup."

■ THE "WILLED silence mark" signifies an intentional silence, the conversational equivalent of building a wall over which you can't climb, through which you can't see, against which you break the bones of your hands and wrists. I often inflict willed silences upon my mother when she asks about my relationships with girls. Perhaps this is because I never have *relationships* with girls – only *relations*. It depresses me to think that I've never had sex with anyone who really loved me. Sometimes I wonder if having sex with a girl who doesn't love me is like felling a tree, alone, in a forest: no one hears about it; it didn't happen.

?? THE "INSISTENT question mark" denotes one family member's refusal to yield to a willed silence, as in this conversation with my mother:

> "Are you dating at all?"
> "☐"
> "But you're seeing people, I'm sure. Right?"
> "☐"
> "I don't get it. Are you ashamed of the girl? Are you ashamed of me?"
> "■"
> "??"

¡ AS IT visually suggests, the "unxclamation point" is the opposite of an exclamation point; it indicates a whisper.

The best example of this usage occurred when I was a boy. My grandmother was driving me to a piano lesson, and the Volvo's wipers only moved the rain around. She turned down the volume of the second side of the seventh tape of the audio version of *Shoah*, put her hand on my cheek, and said, "I hope that you never love anyone as much as I love you¡"

Why was she whispering? We were the only ones who could hear.

¡¡ THEORETICALLY, the "extraunxclamation points" would be used to denote twice an unxclamation point, but in practice any whisper that quiet would not be heard. I take comfort in believing that at least some of the silences in my life were really extraunxclamations.

‼ THE "EXTRAEXCLAMATION points" are simply twice an exclamation point. I've never had a heated argument with any member of my family. We've never yelled at each other, or disagreed with any passion. In fact, I can't even remember a difference of opinion. There are those who would say that this is unhealthy. But, since it is the case, there exists only one instance of extraexclamation points in our family history, and they were uttered by a stranger who was vying with my father for a parking space in front of the National Zoo.

"Give it up, fucker‼" he hollered at my father, in front of my mother, my brothers, and me.

"Well, I'm sorry," my father said, pushing the bridge of his glasses up his nose, "but I think it's rather obvious that we arrived at this space first. You see, we were approaching from – "

"Give … it … up … fucker‼"

"Well, it's just that I think I'm in the right on this particu – "

"GIVE IT UP, FUCKER‼"

"Give it up, Dad ¡" I said, suffering a minor coronary event as my fingers clenched his seat's headrest.

"Je-sus!" the man yelled, pounding his fist against the outside of his car door. "Giveitupfucker‼"

Ultimately, my father gave it up, and we found a spot several blocks away. Before we got out, he pushed in the cigarette lighter, and we waited, in silence, as it got hot. When it popped out, he pushed it back in. "It's never, ever worth it," he said, turning back to us, his hand against his heart.

~ PLACED AT the end of a sentence, the "pedal point" signifies a thought that dissolves into a suggestive silence. The pedal point is distinguished from the ellipsis and the dash in that the thought it follows is neither incomplete nor interrupted but an outstretched hand. My younger brother uses these a lot with me, probably because he, of all the members of my family, is the one most capable of telling me what he needs to tell me without having to say it. Or, rather, he's the one whose words I'm most convinced I don't need to hear. Very often he will say, "Jonathan ~" and I will say, "I know."

A few weeks ago, he was having problems with his heart. A visit to his university's health center to check out some chest pains became a trip to the emergency room became a week in the intensive-care unit. As it turns out, he's been having one long heart attack for the last six years. "It's nowhere near as bad as it sounds," the doctor told my parents, "but it's definitely something we want to take care of."

I called my brother that night and told him that he shouldn't worry. He said, "I know. But that doesn't mean there's nothing to worry about ~"

"I know ~" I said.

"I know ~" he said.

"I ~"

"I ~"

"□"

Does my little brother have relationships with girls? I don't know.

↓ ANOTHER COMMONLY employed familial punctuation mark, the "low point," is used either in place – or for accentuation at the end – of such phrases as "This is terrible," "This is irremediable," "It couldn't possibly be worse."

"It's good to have somebody, Jonathan. It's necessary."

"□"

"It pains me to think of you alone."

"■↓"

"??↓"

Interestingly, low points always come in pairs in my family. That is, the acknowledgment of whatever is terrible and irremediable becomes itself something terrible and irremediable – and often worse than the original referent. For example, my sadness makes my mother sadder than the cause of my sadness does. Of course, her sadness then makes me sad. Thus is created a "low-point chain": ↓↓↓↓↓ ... ∞.

✻ THE "SNOWFLAKE" is used at the end of a unique familial phrase – that is, any sequence of words that has never, in the history of our family life, been assembled as such. For example, "I didn't die in the Holocaust, but all of my siblings did, so where does that leave me? ✻ " Or, "My heart is no good, and I'm afraid of dying, and I'm also afraid of saying I love you. ✻ "

☺ THE "CORROBORATION mark" is more or less what it looks like. But it would be a mistake to think that it simply stands in place of "He agreed," or even "Yes." Witness the subtle usage in this dialogue between my mother and my father:

"Could you add orange juice to the grocery list, but remember to get the kind with reduced acid. Also some cottage cheese. And that bacon-substitute stuff. And a few Yahrzeit candles."

"☺"

"The car needs gas. I need tampons."

"☺"

"Is Jonathan dating anyone? I'm not prying, but I'm very interested."

"☺"

My father has suffered twenty-two heart attacks – more than the rest of us combined. Once, in a moment of frankness after his nineteenth, he told me that his marriage to my mother had been successful because he had become a yes-man early on.

"We've only had one fight," he said. "It was in our first week of marriage. I realized that it's never, ever worth it."

My father and I were pulling weeds one afternoon a few weeks ago. He was disobeying his cardiologist's order not to pull weeds. The problem, the doctor says, is not the physical exertion but the emotional stress that weeding inflicts on my father. He has dreams of weeds sprouting from his body, of having to pull them, at the roots, from his chest. He has also been told not to watch Orioles games and not to think about the current Administration.

As we weeded, my father made a joke about how my older brother, who, barring a fatal heart attack, was to get married in a few weeks, had already become a yes-man. Hearing this felt like having an elephant sit on my chest – my brother, whom I loved more than I loved myself, was surrendering.

"Your grandfather was a yes-man," my father added, on his knees, his fingers pushing into the earth, "and your children will be yes-men."

I've been thinking about that conversation ever since, and I've come to understand – with a straining heart – that I, too, am becoming a yes-man, and that, like my father's and my brother's, my surrender has little to do with the people I say yes to, or with the existence of questions at all. It has to do with a fear of dying, with rehearsal and preparation.

✂ 🏛 THE "SEVERED web" is a Barely Tolerable Substitute, whose meaning approximates "I love you," and which can be used in place of "I love you." Other Barely Tolerable Substitutes include, but are not limited to:

→ | ←, which approximates "I love you."

🌙 ☐, which approximates "I love you."

🔥 , which approximates "I love you."

× ✈, which approximates "I love you."

I don't know how many Barely Tolerable Substitutes there are, but often it feels as if they were everywhere, as if everything that is spoken and done – every "Yup," "O.K.," and "I already know," every weed pulled from the lawn, every sexual act – were just Barely Tolerable.

:: UNLIKE THE colon, which is used to mark a major division in a sentence, and to indicate that what follows is an elaboration, summation, implication, etc., of what precedes, the "reversible colon" is used when what appears on either side elaborates, summates, implicates, etc., what's on the other side. In other words, the two halves of the sentence explain each other, as in the cases of "Mother::Me," and "Father::Death." Here are some examples of reversible sentences:

My eyes water when I speak about my family::I don't like to speak about my family.

I've never felt loved by anyone outside of my family::my persistent depression.

1938 to 1945::□.

Sex::yes.

My grandmother's sadness::my mother's sadness::my sadness::the sadness that will come after me.

To be Jewish::to be Jewish.

Heart disease::yes.

← FAMILIAL COMMUNICATION always has to do with failures to communicate. It is common that in the course of a conversation one of the participants will not hear something that the other has said. It is also quite common that one of the participants does not understand what the other has said. Somewhat less common is one participant's saying something whose words the other understands completely but whose meaning is not understood at all. This can happen with very simple sentences, like "I hope that you never love anyone as much as I love you ¡ "

But, in our best, least depressing moments, we *try* to understand what we have failed to understand. A "backup" is used: we start again at the beginning, replaying what was missed, making the effort to express ourselves in a different, more direct way:

"It pains me to think of you alone."

"← It pains me to think of me without any grandchildren to love."

{ } A RELATED set of marks, the "should-have brackets," signify words that were not spoken but should have been, as in this dialogue with my father:

"Are you hearing static?"

" {I'm crying into the phone.} "

"Jonathan?"

" □ "

"Jonathan ~"

" ■ "

" ?? "

"I :: not myself ~ "

" {A child's sadness is a parent's sadness.} "

" {A parent's sadness is a child's sadness.} "

" ← "

"I'm probably just tired ¡"

" {I never told you this, because I thought it might hurt you, but in my dreams it was *you*. Not me. *You* were pulling the weeds from my chest.} "

" {I want to love and be loved.} "

" ☺ "

" ☺ "

" ↓ "

" ↓ "

" ⚲ "

" ☺ "

" □ ↔ □ ↔ □ "

" ↓ "

" ↓ "

" ▶▶ | ○ | ◀◀ "

" ▨ + ▨ → ■ "

" ☺ "

" ♪ ⊠ "

" ⊠ ⊠ "

" ●⊙♦□○○◆○✣□◎ "

" ■ "

" {I love you.} "

" {I love you, too. So much.} "

Of course, my sense of the should-have is unlikely to be

the same as my brothers', or my mother's, or my father's. Sometimes – when I'm in the car, or having sex, or talking to one of them
on the phone – I imagine their should-have versions. I sew them
together into a new life, leaving out everything that actually happened and was said.

Jerome Stern
Morning News

I GET BAD NEWS IN THE MORNING AND FAINT. LYING ON tile, I think about death and see the tombstone my wife and I saw twenty years ago in the hilly colonial cemetery in North Carolina: *Peace at last.* I wonder, where is fear? The doctor, embarrassed, picks me up off the floor and I stagger to my car. What do people do next?

I pick up my wife. I look at my wife. I think how much harder it would be for me if she were this sick. I remember the folk tale that once seemed so strange to me, of the peasant wife beating her dying husband for abandoning her. For years, people have speculated on what they would do if they only had a week, a month a year to live. Feast or fast? I feel a failure of imagination. I should want something fantastic – a final meal atop the Eiffel Tower. Maybe I missed something not being brought up in a religion that would haunt me now with an operatic final confrontation between good and evil – I try to imagine myself a Puritan fearful of damnation, a saint awaiting glory.

But I have never been able to take seriously my earnestly mystical students, their belief that they were heading to join the ringing of the eternal spheres. So my wife and I drive to the giant discount warehouse. We sit on the floor like children and, in five minutes, pick out a 60-inch television, the largest set in the whole God damn store.

12. Parable

You wonder what your life has been about.
You don't know. You tell yourself parables.

Parable

A CLASSIC DEFINITION OF THE SHORT STORY IS THAT IT'S a narrative that moves through time and space toward a point. Essays, too, come to a point, but the time and space they are moving through is a mental landscape, and it's perhaps even more crucial for an essay than it is for a story to come to not too clear and direct a point, lest the essay seem point-making, point-scoring, didactic, dogmatic.

The six parable-like stories in this section make clearer than most stories do what Hollywood calls the "take-away." The characters, events, and narratives are vectors on the grid of these stories'/ essays' meaningfulness, aboutness, purposefulness. The stories subordinate everything to this "aboutness." What they sacrifice perhaps in vividness they more than make up in clarity, purpose, wisdom delivered.

Contemporary writers and readers tend to be skeptical of any too earnest parable. We live in a society with an infinite number of competing value systems. No one has unique purchase on the truth (with the notable exception of your two intrepid editors). The best way to create an effective parable now is to qualify it, lead with humor, undermine its message at the same time that you're conveying it. Then, paradoxically, we might believe you, buy what you're selling. You're not giving a sermon or writing a legal brief. You're writing a story; in 1,000 words or fewer, create a parable, but remember you're writing for a reader in 2015: be funny, cryptic, self-ironizing, so brief as to appear modest.

Kate Chopin's "The Story of an Hour," written in 1894, is a very direct feminist parable. It works brilliantly and beautifully, through a series of surprising plot twists, each one taking us deeper into the heroine's vertiginous emotional state, each state taking us further on her emotional journey toward, she thinks, freedom. It's earnest and extremely effective. Can contemporary writers write like this? Maybe; maybe not. Posed in an armchair in front of her open upstairs window after hearing news of her husband's death, young Mrs. Mallard breathes in the freshness of the natural world – "the tops of trees that were all aquiver with the new spring life," "the delicious breath of rain," sparrows "twittering in the eaves," "patches of blue sky" – and this collective stirring of the natural world seems to animate her, too: her pulse quickens, she sobs, her bosom rises and falls "tumultuously." Mrs. Mallard's "fancy was running" to a point of sheer ecstasy, imagining a new existence freed from the binds of marriage, "drinking in a very elixir of life" which ultimately proves fatal. When her husband arrives after all, he is the very picture of conventional urban monotony, with his latchkey, grip-sack, and umbrella (to protect himself from what to her are the "delicious" elements). Several other characters observe the scene, but only the reader is privy to the irony, sadness, and transcendence lodged in those final moments.

The point of Donald Barthelme's parable "The School" (1975) couldn't be clearer; it's an allegory of textbook existentialism: we die; life makes no sense except what meaning we will it to have through our own actions. It gets to this meaning through a series of deaths so relentless as to be comic – notice how the deaths edge closer and closer to the unassuming schoolchildren. First the orange trees die, and then the herb gardens, snakes, gerbils, white mice, salamanders, the tropical fish, the puppy, the Korean orphan, the parents, the grandparents, and finally children the same age as the children at the school. The teacher, Edward, mixes down-home language with highfalutin language: "But I think that the snakes – well, the reason that the snakes kicked off was that ... you remember, the boiler was shut off for four days because of the strike, and that was explicable." So when at the end of the story, the children engage Edward in serious philosophical debate about the meaning of life by saying, "But isn't death, considered as a fundamental datum, the means by which the taken-for-granted mundanity of the everyday may be transcended in the direction of –," we understand that this is Edward's projection of his own existential anxiety onto the children: "They asked me, where did they go? The trees, the salamander, the tropical fish, Edgar, the poppas and mommas, Matthew and Tony, where did they go? And I said, I don't know, I don't know. And they said, who knows? and I said, nobody knows." Of the hundreds of stories Barthelme wrote, this one comes closest to articulating his entire vision of the world. This is what you should strive to do yourself – stage your vision, but do it in a subtle, funny, charming enough way that we don't feel bludgeoned by the message.

George Saunders's "Adams" also feels whimsical, funny, silly. The word "wonk" makes many readers laugh. The details are marvelously observed and delightful throughout ("So there's my poor kid, kite in lap all afternoon, watching some dumb art guy on PBS saying, Shading Is One Way We Make Depth, How About Trying It Relevant to This Stump Here?"), but they are all in the service of a very explicit parable about the way in which human beings often take what is most alarming and demonic in themselves and project this "evil" onto someone nearby who is innocent but appears to be threatening. Danger rhymes with stranger. What gives the story its real power is its secondary level. Roger is an approximate anagram of George. Adams is an approximate anagram of Saddam. The story was published in 2004, right in the thick of the Iraq War. Notice all the details that are meant to refer specifically to the run-up to the war (the toxic chemicals, the rifle, the gas tank, the blood on the hands, etc.). Consider writing a parable that is a realistic parable of strife between two or more people but also a political parable. Go to school on Saunders's subtlety, specificity, and comedy.

"Donor" is fewer than 250 words long, but it's an enormous parable about nothing less than love and death. Its effectiveness depends upon the boy's confusing a blood donation with the sacrifice of his life: this is funny to us as adult readers, who at first don't understand his extreme reluctance to give blood; note, too, the effectiveness of Lamott's paragraph break at the moment of the boy's confusion. It's difficult to read this elegant little story without thinking *You don't know what love is*. If you're not capable of the devotion the boy is capable of (in his confusion), it's not love. The story's brevity and wry tone save it from potential bathos.

Linda Wendling's "You Can't See Dogs on the Radio" perhaps seems at first glance to be fluffy, and framed as it is at beginning and end by passages from Wordsworth, the story often baffles students, but look at its many twinnings (the swan and its shadow; spaniels rolling "like the two selves inside every man," the parrot's failed imitation of human speech, Uncle Phil's double-whammy arrest, the Andrews Sisters) and how this twinning is deeply related to its thematic purposes. "Art is life's only twin," Charles Olson says. The story is about the utter uselessness of art – you can't see dogs on the radio, after all – and its absolute necessity. Without art, life reduces to grim pragmatism.

The excerpt from Michaels may seem at first or second glance cruel, and it's politically incorrect, gleefully so; this is what gives it its frisson: it evokes quite specifically how we romanticize what is inscrutable. We project onto darkness our own craving for light.

Kate Chopin
The Story of an Hour

KNOWING THAT MRS. MALLARD WAS AFFLICTED WITH a heart trouble, great care was taken to break to her as gently as possible the news of her husband's death.

It was her sister Josephine who told her, in broken sentences; veiled hints that revealed in half concealing. Her husband's friend Richards was there, too, near her. It was he who had been in the newspaper office when intelligence of the railroad disaster was received, with Brently Mallard's name leading the list of "killed." He had only taken the time to assure himself of its truth by a second telegram, and had hastened to forestall any less careful, less tender friend in bearing the sad message.

She did not hear the story as many women have heard the same, with a paralyzed inability to accept its significance. She wept at once, with sudden, wild abandonment, in her sister's arms. When the storm of grief had spent itself she went away to her room alone. She would have no one follow her.

There stood, facing the open window, a comfortable, roomy armchair. Into this she sank, pressed down by a physical exhaustion that haunted her body and seemed to reach into her soul.

She could see in the open square before her house the tops of trees that were all aquiver with the new spring life. The delicious breath of rain was in the air. In the street below a peddler was crying his wares. The notes of a distant song which some one was singing reached her faintly, and countless sparrows were twittering in the eaves.

There were patches of blue sky showing here and there through the clouds that had met and piled one above the other in the west facing her window.

She sat with her head thrown back upon the cushion of the chair, quite motionless, except when a sob came up into her throat and shook her, as a child who has cried itself to sleep continues to sob in its dreams.

She was young, with a fair, calm face, whose lines bespoke repression and even a certain strength. But now there was a dull stare in her eyes, whose gaze was fixed away off yonder on one of those patches of blue sky. It was not a glance of reflection, but rather indicated a suspension of intelligent thought.

There was something coming to her and she was waiting for it, fearfully. What was it? She did not know; it was too subtle and elusive to name. But she felt it, creeping out of the sky, reaching toward her through the sounds, the scents, the color that filled the air.

Now her bosom rose and fell tumultuously. She was beginning to recognize this thing that was approaching to possess her, and she was striving to beat it back with her will – as powerless as her two white slender hands would have been.

When she abandoned herself a little whispered word escaped her slightly parted lips. She said it over and over under her breath: "free, free, free!" The vacant stare and the look of terror that had followed it went from her eyes. They stayed keen and bright. Her pulses beat fast, and the coursing blood warmed and relaxed every inch of her body.

She did not stop to ask if it were or were not a monstrous joy that held her. A clear and exalted perception enabled her to dismiss the suggestion as trivial.

She knew that she would weep again when she saw the kind, tender hands folded in death; the face that had never looked save with love upon her, fixed and gray and dead. But she saw beyond that bitter moment a long procession of years to come that would belong to her absolutely. And she opened and spread her arms out to them in welcome.

There would be no one to live for during those coming years; she would live for herself. There would be no powerful will bending hers in that blind persistence with which men and women believe they have a right to impose a private will upon a fellow-creature. A kind intention or a cruel intention made the act seem no less a crime as she looked upon it in that brief moment of illumination.

And yet she had loved him – sometimes. Often she had not. What did it matter! What could love, the unsolved mystery, count for in face of this possession of self-assertion which she suddenly recognized as the strongest impulse of her being!

"Free! Body and soul free!" she kept whispering.

Josephine was kneeling before the closed door with her lips to the keyhole, imploring for admission. "Louise, open the door! I beg; open the door – you will make yourself ill. What are you doing, Louise? For heaven's sake open the door."

"Go away. I am not making myself ill." No; she was drinking in a very elixir of life through that open window.

Her fancy was running riot along those days ahead of her. Spring days, and summer days, and all sorts of days that would be her own. She breathed a quick prayer that life might be long. It was only yesterday she had thought with a shudder that life might be long.

She arose at length and opened the door to her sister's importunities. There was a feverish triumph in her eyes, and she carried herself unwittingly like a goddess of Victory. She clasped her sister's waist, and together they descended the stairs. Richards stood waiting for them at the bottom.

Some one was opening the front door with a latchkey. It was Brently Mallard who entered, a little travel-stained, composedly carrying his grip-sack and umbrella. He had been far from the scene of accident, and did not even know there had been one. He stood amazed at Josephine's piercing cry; at Richards' quick motion to screen him from the view of his wife.

But Richards was too late.

When the doctors came they said she had died of heart disease – of joy that kills.

Donald Barthelme
The School

WELL, WE HAD ALL THESE CHILDREN OUT PLANTING TREES, see, because we figured that ... that was part of their education, to see how, you know, the root systems ... and also the sense of responsibility, taking care of things, being individually responsible. You know what I mean. And the trees all died. They were orange trees. I don't know why they died, they just died. Something wrong with the soil possibly or maybe the stuff we got from the nursery wasn't the best. We complained about it. So we've got thirty kids there, each kid had his or her own little tree to plant, and we've got these thirty dead trees. All these kids looking at these little brown sticks, it was depressing.

It wouldn't have been so bad except that just a couple of weeks before the thing with the trees, the snakes all died. But I think that the snakes – well, the reason that the snakes kicked off was that ... you remember, the boiler was shut off for four days because of the strike, and that was explicable. It was something you could explain to the kids because of the strike. I mean, none of their parents would let them cross the picket line and they knew there was a strike going on and what it meant. So when things got started up again and we found the snakes they weren't too disturbed.

With the herb gardens it was probably a case of overwatering, and at least now they know not to overwater. The children were very conscientious with the herb gardens and some of them probably ... you know, slipped them a little extra water when we weren't looking. Or maybe … well, I don't like to think about sabotage, although it did occur to us. I mean, it was something that crossed our minds. We were thinking that way probably because before that the gerbils had died, and the white mice had died, and the salamander … well, now they know not to carry them around in plastic bags.

Of course we *expected* the tropical fish to die, that was no surprise. Those numbers, you look at them crooked and they're belly-up on the surface. But the lesson plan called for a tropical-fish input at that point, there was nothing we could do, it happens every year, you just have to hurry past it.

We weren't even supposed to have a puppy.

We weren't even supposed to have one, it was just a puppy the Murdoch girl found under a Gristede's truck one day and she was afraid the truck would run over it when the driver had finished making his delivery, so she stuck it in her knapsack and brought it to school with her. So we had this puppy. As soon as I saw the puppy I thought, Oh Christ, I bet it will live for about two weeks and then … And that's what it did. It wasn't supposed to be in the classroom at all, there's some kind of regulation about it, but you can't tell them they can't have a puppy when the puppy is already there, right in front of them, running around on the floor and yap yap yapping. They named it Edgar – that is, they named it after me. They had a lot of fun running after it and yelling "Here, Edgar! Nice Edgar!" Then they'd laugh like hell. They enjoyed the ambiguity. I enjoyed it myself. I don't mind being kidded. They made a little house for it in the supply closet and all that. I don't know what it died of. Distemper, I guess. It probably hadn't had any shots. I got it out of there before the kids got to school. I checked the supply closet each morning, routinely, because I knew what was going to happen. I gave it to the custodian.

And then there was this Korean orphan that the class adopted through the Help the Children program, all the kids brought in a quarter a month, that was the idea. It was an unfortunate thing, the kid's name was Kim and maybe we adopted him too late or something. The cause of death was not stated in the letter we got, they suggested we adopt another child instead and sent us some interesting case histories, but we didn't have the heart. The class took it pretty hard, they began (I think, nobody ever said anything to me directly) to feel that maybe there was something wrong with the school. But I don't think there's anything wrong with the school, particularly, I've seen better and I've seen worse. It was just a run of bad luck. We had an extraordinary number of parents passing away, for instance. There were I think two heart attacks and two suicides, one drowning, and four killed together in a car accident. One stroke. And we had the usual heavy mortality rate among the grandparents, or maybe it was heavier this year, it seemed so. And finally the tragedy.

The tragedy occurred when Matthew Wein and Tony Mavrogordo were playing over where they're excavating for the new federal office building. There were all these big wooden beams stacked, you know, at the edge of the excavation. There's a court case coming out of that, the parents are claiming that the beams were poorly stacked. I don't know what's true and what's not. It's been a strange year.

I forgot to mention Billy Brandt's father, who was knifed fatally when he grappled with a masked intruder in his home.

One day, we had a discussion in class. They asked me, where did they go? The trees, the salamander, the tropical fish, Edgar, the poppas and mommas, Matthew and Tony, where did they go? And I said, I don't know, I don't know. And they said, who knows? and I said, nobody knows. And they said, is death that which gives meaning to life? And I said, no, life is that which gives meaning to life. Then they said, but isn't death, considered as a fundamental datum, the means by which the taken-for-granted mundanity of the everyday may be transcended in the direction of –

I said, yes, maybe.

They said, we don't like it.

I said, that's sound.

They said, it's a bloody shame!

I said, it is.

They said, will you make love now with Helen (our teaching assistant) so that we can see how it is done? We know you like Helen.

I do like Helen but I said that I would not.

We've heard so much about it, they said, but we've never seen it.

I said I would be fired and that it was never, or almost never, done as a demonstration. Helen looked out of the window.

They said, please, please make love with Helen, we require an assertion of value, we are frightened.

I said that they shouldn't be frightened (although I am often frightened) and that there was value everywhere. Helen came and embraced me. I kissed her a few times on the brow. We held each other. The children were excited. Then there was a knock on the door, I opened the door, and the new gerbil walked in. The children cheered wildly.

George Saunders
Adams

I NEVER COULD STOMACH ADAMS AND THEN ONE DAY HE'S
standing in my kitchen, in his underwear. Facing in the direction
of my kids' room! So I wonk him in the back of the head and down
he goes. When he stands up, I wonk him again and down he goes.
Then I roll him down the stairs into the early-spring muck and am
like, If you ever again, I swear to God, I don't even know what to
say, you miserable fuck.

Karen got home. I pulled her aside. Upshot was: Keep the
doors locked, and if he's home the kids stay inside.

But after dinner I got to thinking: Guy comes in in his shorts
and I'm sitting here taking this? This is love? Love for my kids?
Because what if? What if we slip up? What if a kid gets out or he
gets in? No, no, no, I was thinking, not acceptable.

So I went over and said, Where is he?

To which Lynn said, Upstairs, why?

Up I went and he was standing at the mirror, still in his goddam underwear, only now he had on a shirt, and I wonked him
again as he was turning. Down he went and tried to crab out of the
room, but I put a foot on his back.

If you ever, I said. If you ever again.

Now we're even, he said. I came in your house and you came
in mine.

Only I had pants on, I said, and mini-wonked him in the
back of his head.

I am what I am, he said.

Well, that took the cake! Him admitting it! So I wonked him again, as Lynn came in, saying, Hey, Roger, hey. Roger being me. And then he rises up. Which killed me! Him rising up? Against me? And I'm about to wonk him again, but she pushes in there, like intervening. So to wonk him again I had to like shove her back, and unfortunately she slipped, and down she went, and she's sort of lying there, skirt hiked up – and he's mad! Mad! At me! Him in his underwear, facing my kids' room, and he's mad at me? Many a night I've heard assorted wonks and baps from Adams's house, with her gasping, Frank, Jesus, I Am a Woman, You're Hurting Me, the Kids Are Watching, and so on.

Because that's the kind of guy he is.

So I wonked him again, and when she crawled at me, going, Please, Please, I had to push her back down, not in a mean way but in a like stay-there way, which is when, of course, just my luck, the kids came running in – these Adams kids, I should say, are little thespians, constantly doing musicals in the back yard, etc., etc. – so they're, you know, all dramatic: Mummy, Daddy! And, O.K., that was unfortunate, so I tried to leave, but they were standing there in the doorway, blocking me, like, Duh, we do not know which way to turn, we are stunned. So I shoved my way out, not rough, very gentle – I felt for them, having on more than one occasion heard Adams whaling on them, too – but one did go down, just on one knee, and I helped her up, and she tried to bite me! She did not seem to know what was what, and it hurt, and made me mad, so I went over to Adams, who was just getting up, and gave him this like proxy wonk on top of his head, in exchange for the biting.

Keep your damn, I said. Keep your goddam kids from –

Then I needed some air, so I walked around the block, but still it wasn't sitting right. Because now it begins, you know? Adams over there all pissed off, saying false things about me to those kids, which, due to what they had seen (the wonking) and what they had not seen (him in his underwear, facing my kids' room), they were probably swallowing every mistruth, and I was like, Great, now they hate me, like *I'm* the bad guy in this, and all summer it's going to be pranks, my hose slit and syrup in my gas tank, or all of a sudden our dog has a burn mark on her belly.

So I type up these like handbills, saying, Just So You Know, Your Dad Was Standing Naked in My Kitchen, Facing My Kids' Room. And I tape one inside their screen door so they'll be sure and see it when they go to softball later, then I stuff like nine in their mailbox, and on the rest I cross out "Your Dad" and put in "Frank Adams" and distribute them in mailboxes around the block.

All night it's call after call from the neighbors, saying, you know, Call the cops, Adams needs help, he's a goof, I've always hated him, maybe a few of us should go over there, let us work with you on this, do not lose your cool. That sort of thing. Which was all well and good, but then I go out for a smoke around midnight and what is he looking at, all hateful? Their houses? Don't kid yourself. He is looking at my house, with that smoldering look, and I am like, What are you looking at?

I am what I am, he says.

You fuck, I say, and rush over to wonk him, but he runs inside.

And, as far as cops, my feeling was: What am I supposed to do, wait until he's back in my house, then call the cops and hope he stays facing my kids' room, in his shorts, until they arrive?

No, sorry, that is not my way.

The next day my little guy, Brian, is standing at the back door, with his kite, and I like reach over and pop the door shut, going, Nope, nope, you know very well why not, Champ.

So there's my poor kid, kite in lap all afternoon, watching some dumb art guy on PBS saying, Shading Is One Way We Make Depth, How About Trying It Relevant to This Stump Here?

Then Monday morning I see Adams walking toward his car and again he gives me that smoldering look! Never have I received such a hateful look. And flips me the bird! As if he is the one who is right! So I rush over to wonk him, only he gets in the car and pulls away.

All day that look was in my mind, that look of hate.

And I thought, If that was me, if I had that hate level, what would I do? Well, one thing I would do is hold it in and hold it in and then one night it would overflow and I would sneak into the house of my enemy and stab him and his family in their sleep. Or shoot them. I would. You would have to. It is human nature. I am not blaming anybody.

I thought, I have to be cautious and protect my family or their blood will be on my hands.

So I came home early and went over to Adams's house when I knew nobody was home, and gathered up his rifle from the basement and their steak knives and also the butter knives, which could be sharpened, and also their knife sharpener, and also two letter openers and a heavy paperweight, which, if I was him and had lost all my guns and knives, I would definitely use that to bash in the head of my enemy in his sleep, as well as the heads of his family.

That night I slept better until I woke in a sweat, asking myself what I would do if someone came in and, after shoving down my wife and one of my kids, stole my guns and knives and knife sharpener as well as my paperweight. And I answered myself: What I would do is look around my house in a frenzy for something else dangerous, such as paint, such as thinner, such as household chemicals, and then either ring the house of my enemy with the toxics and set them on fire or pour some into the pool of my enemy, which would (1) rot the liner and (2) sicken the children of my enemy when they went swimming.

Then I looked in on my sleeping kids and, oh my God, nowhere are there kids as sweet as my kids, and standing there in my pajamas, thinking of Adams standing there in his underwear, then imagining my kids choking and vomiting as they struggled to get out of the pool, I thought, No, no way, I am not living like this.

So, entering through a window I had forced earlier that afternoon, I gathered up all the household chemicals, and, believe me, he had a lot, more than I did, more than he needed, thinner, paint, lye, gas, solvents, etc. I got it all in like nine Hefty bags and was just starting up the stairs with the first bag when here comes the whole damn family, falling upon me, even his kids, whipping me with coat hangers and hitting me with sharp-edged books and spraying hair spray in my eyes, the dog also nipping at me, and rolling down the stairs of their basement I thought, They are trying to kill me. Hitting my head on the concrete floor, I saw stars, and thought, No, really, they are going to kill me, and if they kill me no more little Melanie and me eating from the same popcorn bowl, no more little Brian doing that wrinkled-brow thing we do back and forth when one of us makes a bad joke, never again Karen and me lying side by side afterward, looking out the window, discussing our future plans as those yellow-beaked birds come and go on the power line. And I struggled to my feet, thinking, Forget how I got here, I am here, I must get out of here, I have to live. And I began to wonk and wonk, and once they had fallen back, with Adams and his teen-age boy huddled over the littlest one, who had unfortunately flown relatively far due to a bit of a kick I had given her, I took out my lighter and fired up the bag, the bag of toxics, and made for the light at the top of the stairs, where I knew the door was, and the night was, and my freedom, and my home.

Anne Lamott

Donor

AN EIGHT-YEAR-OLD BOY HAD A YOUNGER SISTER WHO was dying of leukemia, and he was told that without a blood transfusion she would die. His parents explained to him that his blood was probably compatible with hers, and if so, he could be the blood donor. They asked him if they could test his blood. He said sure. So they did and it was a good match. Then they asked if he would give his sister a pint of blood, that it could be her only chance of living. He said he would have to think about it overnight.

The next day he went to his parents and said he was willing to donate the blood. So they took him to the hospital where he was put on a gurney beside his six-year-old sister. Both of them were hooked up to IVs. A nurse withdrew a pint of blood from the boy, which was then put in the girl's IV. The boy lay on his gurney in silence while the blood dripped into his sister, until the doctor came over to see how he was doing. Then the boy opened his eyes and asked, "How soon until I start to die?"

Linda Wendling
You Can't See Dogs on the Radio

The swan on still St. Mary's Lake
Float double, swan and shadow!
We will not see them; will not go,
To-day, nor yet to-morrow ...

– WORDSWORTH, "YARROW UNVISITED"

HOPING TO SOMEDAY ESCAPE THE TAINT OF THE FAMILY'S mediocrity, Dad's Uncle Phil spent a year ("No trouble ... ") rearing twin dogs and parrots for the Doublemint Gum commercials on the radio. (I believe his plan included giving heave-ho to Dad's auntie – she who continuously crossed her arms over her high, severe bosom and warned, "Relying solely on parrots never got anybody anything." But all he mentioned was a lifetime income and a new radio.)

The audition was tough. Yet, there were some good moments, when the dogs rolled over – spaniels that looked and moved "like the two selves inside every man," Dad heard Uncle Phil murmur. But you can't see dogs on the radio.

The tense moment came when the parrots were to sing. But all they'd been able to master was "Double your."

"Pleasure" was too much for them, I guess, as for Auntie.

After the audition, Phil's health declined rapidly. Cardiac arrest hit while being arrested for shoplifting a pinup of the Andrews Sisters under his shirt.

After the funeral no one would take his animals.

"No personality," Dad said, "and no pleasure."

Be Yarrow stream unseen, unknown!
It must, or we shall rue it:
We have a vision of our own;
Ah! why should we undo it?

Leonard Michaels
Journal (excerpt)

KITTREDGE LOVES PRETTY WOMEN, BUT HE IS BLIND, can't pursue them. So I take him to a party and describe a woman in the room. He whispers, "Tell me about her neck." Eventually I introduce him to her. They leave the party together. Kittredge is always successful. Women think he listens differently from other men. In his blind hands they think pleasure is truth. Blind hands know deep particulars, what yearns in neck and knee. Women imagine themselves embracing Kittredge the way sunlight takes a tree. He says, "Talk about her hips." As I talk, his eyes slide with meanings, like eyes in a normal face except quicker, a snapping in them. Kittredge cannot see, cannot know if a woman is pretty. I say, "She has thick black hair." When they leave together I begin to sink. I envy the magnetic darkness of my friend. To envy him without desiring his condition is possible.

13. Metaphysical Contemplation

No matter what you do,
it vanishes in the face of death.

Annie Dillard   This Is the Life

Metaphysical Contemplation

SHORTLY AFTER THE TERRORIST ATTACK ON THE WORLD Trade Center, the editor of the magazine *Image* asked dozens of writers to respond. "This Is the Life" was Annie Dillard's contribution. Fewer than 1,500 words and just a few pages long, it's much the best response to 9/11 over the last dozen years, with the possible exception of David Markson's book-length essay *Vanishing Point*. Both Markson and Dillard address the event extremely obliquely, and Dillard doesn't come even close to mentioning it. Instead, she uses 9/11 as the catalyst for an extremely far-ranging contemplation of the inherent relativism of all cultural "truths" and, given the actuality of death, the irreducible ephemerality of all human experience (each of us is, apparently, "as provisional as a bug"). And yet the essay, like existence itself, is joyful: nothing is meaningful, but everything is significant.

The key to the essay, and to any contemporary contemplation of "ultimate concerns," is the degree to which Dillard contains the contradictions: between ecstasy and despair, herself and the world, life and death. She is aggressively ambivalent. In *The Writing Life*, Dillard advises, "Spend it all, shoot it, play it, lose it, all, right away, every time," which is what she does here: she's utterly unblinking, unapologetically serious (and yet funny) about the fundamental questions of existence.

If, as Rembrandt said, "Painting is philosophy," then certainly writing is philosophy as well. Isn't everyone's project, on some level, to offer tentative theses regarding what – if anything – we're doing here? Against death, in other words, what solace, what consolation, what bulwark? As she does in her collage meditation *For the Time Being*, Dillard here has the temerity to directly address this question of questions. "Assume you write for an audience consisting solely of terminal patients," Dillard says in *The Writing Life*; "that is, after all, the case. What could you say to a dying person that would not enrage by its triviality?"

Lest we have forgotten, Dillard reminds us at the beginning of the essay, "Somewhere in there you die … Forget funeral. A big birthday party. Since everyone around you agrees." This sets the framework for all that follows: everything humans do – "seek to know Rome's best restaurants and their staffs," "take the next tribe's pigs in thrilling raids," "grill yams," "hunt white-plumed birds," "burn captives," "set fire to a drunk," "publish the paper that proves the point," "elude capture," "educate our children to a feather edge," "count coup," "perfect our calligraphy," "spear the seal" – is, in a sense, nothing more or less than a prelude to, distraction from, death. She relentlessly questions her own position as she rigorously investigates the world: "The black rock is holy, or the scroll … Or nothing at all is holy, as everyone intelligent knows."

We know only the culture in which we live, and we abide by its "truths": "The illusion, like the visual field, is complete … Each people knows only its own squares in the weave, its wars and instruments and arts, and also the starry sky." Can we not get beyond our own ethnocentrism? Of course, sort of, but "say you scale your own weft and see time's breadth and the length of space … What, seeing this spread multiply infinitely in every direction, would you do differently? … Whatever you do, it has likely brought delight to fewer people than either contract bridge or the Red Sox." There is a good-sized rock in the garden, there is no way to remove the garden even if you peer at it from above, and all rocks are, *sub specie aeternitatis,* equally significant/insignificant: "However hypnotized you and your people are, you will be just as dead in their war, our war … What new wisdom can you take to your grave for worms to untangle?"

There is, for Dillard, no wisdom, only many wisdoms – beautiful and delusional. As readers, we may grow overwhelmed by the vastness she depicts, but we don't grow *exhausted* – as we might in trudging through a long, boring treatise with equally high stakes. Here, to riff off her metaphor, it is as if Dillard has collapsed, in two pages, the warp and weft of both Space and Time (capital S, capital T) and woven them together for us in the tiniest of squares. Dillard condenses (without diluting) her existential meditations into this tiny but endlessly refracting container of an essay. The short-short, the lyric essay, the prose poem do wonders for the big questions.

How does Dillard communicate a sense of "the infinite" in so few words? Her list-making evokes the expansiveness, the endlessness, the weight that Dillard wants us to experience. We get a sense that she's counting or accounting for the many, the squirming multitudes, in nearly Noah's Ark fashion. Notice how often she uses anaphora – deliberate repetition of a word or words at the beginning of successive clauses – which increases the feeling that she's trying to name everything under the sun (the word "anaphora" is rooted in the Latin word *anapherein*, which is a combination of both "to bring back" and "to carry"). In the following example, you can hear the repetition of the words "beautiful" and "they," and feel the way that the language rhythmically snowballs on itself: "People look at the sky and at the other animals. They make beautiful objects, beautiful sounds, beautiful motions of their bodies beating drums in lines. They pray, they toss people in peat bogs; they help the sick and injured; they pierce their lips, their noses, ears; they make the same mistakes despite religion, written language, philosophy, and science; they build, they kill, they preserve, they count and figure, they boil the pot, they keep the embers alive; they tell their stories and gird themselves."

Dillard also overwhelms us with a seemingly endless supply of questions, often posing several in quick succession: "Try to bring people up the wall, carry children to see it – to what end? Fewer golf courses? What is wrong with golf? Nothing at all. Equality of wealth? Sure; how?" Inundated with question marks, both answered and unaddressed, we sense that for Dillard it's partly the act of asking these questions that makes us human. Notice how she keeps changing gears: establishing the problem, deepening the problem, suggesting "solutions," exploring the permutations of these solutions, arguing against and finally fully undermining these solutions, returning us to the problem.

In 1,500 words or fewer, try to write your own metaphysical contemplation, a statement of your own "philosophy of life." The likeability of Dillard's essay lies in its self-questioning. Convey your vision of life, but also question that vision. Make the questioning integral to your essay. You may also want to employ rhythmic techniques, such as anaphora, to give the prose some momentum. Remember: "Spend it all, shoot it, play it, lose it, all, right away, every time." This phrase should be an anthem for any writer of brief prose.

Annie Dillard
This Is the Life

ANY CULTURE TELLS YOU HOW TO LIVE YOUR ONE AND only life: to wit, as everyone else does. Probably most cultures prize, as ours rightly does, making a contribution by working hard at work that you love; being in the know, and intelligent; gathering a surplus; and loving your family above all, and your dog, your boat, bird-watching. Beyond those things, our culture might specialize in money, and celebrity, and natural beauty. These are not universal. You enjoy work and will love your grandchildren, and somewhere in there you die.

Another contemporary consensus might be: You wear the best shoes you can afford, you seek to know Rome's best restaurants and their staffs, drive the best car, and vacation on Tenerife. And what a cook you are!

Or you take the next tribe's pigs in thrilling raids; you grill yams; you trade for televisions and hunt white-plumed birds. Everyone you know agrees: this is the life. Perhaps you burn captives. You set fire to a drunk. Yours is the human struggle, or the elite one, to achieve ... whatever your own culture tells you: to publish the paper that proves the point; to progress in the firm and gain high title and salary, stock options, benefits; to get the loan to store the beans till their price rises; to elude capture, to feed your children or educate them to a feather edge; or to count coup or perfect your calligraphy; to eat the king's deer or catch the poacher; to spear the seal, intimidate the enemy, and be a big man or beloved woman and die respected for the pigs or the title or the shoes. Not a funeral. Forget funeral. A big birthday party. Since everyone around you agrees.

Since everyone around you agrees ever since there were people on earth that land is value, or labor is value, or learning is value, or title, necklaces, degree, murex shells, or ownership of slaves. Everyone knows bees sting and ghosts haunt and giving your robes away humiliates your rivals. That the enemies are barbarians. That wise men swim through the rock of the earth; that houses breed filth, airstrips attract airplanes, tornadoes punish, ancestors watch, and you can buy a shorter stay in purgatory. The black rock is holy, or the scroll; or the pangolin is holy, the quetzal is holy, this tree, water, rock, stone, cow, cross, or mountain – and it's all true. The Red Sox. Or nothing at all is holy, as everyone intelligent knows.

Who is your "everyone"? Chess masters scarcely surround themselves with motocross racers. Do you want aborigines at your birthday party? Or are you serving yak-butter tea? Popular culture deals not in its distant past, or any other past, or any other culture. You know no one who longs to buy a mule or be named to court or thrown into a volcano.

So the illusion, like the visual field, is complete. It has no holes except books you read and soon forget. And death takes us by storm. What was that, that life? What else offered? If for him it was contract bridge, if for her it was copyright law, if for everyone it was and is an optimal mix of family and friends, learning, contribution, and joy – of making and ameliorating – what else is there, or was there, or will there ever be?

What else is a vision or fact of time and the peoples it bears issuing from the mouth of the cosmos, from the round mouth of eternity, in a wide and parti-colored utterance. In the complex weave of this utterance like fabric, in its infinite domestic interstices, the centuries and continents and classes dwell. Each people knows only its own squares in the weave, its wars and instruments and arts, and also the starry sky.

Okay, and then what? Say you scale your own weft and see time's breadth and the length of space. You see the way the fabric both passes among the stars and encloses them. You see in the weave nearby, and aslant farther off, the peoples variously scandalized or exalted in their squares. They work on their projects – they flake spear points, hoe, plant; they kill aurochs or one another; they prepare sacrifices – as we here and now work on our projects. What, seeing this spread multiply infinitely in every direction, would you do differently? No one could love your children more; would you love them less? Would you change your project? To what? Whatever you do, it has likely brought delight to fewer people than either contract bridge or the Red Sox.

However hypnotized you and your people are, you will be just as dead in their war, our war. However dead you are, more people will come. However many more people come, your time and its passions, and yourself and your passions, weigh equally in the balance with those of any dead who pulled waterwheel poles by the Nile or Yellow rivers, or painted their foreheads black, or starved in the wilderness, or wasted from disease then or now. Our lives and our deaths count equally, or we must abandon one-man-one-vote, dismantle democracy, and assign six billion people an importance-of-life ranking from one to six billion – a ranking whose number decreases, like gravity, with the square of the distance between us and them.

What would you do differently, you up on your beanstalk looking at scenes of all peoples at all times in all places? When you climb down, would you dance any less to the music you love, knowing that music to be as provisional as a bug? Somebody has to make jugs and shoes, to turn the soil, fish. If you descend the long rope-ladders back to your people and time in the fabric, if you tell them what you have seen, and even if someone cares to listen, then what? Everyone knows times and cultures are plural. If you come back a shrugging relativist or tongue-tied absolutist, then what? If you spend hours a day looking around, high astraddle the warp or woof of your people's wall, then what new wisdom can you take to your grave for worms to untangle? Well, maybe you will not go into advertising. Then you would know your own death better but perhaps not dread it less. Try to bring people up the wall, carry children to see it – to what end? Fewer golf courses? What is wrong with golf? Nothing at all. Equality of wealth? Sure; how?

The woman watching sheep over there, the man who carries embers in a pierced clay ball, the engineer, the girl who spins wool into yarn as she climbs, the smelter, the babies learning to recognize speech in their own languages, the man whipping a slave's flayed back, the man digging roots, the woman digging roots, the child digging roots – what would you tell them? And the future people – what are they doing? What excitements sweep peoples here and there from time to time? Into the muddy river they go, into the trenches, into the caves, into the mines, into the granary, into the sea in boats. Most humans who were ever alive lived inside one single culture that never changed for hundreds of thousands of years; archaeologists scratch their heads at so conservative and static a culture.

Over here, the rains fail; they are starving. There, the caribou fail; they are starving. Corrupt leaders take the wealth. Not only there but here. Rust and smut spoil the rye. When pigs and cattle starve or freeze, people die soon after. Disease empties a sector, a billion sectors.

People look at the sky and at the other animals. They make beautiful objects, beautiful sounds, beautiful motions of their bodies beating drums in lines. They pray; they toss people in peat bogs; they help the sick and injured; they pierce their lips, their noses, ears; they make the same mistakes despite religion, written language, philosophy, and science; they build, they kill, they preserve, they count and figure, they boil the pot, they keep the embers alive; they tell their stories and gird themselves.

Will knowledge you experience directly make you a Buddhist? Must you forfeit excitement per se? To what end?

Say you have seen something. You have seen an ordinary bit of what is real, the infinite fabric of time that eternity shoots through, and time's soft-skinned people working and dying under slowly shifting stars. Then what?

Credits

Printed in the USA
CPSIA information can be obtained
at www.ICGtesting.com
JSHW061941280324
60146JS00004B/169